THE
BEGGAR'S
OPERA

THE BEGGAR'S OPERA

PEGGY BLAIR

PINTAIL

PINTAIL
a member of Penguin Group (USA)

Published by the Penguin Group
Penguin Group (Canada)
90 Eglinton Avenue East, Suite 700, Toronto, Ontario, Canada M4P 2Y3

Penguin Group (USA) Inc., 375 Hudson Street, New York, New York 10014, U.S.A.
Penguin Books Ltd, 80 Strand, London WC2R 0RL, England
Penguin Ireland, 25 St Stephen's Green, Dublin 2, Ireland (a division of Penguin Books Ltd)
Penguin Group (Australia), 707 Collins Street, Melbourne, Victoria 3008, Australia
(a division of Pearson Australia Group Pty Ltd)
Penguin Books India Pvt Ltd, 11 Community Centre, Panchsheel Park, New Delhi – 110 017, India
Penguin Group (NZ), 67 Apollo Drive, Rosedale, Auckland 0632, New Zealand
(a division of Pearson New Zealand Ltd)
Penguin Books (South Africa) (Pty) Ltd, 24 Sturdee Avenue, Rosebank,
Johannesburg 2196, South Africa

Penguin Books Ltd, Registered Offices: 80 Strand, London WC2R 0RL, England

First published in Penguin paperback by Penguin Canada, a division of Pearson Canada Inc., 2012
Published in this edition, 2013

1 2 3 4 5 6 7 8 9 10 (RRD)

Manufactured in the U.S.A.

ISBN: 978-0-14-318642-7

Visit the Penguin US website at www.penguin.com

ALWAYS LEARNING   PEARSON

FOR JADE

During times of universal deceit,
telling the truth becomes a revolutionary act.

—GEORGE ORWELL

PROLOGUE

Ricky Ramirez's parents stood on the other side of the door, speaking in hushed tones with the doctors. His grandmother's hand felt like wishbones in his small one. Her eyes were still closed and she breathed shallowly. The hospital room smelled of tobacco and anise, mixed with sweat.

He was surprised more than frightened when she suddenly sat up and pulled his head towards her by the ears. She tugged so hard it brought fresh tears to his nine-year-old eyes. "The dead will come," she rasped. "My gift to you, as the eldest child." He barely recognized her voice. She hadn't spoken for days.

"What dead, Grandmother? Are you coming back?" Dead people *left*, and as far as he knew they never returned.

"No," she smiled weakly. She released her grip and patted his cheek with her soft brown hand. "As much as I would like to see you grow up, little man."

"Then who is coming, *mamita*?" He rubbed his sore ears.

Her body slowly deflated onto the metal bed. She reached for his hand again. "Messengers from the other side. Eshu, the *orisha*, will send them to help you so you can help them. You will be a policeman, Ricky. I see it in your future. Treat them with respect, as they will you. But never forget this: Eshu is a trickster." She whispered her last words so quietly that he had to strain to hear her. "This must be our secret; the gods are too easily angered. Promise me." She squeezed his palm.

"I promise."

She released his fingers one last time and her eyes closed again.

As her hand cooled in his, he knew she was gone, just not where, and he started to cry.

Once he overcame his sadness, the idea of ghosts excited young Ramirez. He wished, at the same time, that his *mamita* had left him something more practical, like a baseball bat.

But as weeks passed, then months, there were no dead, no messengers, and he still had no bat.

His parents explained that his grandmother was old and confused, that she died from a rare form of dementia that caused her to believe things that weren't true. Her legacy, he eventually learned, was one of flawed genes, not sixth sight.

By the time he discovered he was dying, Ricardo Ramirez was the inspector in charge of the Havana Major Crimes Unit of the Cuban National Revolutionary Police.

ONE

From Hector Apiro's thirteenth-floor office in the medical tower, Inspector Ramirez watched a young patrolman slouch against a lamppost on the sidewalk below.

A week earlier, on Christmas Eve, the same bored policeman had worked a corner on the Malecón. He no doubt wished, then as now, for a purse-snatching, a car accident, anything to break the monotony. Instead, according to his statement, he watched a foreign couple bicker as a street child hustled them for money. If he had intervened, would the boy still be alive?

For Apiro's sake, Ramirez almost hoped not.

"That policeman should be more careful where he stands," Ramirez said to the dead woman sitting at Apiro's desk. She had materialized in the parking lot that morning. She wore a frilly southern-belle dress and a wide white bandana bedecked with a giant fabric flower. The several strands of beads around her neck revealed she was — or rather had been — a follower of Santería.

Somehow, she had managed to squeeze her rather large rear end into Apiro's small chair. She sat there uncomfortably, fanning herself in the heat, waiting patiently for Ramirez to finish his business with Apiro and get working on her murder.

"Earlier this month, a building collapsed nearby," Ramirez explained, keeping his voice low, in case Apiro walked in without Ramirez hearing his distinctive hop. "I investigated the deaths; Dr. Apiro examined the bodies."

She nodded politely but suspiciously. Unlike the others, she refused to engage in pantomime. She would be a tough bird to crack, thought Ramirez. Yet someone *had* cracked her, right through the sternum, from the looks of the large knife sticking out of her chest.

Ramirez was surprised cancer hadn't got her first. Even dead, she carried a well-chomped, seven-inch, hand-rolled Montecristo, although she'd never inhale again. Apiro planned to autopsy her remains that afternoon.

Ramirez had wrongly thought the dead would be more accepting of something as ephemeral as a body, but he watched the disappointment build on the woman's face as she scrutinized Apiro's photographs, all hung well below eye level. Perhaps she expected a doctor of Apiro's stature to have, well, more stature. Still, whatever Apiro's defects, they were nothing compared to hers. Apiro, at least, was alive.

Hector Apiro worked part-time as the pathologist on call to the Havana Major Crimes Unit. Ramirez was unsure why the formerly famous plastic surgeon had accepted the unpleasant job. All that Apiro would say was that cadavers never disappeared in the middle of the night. He expected nothing from them and so was never disappointed.

"Believe me," Ramirez said reassuringly, "there is more to Apiro than meets the eye. Whatever genetic or biological defect caused his misshapenness, trust me, it doesn't affect his skill. Only his sensitivities."

The old woman shrugged her shoulders unhappily. That a dwarf would cut her up, however talented, simply added insult to her already fatal injuries.

Despite Apiro's brilliance and kindness, his achondroplasia startled most people. Nature made Apiro's torso normal. His head and hands were unusually large, while his legs and arms were abnormally short. The rest of Apiro's body, so far as Ramirez knew, was unaffected.

Apiro was down the hall, getting a kettle of water to brew a pot of coffee.

Ramirez wanted to go over the events of the past week with his friend before he submitted his final report to the Attorney General. A police report as important as this one required careful reconstruction. With the lies demanded by the Minister of the Interior, it would be as tragic as a Russian novel, but without the humour.

Ramirez sighed. He would start his report with Christmas Eve, the day the past began to overtake the present. In one short week, two murders, a suicide, and an international scandal. Some said Fidel Castro might leave his hospital bed for the first time in months to attend the funerals. Who could possibly have known so many deaths would be triggered by something so commonplace, so ordinary, as a couple arguing on the seawall? Certainly not the patrolman below.

Well, the dead man knew, thought Ramirez, recalling the ghost that preceded this one. But I didn't understand what he tried to tell me. And by the time I did, it was too late.

"I won't make that mistake again," he promised the cigar lady. "Trust me, I will find the person who did this to you. It's just a matter of having enough time before I'm gone."

She nodded slightly, and turned her eyes away.

TWO

SATURDAY, DECEMBER 24, 2006

A half-dozen, dirt-streaked, half-naked boys ran behind Mike and Hillary Ellis as they wandered along Calle Obispo, past the art gallery shops where owners called out to *turistas* to buy their brightly coloured paintings.

The boys, small beggars, chased through the throngs of Canadians and Europeans who had come to Cuba in search of sun and a taste of Hemingway. This one stayed after the others scattered. He skipped beside the couple happily, oblivious to the lies their eyes and mouths exchanged.

The empty metal stands of the outdoor markets shone with the reflection of the setting sun. The small boy's ragged red-and-white shorts flapped in the light breeze as they crossed the Malecón together. They dodged cars and the ubiquitous taxis as they made their way to the seawall, where waves washed lazily along the rocks and young Cuban men flirted with passing women.

The boy pointed again and again to his own mouth, calling out repeatedly in Spanish: "Help me. I am hungry. My mother is a widow. My little sisters are starving."

The woman did her best to ignore him, but the man seemed open to persuasion, so the boy tagged along beside them, begging for money in a language they didn't understand.

"No," she repeated and shooed the small boy away with her hands. "Go away. Oh, for God's sake, Mike, I told you not to give him anything. He's never going to leave us alone now. I'm so tired of these people constantly after us."

Mike reached into his pocket for more coins. He still placed some faith in bribery.

"I don't think giving him a few pesos is going to kill anyone, Hillary," he said, although as it turned out, he was mistaken. "Lighten up. We're on holidays."

"Yeah? Some holiday. I hate this country," she snapped under her breath, even though it was obvious the boy spoke no English. "I can't stand it. All these buildings falling down everywhere. I feel like I'm in Beirut after it was bombed."

"You've never been to Beirut," Mike countered. His jaw was clenched tight as he put another two pesos into the boy's grubby hand. Five in total.

"Here, now that's enough. *No me moleste, por favor.*" Leave us alone, please. The only Spanish phrase he knew, courtesy of the hotel doorman.

The boy wrapped his fingers around the money and hugged Mike tightly for a moment. Mike tried to smile, but his mouth pulled in the opposite direction. The boy didn't seem to notice.

"Get along now," Mike said, and the boy nodded, grinning. The street child stopped for a moment, watching a group of older boys run along the sidewalk on the other side of the seaway. When they disappeared from sight, he finally ran off, clutching his pesos. He weaved between the honking cars like a brightly coloured fish until his yellow shirt disappeared into the deepening shade of a small, high-fenced park near the artists' market. A Ferris wheel and garish carousels spun slowly behind a wall of palm trees.

"You know goddamn well what I meant," Hillary said, openly furious now the boy was gone. They were headed for another argument with all the momentum of a suicide jump. She turned away, rigid with anger. Mike leaned against the seawall, waiting uneasily for her next attack.

Mike was entitled to several weeks of holidays after his disability leave. Chief O'Malley had told him to take his time, have a good long mental-health break. Come back to work when he was well-rested. And make sure to bonk that nice-looking wife of his every day they were away. Mike chose Havana as their surprise destination. He no longer remembered why he thought Hillary would enjoy it, or, frankly, why he cared.

All *she* noticed was the poverty. Families piled into devastated apartments propped up with bits of purloined wood; shaking dogs driven crazy with mange. She started complaining the moment they got off the plane.

Seagulls circled above them, screeching. Others bobbed like small white buoys on the dark waves. She shook her head at him, disgusted. "I don't know why the hell you did that. Gave him more money, after I expressly told you not to."

Mike shrugged helplessly. "They have so little, Hillary. Why get so angry over a few dollars?" But he knew her anger wasn't about that, it was about them. More precisely, about him.

"That's exactly what's wrong with you," she said in a voice as brittle as twigs. "You said a few days in Havana and everything would be better. Well, nothing's going to change who we are, is it? A few more days here isn't going make a difference. I moved my flight forward. I'm going back to Ottawa tonight."

An old car backfired like a gunshot. Mike's heart tightened at the sound. He felt the hard punch of the muscle spasms he'd suffered since Steve Sloan's death. Panic attacks, the departmental psychiatrist called them. Anxiety.

For a moment, he couldn't breathe. He leaned over the seawall and the sharp edges of the rocks pressed into his chest. The water below shone with rainbows of kerosene slick. He swallowed and took a deep breath. He managed to straighten up as the muscle above his heart slowly relaxed. "So you want a divorce? Is that it?"

She evaded his question. "I'm leaving on the nine o'clock flight. You like it here so much, *you* stay."

"And just when did you decide all this?" He grabbed her by the arm, tried to force her to look at him, but Hillary was stubborn. "When did you call the airline? When I was in the shower this morning, after we made love?"

"What difference does it make?" She yanked her arm away. "Either way, I'm leaving."

"Leaving me? Or leaving Cuba while you make up your mind?"

"Don't raise your voice at me, *mister*." She threw her hair back, indignant. He saw tears in her eyes but wasn't sure what they meant. "Coming here was a mistake. You know it, and I know it. I'm going back to the hotel now to pack. I'll call you from my parents' house once I decide what to do."

"You mean you'll have that sleazebag lawyer of yours call me."

"If that's how you want it."

She strode off briskly without a backwards glance. Her silver sandals clattered on the cracked stone. The Cuban men who lined the seawall hissed after her appreciatively.

THREE

The first time it happened, Ricardo Ramirez jumped so high that his head hit the roof of his blue Chinese mini-car. He looked around, but no one in the teeming crowds on the sidewalks seemed to notice the bloodied corpse that sat calmly in the back seat.

Was this some kind of black joke? Was one of his colleagues pretending to be the victim from the crime scene he'd left only moments before?

Ramirez looked up and down the street. He saw nothing out of the ordinary and no one laughed at his confusion. "Is this supposed to be funny?" he demanded. "Who sent you?"

The corpse shrugged his shoulders, conveying his inability to speak.

Ramirez looked at the man more closely for signs of subterfuge. But unless the murder victim had a twin, there was no disputing his authenticity. His neck gaped red where his throat had been slit, and the bruises on his face were identical to those Ramirez had observed on the body just minutes earlier.

"This can't be possible," said Ramirez, trembling.

Hector Apiro and his technicians were still at the crime scene, processing this man's remains. How could he be lying there, dead in an alley, and yet be here, sitting in Ramirez's car?

Ramirez blinked several times, hoping the ghost would disappear, but each time he opened his eyes, the dead man was still there. He waved at Ramirez hesitantly. Ramirez didn't wave back.

The un-dead man followed Ramirez around police headquarters all morning like a stray dog. He vanished from sight only when Ramirez used the toilet. Ramirez walked out, zipping up, to find the ghost waiting in the corridor. He hurried down the hall, the spectre close on his heels.

Apiro had scheduled the man's autopsy for two that afternoon, only twenty minutes away. Ramirez walked as quickly as he could to the morgue without running, trying not to draw attention to himself, again wondering why no one else noticed the bloodied ghost in his wake.

You've been dead for twenty-four hours, thought Ramirez. Apiro is about to cut you up. *What in God's name are you?*

Ramirez darted through the metal door into Apiro's private sanctuary. The dead man stopped outside, frowning. As Ramirez entered the morgue, there was no sign of the apparition.

Ramirez leaned against the door to make sure it was firmly closed. He peered around the small room anxiously. Only Hector Apiro was inside. He stood on the top step of a three-rung stepladder, leaning over a body stretched out flat on the metal gurney he used for autopsies. A proper table would have had runoff areas for blood and other fluids; Apiro made do with metal buckets.

Ramirez hung up his jacket and tried to work his arms through the sleeves of the white lab coat that he was required to wear inside Apiro's workspace. His hands shook and he kept missing the holes. Apiro, busy, didn't notice.

Apiro turned his head to greet him. "Good afternoon, Ricardo. My goodness, you're pale. You look like you've seen a ghost."

"It's nothing, Hector." Ramirez swallowed a few times. "I'll be fine." But he wasn't sure if that was true.

"There's a glass on the filing cabinet, if you'd like to get some water. Autopsies are unpleasant at the best of times, even for me. And if you need to get some air, please, go ahead. This body isn't going anywhere."

Ramirez wasn't so sure of that either.

He approached Apiro tentatively, almost afraid to look in case the body moved.

Apiro had removed the clothes from the cadaver, but it was definitely the same man who had haunted Ramirez all morning. Ramirez half expected the dead man to wink at him, but the eyes that stared at the ceiling were lifeless, waxen.

The thing in the hallway is alive compared to this, Ramirez thought. What in God's name is it?

"He *is* dead, isn't he?" Ramirez asked. But the proof of death lay on the table in front of him and in glass jars on the counter.

"If he wasn't before, he is now," Apiro said, laughing. "I've removed all his organs."

Ramirez fumbled in his pocket for a cigar. "Tell me something, Hector. Do you believe in ghosts?"

"As a man of science, I don't believe in much," said Apiro, holding his scalpel thoughtfully. "Although I am sure such illusions serve a valid social purpose. After all, Catholic priests believe in ghosts, don't they? The consecrated Host? The Holy Ghost?"

"You don't believe in them yourself?"

"In priests, Ricardo?" the pathologist asked. He pivoted his large head and cocked a bright eye at Ramirez. "You know what I think of organized religion. You can imagine what I think of any God who would make *me* in his image."

"But what if someone told you they'd seen a ghost? Someone credible," Ramirez pressed. "Unlikely to make things up."

"Ah, now, Ricardo, believing in ghosts is one thing. Seeing them is another. I would suspect that person had developed a medical problem. There are certain illnesses — tumours, toxicities like lead poisoning, for example — that can cause hallucinations. As well as some mental illnesses like schizophrenia and senile dementia. Even a stroke can sometimes have that effect."

"What about the *santeros*?" asked Ramirez. He pulled a stool over and sat down to steady his legs. "They claim to communicate with the dead. My grandmother was Vodun. On my father's side."

Slave traders brought Ramirez's Yoruba ancestors from West Africa in the 1800s to harvest Cuban tobacco and sugar. The Yoruba followed their own religion, Vodun, as well as the Catholicism forced upon them by their owners.

Or at least they pretended to. They cloaked their religion with Catholic rites, but never gave up their own practices. The resulting mix of Catholicism and Vodun — Santería, or Lukumi — included a belief in multiple gods, and regular and animated interaction with the spirit world.

Apiro nodded doubtfully. "Superstition, I think. In that sense, Santería is no different than other religions. I agree with Castro on that point. We were both trained by Jesuits, and we both became atheists. Perhaps there is a connection."

Ramirez cringed as Apiro probed the neck wound with his gloved fingers, but the body didn't twitch. Definitely dead, thought Ramirez. No doubt about it.

"Your grandmother believed in ghosts?" asked Apiro. He leaned against the top rung of his ladder as he waited for Ramirez's response.

Ramirez inclined his head slightly, remembering his promise of secrecy. His grandmother had spoken to him of a gift across generations, of messengers from the other side. A gift that waited for him outside the door, the bright slash of his wound coiled around his neck like a red bandana.

"My parents said she died from an unusual form of dementia. But she knew where she was, and who we were, right up to the end. I was there when she passed away."

"She probably had a disease called DLB, then," said Apiro. "Dementia with Lewy bodies. It can cause extremely compelling hallucinations. Quite often those who have it know their visions are not real; they may even find them amusing. Socks that turn into kittens, for example. Although in Cuba, kittens that turned into socks would be more useful. I personally think it's more difficult to deal with than Alzheimer's because of that self-awareness. It's a terrible illness, Ricardo. I'm sorry to hear she suffered from it."

"Is that the only symptom of the disease, Hector?" asked Ramirez, his hands shaking as he lit the cigar. "Delusions?"

"Hallucinations and delusions are not quite the same, Ricardo. Hallucinations occur when one sees things that don't exist. A delusion is when one believes them. But no, there are certainly others as the illness progresses," said Apiro, turning back to the corpse. "Insomnia is quite common in the early stages. Then tremors in the extremities. The cognitive deterioration comes much later on. Unfortunately, it is impossible to diagnose the illness with certainty until one autopsies the brain, although CT scans and MRIs can be useful if there is a reason to suspect it. She did well to live so long, your grandmother. The disease can be of quite early onset. It often strikes people in their forties and fifties."

"My God," said Ramirez. His heart sank. He had suffered from insomnia for months, ever since his promotion. And now apparently from hallucinations, too. "What's the prognosis?" Ramirez was almost afraid to ask.

"Fatal. Usually within five or six years."

"Is there no treatment?"

"Nothing, I'm afraid." Apiro looked up and searched his friend's eyes carefully. "Are you worried that your father may have it? It is not usually considered hereditary, but I could try to arrange an MRI. It could take months, maybe a year, to get an appointment. There are only two machines in Havana and limited supplies. And like most things, the tourists come first."

Ramirez shook his head. His father was old but healthy. He didn't know how to tell Apiro that he was the one seeing ghosts, not his father. And what was the point of an MRI if there was no way to conclusively diagnose the illness, and nothing Apiro, nothing anyone, could do about it anyway?

Ramirez breathed in and out rapidly, deeply stunned. Francesca was four months pregnant with their second child. What should he do? He couldn't tell his wife that he would probably die before their unborn baby started school. Francesca would kill him herself.

Apiro stepped down and snapped off his gloves. "If you give me your grandmother's name and her date of birth, I can check our records to see what the autopsy revealed. When did she die?"

"In 1973, when I was nine. She must have been in her nineties by then. But I don't know her exact birthday, Hector," Ramirez answered slowly, his thoughts heavy as cement. "She was Yoruba. Born a slave."

Until the late 1800s, slaves were considered property, and birth certificates were never issued for them. But his grandmother was a free woman when she died. A person, no longer a thing, under Cuban law. "Would they have done an autopsy that far back?"

Apiro nodded. "If they suspected Lewy body dementia, yes. It's been a matter of medical interest for at least a hundred years. It may take me some time, Ricardo, but I'll find out, I promise."

Those old records were Ramirez's only hope.

But they weren't computerized, and Apiro called him later that day to say that until they were, he had no way to find a pathology report for a former slave who died more than three decades earlier.

The dead man disappeared a few days later, after Ramirez found his killer, and Ramirez never saw that particular vision again.

But a month or so later, another dead man appeared in the hallway outside his apartment. Like the first ghost, this one was silent. He communicated with Ramirez through shrugs, raised eyebrows, and somewhat clumsier charades. He, too, vanished after Ramirez solved his case.

With increasing frequency as his disease progressed, Lewy body hallucinations popped up in Ramirez's office, his car, and his apartment. The dead people he conjured never spoke, only gestured or made motions in the air. They always disappeared once their killers were identified.

To his surprise, Ramirez managed to get used to them. He even found the products of his dying synapses occasionally amusing, as Apiro said they might be.

His hallucinations looked over his shoulder, grimaced slightly at his mistakes. They were unfailingly polite. They stayed out of the bathroom and the bedroom, and if Ramirez suggested they leave, they left. All it took was a meaningful glance.

Eventually, Ramirez convinced himself that they were simply manifestations of his overworked subconscious. Images manufactured by his tired brain to help him process clues he might otherwise miss. Sometimes he talked to them about his investigations, and they always listened attentively, either nodding in agreement or shaking their heads if they had other ideas.

He didn't tell Francesca about his illness. He didn't know where to begin. After all, he felt fine physically, although tired from lack of sleep. If anything, his police work was better, more focused, despite the nights he tossed and turned.

His little Estella was almost five years old, no longer a baby, when Ramirez's hands began to tremble uncontrollably.

Ramirez knew then that his time was running out.

FOUR

As evening approached, the sky deepened to the same shade of azure as the ocean. Wispy clouds floated above the cooling air.

Cuba was mostly closed to the outside world, a once-vibrant country slowly strangling under an American embargo. Even now, just before the dinner hour, no foreign fishing boats disrupted the radiant surface of the water, only the lazy line of a single tug far off in the distance. It hauled a dark shape that Mike Ellis couldn't quite make out.

It was the end of another gorgeous day. No portents of disaster, no looming storm clouds, nothing to warn Ellis that the fiction he had struggled to maintain — his marriage — would end right there on the seawall.

The distance between sky and sea slowly disappeared. Only a thin edge of light hinted at the boundary between air and water. Fishermen bobbed in truck tires on the ocean waves, casting night lines from their rubber boats.

A few toughened men with callused hands and bait cans at their feet stood along the seawall holding fishing lines. Hazy rings of cigarette smoke curled around their heads in the light dusk. People laughed, enjoying the fresh ocean breeze. Cars honked hellos to each other along the Malecón. Ellis felt completely out of place: guilty, wounded, and alone.

A young black Cuban man wearing a T-shirt and shorts, with a striped shirt tied around his waist and his baseball cap on sideways, stood in front of Ellis, blocking his path.

"Hey, where you from, mister?" the man said, smiling widely. "You from Canada? Got some soap?"

"Not now." Ellis forced his way past the man. "Leave me alone."

"What's wrong, Señor? It's a beautiful day; you should be smiling."

The Cuban looked at him with concern, or perhaps pity. He put his hand on Ellis's shoulder. Ellis knocked it off. The man took a step or two backwards. He put his hands out in front of him to ward off Ellis's anger before he turned to follow another tourist.

I need a drink before I lose it, thought Ellis. More than one. A tankful. What the hell; I'm not driving.

He decided to head over to Hemingway's favourite bar, El Bar mi Media Naranja. It made him feel a little better somehow, knowing that even a macho guy like Hemingway had problems with women.

FIVE

The bartender was burly, with thick ropy arms and a flattened nose. Mike Ellis had finished his second *añejo*, straight, no ice, and the man was generous with the bottle.

The seven-year-old rum tasted like sweet hot water. Ellis downed the next one quickly, tapped the counter again. He took his jacket off and laid it on the stool next to him, felt the warm flush of alcohol begin to calm him down.

So she's finally done it. She's really gone. Ellis had tried hard to rebuild a marriage that was, at its heart, as beyond repair as the collapsed shells of buildings all around him. *Damn her.* Every Christmas from now on would remind him of the way his soon-to-be-ex-wife abandoned him in Old Havana.

Ellis could still hear Steve Sloan's voice, could feel the big arm Sloan threw around his shoulder the night before he died. He could almost taste the cold beer Sloan shoved in his hand in the smoky, noisy bar when Ellis said he didn't know what to do.

"We've all been there, buddy. I'm a serial offender." Sloan was only thirty but already married and divorced twice. "I shouldn't have married either of them. Just be glad you two never had children."

But Sloan didn't know then that Hillary was pregnant.

Even in a short-sleeved shirt, Ellis was hot. A mahogany ceiling fan gently moved the air above the bar. A row of framed photographs hung on the wall. Beneath it, a large mirror ran the length of the counter. He looked at his reflection, watched the other patrons pretend not to stare at his thick scars.

"What's your name?" Ellis asked the bartender.

"Fidel," the man answered, smiling. "Like him. Castro." The bartender put another drink in front of Ellis and inclined his head to a faded brown-and-white photograph of the young Castro. Bearded, tall, craggy, almost handsome in his flat-billed hat and khaki jacket. The heroic populist had vanquished a dictator, thought Ellis, only to become one. Castro had either saved Cuba or destroyed it, depending on your perspective.

"*Gracias*, Fidel." Ellis toasted the bartender and emptied the glass.

Fidel pointed with his shoulder to the row of bottles behind him. He raised his eyebrow. Ellis nodded.

Fidel brought over a dark-brown bottle of Havana Club. The bartender hadn't asked him about his injuries, but he could see the man eyeing him discreetly from time to time, wondering what happened to his face.

Fidel busied himself washing glasses behind the bar, lining them up beside the ones he'd already prepared with lime juice and sugar. Waiting for the tourist onslaught.

Six o'clock. Lots of time to get drunk. Ellis had in mind *shit-faced*, as Sloan would say. He wanted to obliterate the past, erase it from his memory. Forget about the shooting, and how badly he'd screwed things up. *Fuck Steve.*

The departmental shrink said he suffered from survivor's guilt. The psychiatrist had no idea what it was like that night in that hallway, what really happened.

Anxiety. Well, that was one word for it. Just not the one Ellis would choose. He stared at his empty glass and ordered another bottle.

"I'll have a mojito, please, Fidel," the woman said.

The bartender smiled, admiring her looks, her streaked blonde hair and her low-cut blue top. She wore a tight beige skirt that accentuated her long, shapely legs. Ellis watched her skirt ride up as she pulled herself on the stool next to his. She wore silver strappy sandals with very high heels.

The bartender wiped down the bar in front of her. The woman was tall and slim, dressed a little like his wife, Ellis realized. The resemblance depressed him.

Fidel crushed some fresh mint leaves into a glass full of ice and lime juice, added more sugar, poured in the rum, and passed the drink to Ellis's lovely neighbour across the wide brass rail. She put it on a cork coaster that said "Home of the Famous Hemingway Mojito," where it left a ring of condensation.

"*Gracias*, Fidel." The woman turned to smile at Ellis. She hadn't seen the scars, couldn't see them, sitting as she was, on his good side, where everything looked normal.

Ellis glanced at himself in the mirror. His mouth was pulled to the side, perpetually sardonic, the scar on his forehead a fine white slash below the hairline where the knife had caught. He remembered the warm blood running down his chin, how it mingled with his tears. He drained his glass.

Black-and-white photographs of Hemingway hung above his reflection, along with the iconic photographs of Castro. In the early shots, Hemingway was still handsome, not yet bloated with booze. Later on, he had a trim white beard. He often stood beside a younger, thinner Castro.

Nothing in the photographs gave away Hemingway's lost

battle with depression or the voices he'd already started to hear by the time those pictures were taken. Hemingway's scars were inside, where no one could see them. Ellis wasn't sure if that worked better.

Fidel refilled his empty glass: the amber liquid glowed in the light. Ellis looked in the mirror again. Sometimes women told Ellis he looked sexy, that the injuries added character to his face. But he knew better. He saw the fear in his wife's eyes whenever she looked at him. Hillary was scared of him. He felt it that morning when they finally, reluctantly, made love. She was afraid he knew about the affair.

But *he* was the one who got away with murder.

SIX

The woman sipped her drink, then rested the glass on the counter. She wiped her hands dry on her skirt. The deep mahogany wood of the bar displayed her reflection. She had pink nails that matched the sunglasses pushed on top of her thick hair.

Outside, it must have been close to thirty degrees. The sun was an orange tennis ball rolling slowly into the ocean.

"Are you alright, Señor?" she asked with what seemed like genuine concern. She had a deep, husky voice. A whisky voice. There was a faint sheen to her skin.

Ellis took a closer look at her. Early to mid-twenties, he guessed. Astonishingly pretty, with her clear skin and large brown eyes. His type of woman, or at least had been once, long ago.

She smiled at him again and he realized she was a prostitute. One of the thousands of Cuban *jineteras* who looked for foreigners to ease their impoverished lives for a few hours or a few nights. He would have preferred someone attracted to him, not his wallet. But tonight, just this once, he might settle.

"I'm fine, thanks," he said. He tried to smile at her, to let her see his ruined face, in case she changed her mind.

She didn't avert her eyes. Instead, she caught his with a look of frank interest. She said softly, when he turned away, "I am sorry. I did not mean to make you feel uncomfortable."

She spoke with a breathy, seductive tone that hinted at the opposite. That she hoped for discomfort; that what she really wanted was to knock him off his seat and mount him right there on the floor. His mouth felt suddenly dry. He reached for another drink.

She moved her stool a little closer, played with her glass, ran her fingernail around the top. She glanced at him from time to time with a demure smile. Her body language said there was no rush.

"Can you look after my bag for me while I go to the ladies' room?"

"Of course," he agreed. He watched her sashay to the washroom at the back of the bar. She left her striped tote behind, planted on her seat like a flag of discovery, so the women in the bar would know he was taken.

Men's eyes followed her. Even the Hemingways on the wall seemed to trace her slim body with their eyes as she moved fluidly out of sight.

A South Asian man sporting a straw hat pulled up a stool on Ellis's other side. It was the only empty stool left in the small bar. The man was dark, thickly furred. Hair poked out of his collar.

"Where are you from?" asked the man. He leaned against the bar, facing the washrooms at the back where the woman had disappeared.

"Canada."

"I'm from London. England, that is. Great place, isn't it, Cuba?"

Ellis nodded.

"Been here long?" the man asked, as Fidel placed a mojito in front of him.

"About a week."

"Yeah? Where are you from in Canada?"

"Ottawa."

"That's the capital, right?"

"Yes." Ellis took another gulp, then put his glass down. Something about the man put him off. He answered tersely, giving nothing up freely.

"Cold." The man pretended to shiver. "Eskimos. Snow and ice. I've never been there. What do you do in Canada?"

"Police work."

"Really," the man said, clearly interested. "So you're a copper. You look like one, now that I think about it. What kind of work do you do?"

"Sex crimes at the moment. And child abuse."

"Ah," he said. "That must be interesting for you. Busy, is it?"

"Very," Ellis agreed. But it crossed his mind that not many people would describe his line of work as "interesting."

"I work in the modelling business."

The man turned around to face the mirror. They watched the woman's reflection as she languidly made her way back to the front of the bar. "Where are you staying?" the man asked as she approached.

"The Parque Ciudad Hotel."

"Ah," the man said. "Beautiful place. Do you like it?"

"The staff is extremely accommodating."

"There's a new wing they finished recently. Very nice, I hear."

"Yes. That's where my room is."

The woman slid back on her stool and put her hand on Ellis's shoulder while she stabilized herself. He thought he saw her eyes flicker to the South Asian man and narrow, but he wasn't sure. Her expression lasted only a moment.

"You are very strong," she said to Ellis, but he thought for some reason that the comment was directed to the other man.

The dark man held her eyes as she slipped her arm through Ellis's and slid closer. Fidel brought the stranger another drink.

"My turn to go," said Ellis. "I'll be back shortly," he promised, but he felt uneasy leaving her alone.

As Ellis walked back from the men's room, he could see the two of them in the wide mirror. The dark man leaned over Ellis's stool and put his face in front of the woman's. Ellis saw him draw his finger across his throat and mouth something to her. She squirmed on her seat. When Ellis sat down, he saw she was trembling. *What the fuck?*

"Do you know this man?" he asked. He tried to imagine what the man had said to scare her so badly. She too quickly shook her head and he didn't believe her. He turned to confront the man. "Maybe you want to leave the lady alone, pal," he said, almost snarling.

"I'm just having a drink," the dark man responded. "Making conversation with the lady. If that's what you want to call her."

But his rudeness to the woman made Ellis suddenly angry again. He tensed up, ready to fight. He and Steve Sloan would have drawn lots to see which one of them would get to beat the shit out of an asshole like this one.

He lowered his voice and said menacingly: "Listen, pal. You stay the fuck away from her, okay? Tonight, she's with me. Got it?"

"Like I said, I just came in for a drink," the man replied. He threw some bills on the bar. "Here, I've got your tab covered. No hard feelings, right mate? Just a little misunderstanding. I'm leaving. No need to be upset."

"Good plan," Ellis said sarcastically.

The man threw back his drink and slipped off his stool. He had been sitting on Ellis's jacket, which made Ellis like him even less.

"Thank you," said the woman, clearly relieved by the man's departure. "That was awkward. There are many men in Cuba who do not appreciate women like me."

"I find that hard to believe. He was just jealous. Forget about it."

Ellis drained his glass, tilting his head back, letting the sweet brown liquid slide down his throat. Aged rum. Nirvana.

For the first time in months, Steve and Hillary slipped away.

SEVEN

The woman put her hand over Ellis's and squeezed it a little. She was seducing him and he was surprised to find himself responding. He hadn't felt attractive for a long time. He reached for the bottle and poured himself another drink, neat. He poured one for her, too, as they chatted. She was articulate and charming. She told him she was in the tourist business. She winked at him, knowing he knew exactly what she was and didn't care.

"What do you do for a living?"

"I'm a police officer. In Canada." He told her that he had just started a new job in the Child Abuse and Sex Crimes Unit. That he had been on leave before then, because of his injuries.

"Because of these?" she said and touched the place on his lip where the thick scar puckered.

"Yes. That was part of it." He liked that she didn't ask questions about them. "Do my scars frighten you?"

"No, not at all," she said "They make your face more interesting. They give it character."

"I've heard that before. But I never believed it." He tried to grin, his mouth lopsided in the mirror.

"I understand scars, believe me. I did not mean to offend

you earlier by staring." She put a gentle hand on his face, ran her fingers lightly across the scar that ran from his forehead to his upper lip. He pulled her hand away and she took his fingers, ran her tongue lightly over them. He became aroused.

He reached for the bottle again, more to distract himself than anything else, but it was empty.

"Here," she said, and pushed her drink towards him. "Finish mine. Please, I haven't touched it. Are you here on your own?"

"I am now," he said. "My wife went home today. Early."

He drained the drink, held the empty glass. He looked at the back of his hand, the knuckles scarred from years of breaking up other people's fights. A trickle of sweat ran down the back of his shirt. The ceiling tiles swirled above.

Man, I am really getting drunk.

"Too bad," said the woman. "Is that why you wanted company?"

He felt her warm hand on his leg. She ran one finger slowly along his thigh. "No one should be alone in such a beautiful city as Havana. You do not want to be alone, do you? We should find somewhere to go."

He didn't answer right away. He considered whether he wanted to spend the night with a woman and forget his real life for a few hours.

For a moment, the notion of AIDS crossed his mind. Then his wife's face came into focus. He shoved that mental image away. Hillary was gone. They were finally done with each other. He was alone in Old Havana, and no, he didn't want to be. What the hell. Why not? *Fuck Steve.*

"Some company would be nice," he decided, still apprehensive. "But wait a minute, okay? I have to go to the men's room first." He wanted to find a condom machine. He hadn't used a condom in years; wondered how it would feel.

He stumbled off the seat. The ceiling tiles slipped with him and the walls were curved now. He held on to the backs of chairs, then the wall, as he weaved down the narrow hallway to the washrooms at the back of the bar. His shirt clung to his back. The bar had become unbearably hot.

Ellis pushed open the door and walked over to the sink, where he caught sight of his damaged face in the mirror. He splashed some water on the back of his neck. He put his hands on the sink to steady himself as the walls slowly revolved around him like a children's carousel. There was a condom machine, but it was empty.

He began to walk back to the woman, running his hand along the wall to keep upright. He bumped into a man in the hall, knocking him a little to the left. The man scowled, brought his ugly, scarred face close to Ellis's. Ellis recoiled, until he realized he'd stumbled into a mirror.

I'm plastered, he thought. He managed to get back to his stool without offending anyone else. His jacket was on the floor. He picked it up, but almost fell as he bent over. He straightened up unsteadily.

"My, you *are* drunk, aren't you?" the woman said, laughing. "I had better get you into bed. Where are you staying?"

"The Parque Ciudad," he said, surprised he wasn't slurring, but then the drunks he arrested for impaired driving never thought they slurred their words either. "Do you know where that is?"

"Yes, of course I do, lover." She put her mouth close to his ear and whispered softly, "You understand, Señor, I never kiss. It is nothing personal."

He pulled on his jacket; the air was cooler outside. He staggered, had to concentrate to keep his balance. She gripped his arm tightly, used her hip to keep him upright. The cobblestones were uneven under his feet. His mouth tasted bitter, his tongue too thick to speak easily anymore. Every now and then, he stumbled, but she caught him. She was stronger than she looked.

He heard the sounds of mariachi bands, trumpets, guitars, and maracas. The music seemed distorted, loud. There was even a bagpipe. He tried to speak, to comment on the fact that there was a Scottish bagpipe in Cuba, of all places, but his brain and mouth were no longer connected. He laughed, but no sound came out.

Firecrackers popped in the distance. He winced at the noise, watched the colours fall from the sky in trails like the jet streams of the Canadian Snowbirds. He couldn't remember ever being this loaded.

He realized he didn't know her name. If she'd told him, he'd forgotten. It seemed better somehow not to ask. He was embarrassed that they were about to make love and he couldn't remember her name. He wasn't sure where they were going, but that didn't seem to matter either. *What is her name?*

He didn't know how long they walked, the woman holding much of his weight, encouraging him, laughing lightly, easing him along the path until his hotel emerged from the darkness.

EIGHT

Inspector Ricardo Ramirez planned to sleep in late on Christmas Day, make love to his wife and play with his children. Maybe listen to his Christmas gift from Francesca, a CD of the terrific Cuban soprano Lucy Provedo.

He did not expect to spend the morning investigating the death of a small boy pulled from the ocean like a fish. Or the afternoon watching Hector Apiro practically straddle the child's battered body.

Like most Cubans, Ramirez and his family had stayed up late on Christmas Eve. His apartment was the only one able to hold all nine of his extended family on the night of such a major celebration without serious risk of collapse. For years, Fidel Castro had banned Christmas because it interfered with the sugar cane harvest. But Castro changed his mind just before the Pope's visit some years before, and so Christmas was once again legal, even if religion was officially discouraged.

After the children went outside to play, the adults relaxed with music, beer, and rum. Then they all walked to Revolution Square along with hundreds of thousands of other Cubans for the midnight mass. As church bells rang, a huge television screen displayed the Pope's address. Despite Cuba's official atheism, most Cubans believed in Catholicism a little, just in case. In Cuba, Catholicism was a hedge.

They walked back to their apartment, dropping relatives off along the way. Ramirez lay awake now, listening to his wife's soft snores, thinking how much he already missed her.

He kissed her hair before he finally fell asleep. Slept restlessly, fitfully, until 6 A.M., when the phone rang and startled him. Beside him, Francesca stirred. "I hear bells ringing, Ricardo. But it is too early for church."

"It's just the phone, *cariño*," he whispered. "Go back to sleep. I will answer it."

He got up and knocked his head against a bell. Francesca had decorated the apartment with metal Christmas bells and homemade stars that hung from everything, even the overhead lights. Ramirez ducked to avoid losing an eye.

He pulled on his underwear and walked to the kitchen. He stubbed his bare toe on a chair as he stepped around the stranger waiting for him in the doorway. *Coño*, he cursed silently, and hopped on his other foot until the pain subsided.

The dead man shrugged apologetically. He held his hat with both hands. A middle-aged man with light brown, weathered skin. Unlike his other hallucinations, Ramirez was quite sure he'd never seen him before. He wasn't a victim in any of Ramirez's files.

Ramirez grabbed the phone to stop the relentless ringing and fumbled as he put what he thought was the receiver to his ear. Still sleepy, he wondered why he didn't hear anything except a distant buzzing. He finally managed to get it turned around the right way.

The dead man hovered nearby. It seemed rude to leave him waiting indefinitely. "My day off," Ramirez whispered, his hand over the mouthpiece.

The man looked disappointed but showed himself out.

An honest mistake, thought Ramirez. Christmas Day, unlike Christmas Eve, was a working day in Cuba. For the first time in years, however, Ramirez had the day off.

"Yes?" he said, careful to keep his voice down, but he knew who it was and guessed that his record for working Christmas Days would remain unbroken.

He heard the voice of the morning dispatcher. "Inspector Ramirez? I am terribly sorry to wake you, but a boy's body has been found in the ocean across from the medical towers on the Malecón. It looks suspicious. Dr. Apiro is at the scene."

"Tell me what you know so far." Ramirez scrambled to find a pen and some paper.

Ramirez's office processed only some twenty homicides a year, in a city of over two million inhabitants. Child abuse was not uncommon, if under-reported. But the murder of a child was extremely rare; years since his section investigated one.

His black notebook was in his pants, in the bedroom, on the floor. Ramirez did not want to wake Francesca again by re-entering their bedroom and rummaging around or there would be another murder for someone *else* to investigate.

He found one of his small daughter's drawings and began to scribble notes on the back. It would have to do.

"A fisherman, Carlos Rivero, discovered the body around twenty minutes ago. He was setting up his bait cans when he saw something floating in the water. He screamed for help. Another fisherman ran over and they lifted the body over the seawall. That is when they realized the boy was dead. It took a few minutes for Señor Rivero to find a policeman because of the holiday last night."

It wouldn't take long to overcome that problem, thought Ramirez. There would soon be dozens of policemen at the scene.

They swarmed to any incident as quickly as cockroaches fled from light. But according to Dispatch, the patrolman who arrived first acquitted himself well.

Officer Fernando Espinoza confirmed that the boy was dead, then made a note of the time of his arrival and took statements from witnesses while memories were fresh. Espinoza looked for signs of violence on the body, which he carefully recorded in his notebook. Only then did he search the small body. He found a wallet hidden in the boy's underwear. It held a Canadian passport and a badge.

The dispatcher gave Ramirez the name and birthdate of the man in the passport: Michael Taylor Ellis, born August 29, 1969. And according to the badge, Señor Ellis was a detective with the Rideau Regional Police in Ontario, Canada.

"Drowned?"

"Dr. Apiro says blunt force trauma."

It was Espinoza's first homicide, but it appeared that he had used uncommon sense. Instead of disturbing the scene further, he asked Dispatch to contact Ramirez for further instructions.

"Which is why I had to wake you up on your day off," the dispatcher explained. "Again, my sincere apologies, Inspector Ramirez."

"You did the right thing, Sophia. I was afraid I would end up working today. I have learned over time that what I most fear often happens. Radio that young officer back and patch him through, will you? And by the way, *Feliz Navidad*."

"Thank you, Inspector," Sophia said, and then less certainly, given the circumstances, "I hope you and your family have a Merry Christmas as well."

Ramirez was undressed and scruffy with a light morning beard, but he was waking up rapidly. His plans for Christmas Day were shattered. There had been enough left of the chicken from last night's dinner to invite his relatives back for a second time tonight. The dinner on Christmas Eve was the first meal with meat that he'd tasted in months. The disturbing nature of this call made it unlikely he would enjoy two.

The line crackled as the dispatcher connected Espinoza and said goodbye.

"Officer Espinoza?"

"Yes, sir?"

"You've done a good job so far. Now make sure you preserve and protect the scene and keep onlookers as far back as possible. Do you have any yellow barrier tape?" Ramirez hoped that Patrol had some. If they were out of tape, it could take months to find more.

"I will call for some, sir."

"Good. I will be at the scene as soon as I get dressed. You are the officer in charge until then." Ramirez could almost see the young man's face break into a smile as the patrolman contemplated a day of real police work.

A dead child. Ramirez wondered when the boy would drop by.

NINE

Mike Ellis woke up around five in the morning. His head cracked with pain. He didn't realize that Hillary's things were gone until he went into the bathroom to get a glass of water and an aspirin. For a split second, his adrenalin spiked at the thought that someone had broken into their hotel room.

Then he remembered their argument. The way Hillary left him standing on the Malecón, arguing with himself. He walked back to the bed. Her side was empty, the pillowcase smooth.

Damn. He pulled open the closet doors and the drawers. She had taken all her belongings except her birth control pills, which sat on the bathroom counter. Maybe that was deliberate. Her way of telling him sex between them was over, that she didn't need to protect herself from his sperm any longer.

The small combination safe in the closet was open. All the Cuban money in it was gone. Only his travellers cheques remained. The miserable bitch, he thought, incredulous.

He straightened up too quickly and felt his head reel again. He went back to the bathroom sink and splashed some water on his face, looked at the horror in the mirror.

His scars were an angry shade of red, even uglier and more

raised than usual. He gulped down a glass of tap water, then another. His mouth had the taste of copper pennies; he couldn't feel his lips.

What the hell happened last night? After he got back to the hotel, Christmas Eve was mostly a blank. He wondered how much money it took him to get that drunk and hoped he had some left.

He found his pants folded neatly on a chair by the desk, but he didn't remember putting them there. He checked the pockets. Empty. Then he searched the pockets in his jacket, the floor, the desk, and the hotel safe again. Nothing. *Where the hell is my wallet?*

That's when he panicked. He thought of the woman from the bar. *She took my fucking wallet.*

Ellis lay down again on the king-size bed and tried to remember the night before. Did she come to his room? Did they have sex? What if she had AIDS?

But he recalled only vague images that lost more detail the longer he was awake. Nothing. His brain was as frozen as the right side of his face. He made it to the bathroom in time to throw up. *My God, Mike, that was one helluva bender.*

No wife, no wallet, no identification, no money, and God only knew what other risks he'd exposed himself to. Here he was, stuck on an island in a communist dictatorship, unable to prove he was a Canadian if he had to. In a country where just being American was illegal.

Shit. Shit. Shit. He'd have to cash his travellers cheques at the currency exchange wicket in the hotel when it opened and report his missing credit card to Visa. He tried to remember what else he'd lost besides his wallet and his wife. His health-care card, driver's licence, passport. Some American money. Maybe some tourist pesos. His police ID.

Shit. Double-shit. O'Malley would not be happy. His badge was in his wallet, and badges were supposed to be guarded as carefully as guns.

He wasn't sure how to replace his lost passport; didn't even know if there was a Canadian embassy in Havana. The Foreign Affairs website recommended making a photocopy; he had one in his suitcase. He wasn't sure if that would help, but until the government offices opened, there wasn't much he could do.

He stumbled when he got up, his legs wobbly beneath him. He showered, put on his jogging pants and a sweatshirt, tied on his running shoes. He'd started running years before, after he and Sloan became partners. Afraid that driving around in a patrol car every day would make him soft. He remembered the old joke: a hard man is good to find.

He took the back stairs to the hotel exit and walked up Agremonte towards the Malecón until his legs felt more steady, then turned left and began a slow jog towards the centre of town. Some of his sluggishness ebbed away as he regained control of his feet. He pounded along the seawall. There was a light breeze and he eased into the rhythm of the run.

He stopped just shy of the tall medical towers, the centre of Cuba's plastic surgery business. A dozen or more police cars blocked the seaway. The sidewalk crawled with at least twenty policemen, although it was still too early in the morning for rubberneckers, as they called gawkers back home. He saw technicians in white overalls. A small man kneeled next to a body on a tarp. He wondered if someone had drowned.

Ellis thought of asking one of the policemen how to report his stolen wallet, but he didn't want to get in the way if they were dealing with a death, and he wasn't sure if anyone spoke English anyway. As he swung back towards the Parque Ciudad, it occurred to him that Miguel could probably tell him what to do.

TEN

Inspector Ramirez called his subordinate, Detective Rodriguez Sanchez, at home. He heard the fatigue in his colleague's voice and immediately knew that Sanchez had been up late the night before as well.

"Merry Christmas, Rodriguez. I am sorry to wake you, but it appears we have to work today." He briefed the younger man about the situation. They punctuated their words with failed attempts to stifle yawns as both tried to feed oxygen to their tired brains.

Although only in his early thirties and a relative newcomer to the Major Crimes Unit, Sanchez was Ramirez's best investigator. Ramirez had recently assigned Sanchez to the sex tourism websites that had started to show up in their monitoring of internet transmissions to and from the outside world. Given the hours Sanchez spent involved in virtual policing, Ramirez thought he might actually enjoy being involved in a real-life, down-to-earth, homicide investigation again. Even one so early in the morning.

"You still have contacts at the airport, Rodriguez?"

"Yes, of course. I was just there last week."

"Good. Then I need you to go back and check the registries. This man, Señor Ellis, had to disclose where he was staying when he checked through Customs. I want the name of his hotel. Get copies of the surveillance tapes from when he first cleared Customs as well. Oh, and Rodriguez, check the dogs, will you?"

"I have a car today, but no fuel. I will take a bus, or hitchhike. Faster than waiting for someone from Patrol to pick me up."

Ramirez sighed. The fuel shortages were a problem for the whole division. They managed by rotating cars and using whatever other transportation they could find.

Sanchez had no personal car. If he had run out of fuel rations for his police car for December, he couldn't get more until January 1. Ramirez wondered what would happen if all the Havana police cars ran out of fuel. Slow-speed foot chases? He might have to find his men bicycles.

It was another reason he assigned Sanchez to computer work; Sanchez could do it from the office. Few government buildings, other than theirs, had authorized internet connections. Some of the higher-end hotels, like the Hotel Nacional, had internet access, but only for foreign tourists. Otherwise, with limited exceptions, the internet was illegal in Cuba.

"Call Dispatch when you finish at the airport and ask Sophia to send a car to pick you up. I'll wait for you at the scene. Later today, trade cars with someone else on the squad: you'll need one."

"Half an hour," Sanchez said, and hung up.

Ramirez shaved quickly, then dressed in his patrol blues. He always wore his blue-and-grey uniform to crime scenes. There was a pragmatic reason for this. Ramirez could get his uniforms laundered at government expense, but not his suits. Dry cleaners were for *turistas* only. Besides, Francesca had scolded him when he was first appointed to head up the Major Crimes Unit and came home with stains on his clothing of somewhat dubious origin. "I have no laundry soap, Ricardo," she said sharply, "and I am not a technician. I prefer not to clean up your crime scenes."

His wife would be distinctly unhappy to know how many of his crime scenes followed Ramirez home. But he made a point from then on of wearing his uniform at such times and discovered that his men liked it, too. It made him seem like one of them instead of their superior.

Ramirez kissed his sleepy wife goodbye and apologized for having to leave. "I will be home as soon as I can. I promise to make this up to you when this case is completed. Please put aside some chicken for me if any is left, will you?"

His daughter and young son were asleep, arms splayed out across each other in their bed. He kissed each of them lightly, afraid of waking them up. They would have to open their gifts without him. He hoped they enjoyed their small presents. He had done his best to find them toys, never easy with the embargo.

ELEVEN

Inspector Ramirez arrived on the Malecón to find Hector Apiro kneeling beside a small body on a plastic tarp. The dead man walked closely behind him, a worried look on his face, perhaps concerned that the investigation of his own death would be delayed by this tragedy. Ramirez gave him a look to let him know that, yes, the child was his immediate priority.

The dead man backed away, twisting his hat in his hands, but he lingered, nervous and expectant, the way a teenage girl might wait by the phone.

"Merry Christmas, Hector," Ramirez said to the pathologist. He wondered how Apiro had celebrated Christmas Eve.

Even though Apiro was Ramirez's closest friend, Ramirez had never been to his apartment and Apiro had never accepted an invitation to his, not even to join them for last night's festivities. The small man lived alone. He once told Ramirez he never expected to marry.

"I allowed myself to imagine, years ago, that I might find love someday. I got over that illusion quickly. There was a patient. It was stupid of me. You can imagine the ethical complications, Ricardo, even if she had felt the same way. That's the only real problem with being a dwarf, you know, once you get past the height issues. One's dreams, even shattered, aren't as small as others might think."

Ramirez knew Apiro would spend all Christmas Day processing the crime scene and the child's remains, making sure the evidence was rock solid.

The small man looked up and smiled. "And Merry Christmas to you, Ricardo. How was your dinner last night?"

"Very good. I had almost forgotten what chicken tasted like."

"Ah, chicken. I remember 1998, when the Pope came to Havana. Castro found everyone a chicken that Christmas. I wondered if Castro was a *babalao*. Because there were no chickens anywhere before the Pope's visit, yet Castro found thousands."

Ramirez chuckled. A *babalao* was a high-ranking Santería priest, a magician who offered animal sacrifices as part of his dark magic. Castro had indeed pulled chickens from thin air.

"Tell me, Hector, which one of those men is Espinoza? I put him in charge of the crime scene this morning."

"He's the young one over there." Apiro pointed towards a policeman, hardly more than twenty, who looked both proud and apprehensive at the same time.

"I'll be back in a few minutes."

Ramirez walked over to the stocky patrolman, who was attempting to make himself look taller by standing on the balls of his feet. "Officer Espinoza? You did well today."

"Thank you, Inspector." The young man blushed. He handed Ramirez a clear plastic exhibit bag containing the wallet and the Canadian passport. "Inspector Ramirez," Espinoza added, an undercurrent of excitement in his voice, "I believe I have identified the deceased."

Ramirez smiled somewhat to himself. Calling victims "the deceased" was the way that new officers distanced themselves from the dead. But in his world, the dead were not distant at all. He glanced at the seawall, where the dead man lifted his hand in the air hesitantly, trying to catch the inspector's attention.

Espinoza explained that he had radioed the other officers who worked foot patrol in Old Havana while he waited for Ramirez to arrive.

"I asked if any of them saw a Cuban boy of eight or nine years, dressed in red shorts with a small pattern, either this morning or last night. Officer Lopez said he would check the Ferris wheel — it is a magnet for children around here. He just radioed me to say that the ride operator is in the process of opening up the park. He says the man seems very nervous."

Not surprising, thought Ramirez. Most Cubans were frightened by a visit by the police.

"Perhaps he is concerned that the presence of the *policía* will deter potential customers. What did Lopez find out?"

"There *was* a boy dressed in red shorts that ran around with a small gang of boys yesterday. Chasing after tourists for money."

"Have Lopez take a statement, will you?"

"Already done, sir."

"Good. Did the witness know the boy's name?"

"No, sir. But one of the officers who usually stands in front of the Palacio de los Marqueses de Aguas Claras stopped some boys in the late afternoon and warned them to be less aggressive with tourists. He remembers one had a yellow shirt and red shorts with a white print. He recorded his name in his notebook and threatened to contact the boy's parents if he didn't stop bothering the *extranjeros*. It could be the same boy."

"It probably is."

Ramirez recorded Espinoza's badge and section number in his notebook and considered having him transferred to his own section. Foot patrol officers who could think independently were as rare as chickens. Most were nearly brain-dead with boredom.

He thanked the young patrolman, then picked up his radio and had Dispatch contact Detective Sanchez.

"Rodriguez, I need you to do one more thing before you come here," Inspector Ramirez said. "Get in touch with Interpol, will you? I want a criminal record check on Señor Ellis."

Ramirez pulled his daughter's crumpled drawing out of his pocket and provided Sanchez with the Canadian's full name and date of birth. He was glad he had managed to find a pen. Finding a pencil could take years.

"Tell me, is that Señor Rivero, the fisherman?" Ramirez inclined his head to a gnarled man in his late sixties or seventies who stood nearby, a metal bait can at his feet. The man looked shaken and somewhat bewildered.

"Yes. I asked him to wait, in case you had any questions."

Ramirez walked over to Rivero. The older man was shaking. From wading into the cold water, no doubt, but likely also from his find. A child's body was not what Rivero got up so early that morning to catch.

Words poured from the old man like water. "When I saw the bright red fabric puffed out with air in the current, I thought that someone lost a jacket. It looked like a flower, blooming in the waves. Then I saw a small brown hand floating above the water and realized what it was."

The fisherman's knees were bleeding, scraped on the jagged rocks as he dragged the boy's body from the water. His face was ashen. He was clearly in shock. Ramirez put his arm around the man's shoulder and gently escorted him to Apiro.

"Thank you, Señor Rivero, for everything you have done here. Believe me, it is much appreciated."

"There was nothing I could do." The man shook his head, his eyes red from tears. "He was already dead. So small, just a boy."

"Hector, can you put a bandage on that knee for Señor Rivero? And if you have a thermos with you, I think Señor Rivero could use a coffee to warm him up."

Apiro nodded and smiled at the man kindly as he reached into his kit. Ramirez knew he would make sure Rivero had a shot of rum before he left as well. "Dr. Apiro will take care of your injuries. Is there anything else we can do for you?"

"No, Inspector, thank you."

"Let's hope the rest of your day is less upsetting. But you should feel very proud of the way you behaved today; you did well to brave the cold water."

Many Cubans would have walked the other way when they saw the body in the water. Afraid they would be blamed somehow for the child's death.

Ramirez looked more closely at the child's body. The boy was shirtless, malnourished, like so many Cuban children. Ribs poked through his skin. His right eye was heavily bruised.

Apiro gently turned the boy over. There were flat purple bruises on his back. He used his gloved hands to pull down the boy's shorts and underpants.

"Look here," he said, pointing out injuries to the rectum, small tears.

"Rape?"

"At this age, not likely to be consensual," the doctor murmured. "There was a strong degree of force involved in this assault. It would have been very painful for this child to sit down for some time, excruciating to go to the bathroom."

"Do you know how he died?"

"I can't say yet for sure, but based on this," Apiro pointed to some swelling at the back of the head, "I would guess he was hit with something hard."

"And the bruises on his face and back?"

"Hard to say. The ones on his face could be from the rocks. I will have to assess the bruises at the autopsy to know for sure. My guess, though, is that they were ante-mortem injuries. Caused before death, not after."

"From blows?"

"Ah, Ricardo, I cannot be sure with a boy of this age. Boys play, they climb trees, they run into things, they push each other, they fight. But once I see everything and evaluate all the known facts together, I will have a better idea. I will do the autopsy this afternoon. I have to, really," he said wistfully. "Our refrigeration unit is not working properly."

"Bad luck," Ramirez said, thinking of the conditions Apiro would have to work in once the afternoon heated up.

The pathologist grinned. "Bring your cigar."

TWELVE

A giant Christmas tree sparkled in the lobby. It was decorated with long strings of flashing blue and green lights that lit up at different times so the entire tree changed colour as if by magic. The twinkling lights hurt Mike Ellis's eyes. He took the elevator up to his room and undressed, took his time showering for the second time that day. His eyes stung from the water, but at least his legs felt like they were his own again.

Ellis dried himself off and walked naked across the room, pulled the curtains tightly to keep out the light. He found a pair of chinos in one of the drawers. He put on a clean pair of briefs, a golf shirt, slid on socks, shoes, grabbed his sunglasses, and rode the elevator down to the lobby.

The skylight over the restaurant below him dripped with the residue of early morning rain, but the open sky above was pure blue. Another beautiful, ruined day.

It was just after eight, but the currency exchange desk was open. He cashed his travellers cheques, folded the money, and put it in his back pocket.

As he entered the lobby, Ellis looked over at the concierge desk and saw Miguel. The doorman moved towards the door as

Ellis approached, ready as always to let him out, his white gloves immaculate, his hat set exactly straight. A handsome young man.

"Merry Christmas, Señor Ellis," Miguel said, smiling, and pushed the revolving glass door. But instead of walking through it as he usually did, Ellis stopped.

"Merry Christmas to you, Miguel," he said and tried to smile back, but his lip no longer moved on the side where the knife had snagged. "Listen, I lost my wallet somewhere last night. Probably somewhere around El Bar. You know, Hemingway's bar. Any idea what I can do about it?"

"I will call the police for you, Señor, and let someone know to contact you here so you can file a report. I am not sure what office handles it. Do not worry, I will take care of it for you."

"Thanks. I don't imagine they can do too much, but it had my passport in it." He gave Miguel the details and a ten-peso note. "This is to thank you for everything you've done for me. And also because it's Christmas."

"Thank *you*," Miguel said and quickly slipped the money into his own pocket. He gave Ellis a huge smile and a handshake so hard it hurt.

Five pesos was almost a month's wage in Cuba. Ten CUCs, the tourist currency in pesos, was a great deal of money. But Miguel had been helpful to Ellis and his wife throughout their stay. He arranged their tour for them, cautioned them about *jineteros*, the street hustlers who would try to scam them, even taught them a little Spanish.

"You are too generous, Señor Ellis. I am truly sorry about your wallet. But our police are very efficient. Do not worry, I am sure they will find it for you."

"Is there somewhere nearby that I can get breakfast?"

"The Hotel Machado is quite good, Señor. Through the park, on the right-hand side."

Outside, a cluster of horse-drawn carts sheltered in the cool shade of the Parque Ciudad, City Park, trees. The browbeaten, blinkered horses flicked their manes in the heat, shaking their large heads back and forth. They looked as miserable as Ellis felt.

A row of taxis lined the street. Three or four drivers called out, asking if he wanted a ride. He declined.

The Hotel Machado was easily identified by the distinctive large blue letters on the second level that announced its name. The outdoor café faced away from the sun, fronting the park.

Ellis ordered black coffee and gulped it down. It went down smoothly and helped to soothe his jangled nerves. He caught the waiter's eye and ordered brown rice, eggs, and beans.

It was getting hot out already. He watched some boys play in the park. They had a plastic bottle and kicked it around like a soccer ball. One boy wore running shoes without laces that were far too big for him. The others were barefoot.

Despite being in Havana for a week, Ellis was still startled by the poverty.

The taxi driver explained to them on the ride in from the airport how anxious the Cuban people were for Fidel Castro's death, how tired they were of living in Third World conditions. Thanks to free public education, most of the service workers, even the prostitutes, had graduate degrees. Some were doctors, engineers. They wanted more from their lives than *this*.

"Have you heard the joke?" the cab driver said. "A Cuban woman is happy that her new boyfriend is a taxi driver, but heart-broken when she finds out he is only a neurologist." He laughed, hit his steering wheel with his hand. "Look at me. I have a degree in particle physics and I drive a taxi because we have no laboratories in Cuba. Nothing is simple here, believe me. Nothing."

"How safe is it in Havana?" Hillary asked. "Can we walk around at night?"

"Of course, but be careful to keep your hands on your purse, Señora. There are pickpockets everywhere. But don't worry," the cabbie assured her. "Apart from that, this is the safest country on earth. Look at all the police. They come here to work from all over the island. We call them *palestinos*, because they never leave. They have the most boring job in Cuba. Believe me, they have to invent crimes just to have something to do."

The taxi driver was right, Ellis realized, as the waiter refilled his cup. There were young policemen with blue pants and berets on every corner, sometimes more than one. They looked like restless children carrying guns. It wasn't reassuring.

THIRTEEN

Inspector Ramirez and his apparition watched sadly as the small remains were loaded into the white van that carried bodies to the morgue.

Ramirez sighed. Cases involving children were the hardest. The file would be difficult for everyone in the unit, especially those with children. Including himself. His son, Edel, was around the same age as the boy.

Sometime later that day, Ramirez would have to explain to grieving parents that their son had died. He wanted to be able to tell them he had a suspect under arrest and en route to the firing squad. He glanced at the dead man, surprised to see him wipe away tears.

A patrol car pulled up. Detective Rodriguez Sanchez stepped out. He looked tired; his complexion rougher than usual. He handed Ramirez the surveillance tapes he had requested. As the two men spoke, the technicians began to brush the sidewalk for evidence using tiny combs.

Ramirez and the dead man stepped to the other side of the barrier tape, making sure to get out of their way. Ramirez opened the plastic exhibit bag Espinoza had turned over and removed the passport. He flipped gingerly through the wet pages. He winced at the man's scars, magnified in the unsmiling black-and-white photograph. It looked like Michael Ellis had been in a serious accident. His face was cut up like a jigsaw puzzle.

"Not so pretty," said Ramirez, showing the picture to Sanchez. "Did you find out where he's staying?"

"The Parque Ciudad Hotel. But listen to this, Inspector. Dispatch called me a few minutes ago, on my way here. She received an anonymous call that a man with a scarred face approached some young boys in the Parque Ciudad yesterday demanding sex for money. It must be the man in the passport. I think we should go to the hotel and interview him now, before he goes out for the day."

"How convenient that we have a complaint this early in our investigation," Ramirez commented dryly.

Under Cuban law, the police had only three days to complete their investigation into a felony offence. The legislature had imposed this requirement most likely because flights left the island several times daily. Otherwise, suspects could flee the country before investigations were completed. Cuba had very few extradition treaties with other countries, only a few informal agreements.

Because of this, the Major Crimes Unit had to move rapidly when outsiders were suspected of criminal acts. His men usually met the timeline, despite the department's continual lack of resources, like the fuel Sanchez had run out of and the forensic supplies Apiro somehow managed to do without.

Once they arrested a suspect, Ramirez had to turn his case file over to a prosecutor within seventy-two hours, along with a draft indictment. If he couldn't meet those timelines, he was required to let the suspect go, guilty or not. Most *turistas* were unaware of the law, allowing many Cuban officials to line their own pockets by accepting money from foreign suspects in lieu of uncertain charges. "Win-win," as they said in America.

If Ramirez needed more time, he was required to develop a plan that outlined what was left to do. The prosecutor then had to persuade a sometimes reluctant juridical panel to deny bail based on that plan. Panels could be skittish when tourists were involved.

Life was considerably easier for Ramirez if he could work within the three-day time frame. He preferred to keep things informal at first, to stop the clock and make sure they had enough time.

Sanchez, on the other hand, thought it was more efficient to frame the guilty, that it allowed for a speedier investigation, given their tight deadlines. Ramirez had never really believed that he was joking. He half-suspected Sanchez of calling in the complaint himself.

"Too bad the call was anonymous. Did Dispatch get a number?"

"A cellphone, no display."

"Anything distinctive about the voice? Male or female?"

"I asked. She forgot to make a note of it."

"That is unfortunate," Ramirez said. "But there are *cederistas* everywhere."

It was not uncommon for members of citizen watch groups to call about crimes without identifying themselves. The use of a cellphone was unusual, however. It was illegal for unauthorized Cubans to have one, and very few had authorizations. But Sanchez had no cellphone either, just the phone at his apartment and his police radio, which meant the complaint must have originated elsewhere.

"Then perhaps this Michael Ellis is our man," said Ramirez, although he did not like the idea of accusing a foreign police officer of a serious crime based only on an anonymous call. "Let's go see what he has to say."

FOURTEEN

Inspector Ramirez parked across from the new hotel that sat on prime real estate at the edge of Old Havana on the north side of the beautiful, well-treed Parque Ciudad. He and Detective Sanchez crossed the street. A uniformed doorman let them in through the revolving front door.

The dead man hesitated. It was illegal for Cubans to enter tourist hotels unless they worked there. But there were no laws prohibiting dead or imaginary Cubans from doing anything. Ramirez believed it was one of the few legal restrictions the Cuban government had failed to implement. He expected the amendment any day.

Given that legislative gap, the dead man accompanied the two policemen inside. He stopped to admire the giant Christmas tree that dominated the entry as the two investigators walked to the reception desk.

Ramirez and Sanchez identified themselves to the young woman working at the counter, although it was obvious they were police: Ramirez still wore his uniform. He asked the woman, barely out of her teens, in what room Señor Michael Ellis was staying.

She checked. "Room 612, sir."

The doorman approached them as they were about to take the elevator up to the sixth floor.

"I overheard you asking about Señor Ellis," he said. "I was just about to call you. Señor Ellis told me this morning that he lost his wallet last night. He asked me to report it to the police. He has just left the hotel — you've missed him by only minutes."

"Has he checked out?" Ramirez asked and pulled out his notebook.

"Oh, no, sir, he will be back soon, I expect. I recommended the Hotel Machado to him. I think he plans to eat breakfast there."

"Were you here when he came in last night?" A suggestive question, Ramirez knew. In court, only the judges and lay members on the panel could ask leading questions. As the investigator now, however, he had full freedom as to how he gathered evidence.

"I am always here," said Miguel Artez sadly, with a small smile. "Yes. I was here when Señor Ellis returned, although he did not mention his wallet to me then. He was quite drunk when he came in. He may not have realized it was lost until this morning."

"What time was that?" Sanchez asked. "When he came in."

"Around eleven, I think. Perhaps eleven-thirty. I ended my shift at midnight. Not long before then."

"Was he alone?" Ramirez inquired.

"I think so." Artez reflected for a minute. "Yes, definitely. His wife left during my shift yesterday. In the evening. I called a taxi to take her to the airport. I helped her with her luggage."

"No child with him?"

"No," said the doorman, surprised. "They were here on their own."

"Is he staying by himself now?" Sanchez asked.

"Yes, of course. Señora Ellis was a very nice woman," the doorman emphasized. "Very beautiful. I was sorry when she left Cuba so early, by herself."

Sanchez took the doorman's name, address, and date of birth, and recorded them in his notebook. He stepped aside to speak to Ramirez privately.

"I think we should search Señor Ellis's room before we talk to him. We have enough evidence, with his wallet on the body and that complaint about the children in the park."

Ramirez considered this. Sanchez was right. Once they had grounds to suspect a crime had been committed, the police could search a state-owned hotel without a warrant. The grounds were not particularly strong but enough to meet the legal test.

Ramirez returned to the reception desk and asked the young woman for a key to Señor Ellis's hotel room. She handed him a plastic card.

At first, he was not entirely sure what he was supposed to do with it. The only hotels he had stayed in were in Moscow. In those days, a dour key lady had doled out steel keys grudgingly, as if they were cabbages.

Inspector Ramirez and Detective Sanchez walked down the pink hallway with its blue-tiled floor to Room 612. Ramirez rapped on the door; Sanchez drew his gun. When there was no response, Ramirez slid the hotel key up and down in the narrow key slot below the door handle until a green light flashed and the lock clicked.

He opened the door slowly and cautiously let them in, but the room was empty. The dead man followed them inside.

The room was messy; the bed unmade. The drapes were pulled tightly shut. Ramirez turned on the lights and opened the curtains to let the morning light stream through the glass.

Sanchez put his gun away and they both snapped on thin latex gloves. The gloves were made by the same manufacturer in China that produced condoms, with much the same unfortunate effect, given the burgeoning Chinese population. They frequently had holes in them.

"No sign of a wife in this room," Ramirez commented. The dead man smiled slightly.

Perhaps the ghost was a bachelor, thought Ramirez. The irony of Ramirez's business was that most murders were domestic. Spouses, lovers, people who cared for each other were most likely to kill each other, but it also meant that someone noticed if a loved one disappeared. A single man could be missing for months before anyone paid attention. *Who are you?*

"No," said Sanchez, and it took Ramirez a moment to realize that Sanchez was speaking to him. "I checked when I was at the airport. Michael and Hillary Ellis arrived on December 18. They were supposed to leave on January 2. The airport records show that she flew back to Ottawa last night on the 9 P.M. flight. The doorman is right; she left very early. A week early, in fact."

"What time did you say her flight out was again?"

"Nine o'clock. Twenty-one hundred hours."

"Hmmm. That *is* interesting."

Ramirez opened the folding door to the closet in the hallway. It contained a stand on which a single green suitcase rested. He opened it. It was empty but for a single piece of paper. A photocopy of the same passport they'd found in the wallet.

A wall-safe above the suitcase was locked. There was nothing else to see. Ramirez took the photocopy and closed the closet door.

A man's jacket was slung over a chair beside the wooden desk in the bedroom. A pair of pants lay crumpled on the floor. Ramirez checked the pockets of both, but there was nothing in them.

"Look at this," Sanchez called out. Ramirez walked over to the opposite side of the room. Sanchez pointed to a broken capsule lying on the carpet near the bed between the wall and the window. The dead man pointed to Sanchez.

"Bag it," Ramirez instructed.

Sanchez pulled a plastic bag from his pocket, put the capsule inside, and sealed it. He initialled the bag and handed it over. Ramirez put it in his pocket.

He walked into the bathroom and flipped on the light. "Señora Ellis must have left quickly."

"Why do you say that?" Sanchez asked, puzzled.

Ramirez walked back out. He held up the plastic disk of birth control pills, grinning. "No Cuban woman would go anywhere without these."

Ramirez saw nothing out of the ordinary in the bathroom. A man's electric shaver, a small hotel bottle of shampoo, a square of soap.

"So tourists get free soap and shampoo when they stay here," said Ramirez.

He smelled the soap, thought how much his wife would appreciate scented toiletries instead of the one grey bar of sudless acidic soap she lined up to get once a month as part of their rations.

"Look what I found under the mattress," Sanchez called from the other room. He flourished several Polaroid photographs along with a CD.

Ramirez looked at the Polaroids and felt sick. They were pictures of a young boy fellating a man; in another, the boy was bent over. The same boy in each shot. He could imagine what was on the CD.

It wasn't possible to identify the man in any of the pictures; the camera had focused on the boy. But there was no question about the child's identity: it was the boy Carlos Rivero had pulled from the water that morning.

The inspector's cellphone rang. It was the female member of his investigative team, Natasha Delgado, updating him on the results of their canvassing. Once again, his team had done well.

"We found several men on the Malecón who saw a foreigner with a scarred face," said Delgado. "One remembers seeing him walking with a Cuban boy who wore red shorts, accompanied by a blonde woman. Another said the *extranjero* pushed him after he tried to talk to him, that the foreigner was visibly angry."

"Good work, Natasha. Get Dr. Apiro and his crew over here right away." He snapped his cellphone closed. "Treat this as a crime scene," he instructed Sanchez.

The men walked out into the hall. Ramirez checked that the door was locked. He gave Sanchez the plastic room key and left him standing in the hallway to make sure no one entered.

The dead man stood beside Sanchez. He held his hat over his heart like a mourner at a funeral.

Ramirez took the elevator down to the lobby to wait for Apiro. Once the forensic process began, protocol required that the police turn evidence-gathering over to the forensic team to avoid contamination.

Apiro arrived a few minutes later, his black kit in hand, and Ramirez explained what they had found.

"Thank you, Ricardo. I'll take over from Detective Sanchez."

"Tell him I'll wait for him outside."

It wasn't the first time Ramirez had seen photographs like this, but they always disturbed him. He wanted to breathe in some fresh air, get the bitter taste of bile out of his mouth. He tried not to think of his own children.

A few minutes later, Sanchez joined Ramirez on the sidewalk. "I can walk over to the Hotel Machado and bring the suspect back to you for questioning," he suggested.

"No," said Ramirez. "Better if we drive. In case he tries to run."

FIFTEEN

As Mike Ellis waited for the waiter to bring his bill, a short Cuban in an open-necked white shirt with a slightly pockmarked face walked towards his table. A number of heads turned to look. Ellis's heart skipped. He wondered how the plainclothes officer had found him, until he recalled that Miguel had promised to call the police about his wallet. He forced himself to relax.

"Señor Ellis?"

"Yes?"

"I am Detective Sanchez of the Cuban National Revolutionary Police. You wanted to file a report with us about losing your wallet?

"Yes, I did."

"We have found it. Will you accompany me to the police station, please?"

"Of course," Ellis said, and felt some of his tension ease. "That's great news."

Ellis left a few pesos on the table to cover his bill along with a generous tip. They walked to a very small blue car parked across the street. Ellis didn't recognize the make. It had no police markings and the windows were rolled down.

Sanchez opened the door to the back seat. Another man with the light blue-and-grey shirt and dark pants of the Cuban police force sat in the driver's seat.

The car was far too small for someone of Ellis's size, and he bumped his head on the door frame as he got in. He winced at the fresh jolt of pain. He lowered his head and folded himself into the car, squeezing his legs behind the front seat until they were bent almost to his chest.

Like police cars everywhere, the doors couldn't be opened from inside, but in this case it appeared that was due to rust, not protocol.

"I didn't think the Cuban police would have time on a holiday weekend to look into such a small matter as a lost wallet. That's very impressive. Thanks. Where did you find it?"

Neither man answered.

Ellis looked out the window as they drove down roads jammed with honking hansom cabs and taxis. They stopped for a red light beside a *camello*, one of the oddly shaped buses made from truck parts and salvaged buses for which Havana was famous. For a second, the large bus, crowded with hundreds of weary Cubans, blocked out the sun.

Ellis ran a hand over his scars, remembering how dark it was when Steve Sloan died in his arms.

Sanchez and Ellis walked up to the second floor of police headquarters. The building was not at all what Ellis expected. Unlike the Soviet-style government buildings he'd seen elsewhere in Havana, it resembled a turreted medieval fortress with a beautiful stone exterior.

Sanchez opened the door to a dark room. He flipped on fluorescent lights, which flickered from time to time. Ellis guessed that the power supply wasn't particularly reliable. As directed, he sat down on a hard red plastic chair with metal legs.

The room had grey walls with large cracks, but it was cool compared to the blistering heat outside. There was a mirror on the wall. Ellis assumed it was two-way glass like they had in the Rideau Regional Police interview rooms back home so that investigators could watch suspects being questioned without being seen themselves.

Sanchez closed the door. He sat across from Ellis and pulled out a small tape recorder, which he placed on the Formica table between them. He pushed the "record" button.

"We will tape this interview." He didn't ask for permission, and Ellis was surprised that a report of a stolen wallet required this much formality.

"This is an interview with Señor Michael Ellis," Sanchez said into the small microphone. "You are from Canada, correct?"

"Yes, that's right," said Ellis. "I'm from Ottawa. Ontario."

"Do you speak Spanish, Señor Ellis?"

"No. Only a few words."

"Very well. Then we will proceed in English." Sanchez spoke with a heavy Spanish accent, but his English was very good. "It is Sunday, December 25, 2006. This interview is being conducted by Detective Rodriguez Sanchez of the Major Crimes Unit, Havana Division."

Sanchez brought out a plastic evidence bag, opened it, and put the contents on the table in front of them. "Is this your wallet?"

It was soaking wet, and there were white salt stains on the brown leather, but Ellis recognized it immediately. "Thank God. Where was it?"

"We found it on a young boy earlier today." Sanchez waited for Ellis to respond.

"That little bugger," Ellis exclaimed, and laughed as he realized what happened. It wasn't the hooker after all. He felt surprisingly relieved. "He must have lifted it from my pocket. He followed my wife and me around yesterday, begging. After I gave him some money, he hugged me. He must have been a pickpocket. The cab driver warned us to watch out for them. It never occurred to me to look out for a child."

"Did you have any other contact with the boy?"

"No," Ellis said, "I didn't even notice my wallet was missing until this morning."

"Do you remember anything about him?"

Ellis thought back to how crazy the night had been. "I think he had red shorts and a bright coloured shirt. Yellow, maybe? He was with a group of boys that begged us for money in Old Havana initially, then he followed us — my wife and me — along the seawall after the others took off."

The Cuban detective waited, a slight buzz coming from the recorder. Ellis could think of nothing else to add.

"May I?" He reached for his wallet and opened it. His badge was inside, and although his passport was sopping wet, at least he had one again. He wasn't surprised to see that the money in it, the equivalent of about a hundred U.S. dollars, was gone. "That's about all I remember."

"Do you remember seeing a man on the Malecón after you met with this boy?"

"Pardon me?"

"Was there a man who spoke to you?"

"I saw a lot of men on the seawall on my way to the bar." Ellis tried to think where Sanchez was going. "There may have been someone I talked to for a moment, but I really don't remember. I got pretty drunk later on."

"Why was that?"

"My wife — well, it's a long story. She went back to Canada last night. I decided to go out for a few drinks."

"There is a man who saw you on the Malecón who says you were extremely angry after the boy ran off."

The question made Ellis uneasy. It suggested the police had investigated *him*, not the theft. "My wife had just told me she was leaving Cuba early. We had a bit of an argument. But it's not like we were yelling at each other or anything. Quite the opposite."

Their fights were too often like that, he thought. Holding back, hiding what they really wanted. Who they really were. But what could he tell her? Not the truth.

The detective's next question interrupted his thoughts. "Your wife is not in Havana any longer?"

"No. Like I told you, she left last night." Ellis tried to change the subject. "There's nothing missing from my wallet except some money. Can I have it back now?"

He reached for it again, but this time Sanchez pulled it away. "It is evidence of a crime, Señor Ellis. I told you, we found it on the boy."

"Oh, come on," said Ellis, chuckling uneasily. "That kid is what, seven, eight years old? If that's what this is about, I don't want to press charges. I'm just glad you found it. No real harm done."

Sanchez said nothing. Ellis knew the technique. Suspects were uncomfortable with silence; it tended to draw them out. He suddenly sensed that this was about something other than his wallet and felt his heart jump. *Did they know?* He had to assume they didn't. How could they? Even his own wife didn't know.

"I'm being questioned as if I've done something wrong. Was it a crime to give the boy money?" Ellis asked.

"This is Cuba, Señor Ellis. No crime exists until we have completed an initial investigation."

Ellis sat back, trying to think how to approach the ambiguities of that response. He decided to fake confidence.

"Detective Sanchez, I am a police officer with a Canadian police force. A detective just like you. If there is more to this story than what you've told me so far, maybe I can help. If not, I really do have other things I'd like to do, if you don't mind. I'm on holidays." He stood up. "I appreciate your help. But I don't want to press charges against that little boy. I would never have asked Miguel to file a police report if I'd known he was the one who took it."

"This interview will be over when I say it is. Please," Sanchez gestured, "sit down. I have complete discretion in this regard. Trust me."

Ellis sank back onto the chair. He was starting to feel anger and fear on top of confusion.

"You became quite drunk last night at a bar, Señor Ellis?" Sanchez continued.

"Yes, I told you that already."

"And you say the boy took your wallet from you earlier in the day?"

"I'm guessing that's what happened, yes."

"Then how did you pay for your drinks?" Sanchez asked.

He hadn't thought about that, but Sanchez was right. "Then I must have lost my wallet afterwards. Or left it somewhere. Maybe even at the bar."

"And the wallet just happened to end up on the boy?"

"Apparently, if he had it. But what difference does it make?" asked Ellis. "I've already said I don't want to press charges either way."

But even as he said it, he began to worry. If the boy didn't take his wallet that afternoon, how did he get it? And how did Ellis pay for his drinks?

For a moment, Ellis wondered if the Cubans had found his police service records, but pushed that notion aside. No, he was in trouble for something that happened here, not in Ottawa. But he didn't know what, so he had to be careful.

Sanchez leaned over, then slapped a Polaroid photograph of a young boy on the table. "The boy, Señor Ellis. The boy you gave the money to. His name was Arturo Montenegro. He was not quite nine years old." Sanchez leaned back in his seat, watching for Ellis's reaction.

Small boy, round face. "Yes. That looks like him. Is that it? I broke the law by giving him money? I'll pay the fine then. Trust me, I had no idea you people took this kind of thing so seriously."

Detective Sanchez gave Ellis a look that merged disgust with surprise. "The rape and murder of a child, Señor Ellis, is taken very seriously in Cuba. We punish it by firing squad."

SIXTEEN

Inspector Ramirez had watched the Canadian closely from his side-view mirror as he drove to the police station. His car had no rear-view mirror, and it was impossible to find a replacement for a Chinese car in Havana these days.

He looked for signs of guilt in the man's demeanour, but all he saw was a typically nervous, if uncomfortably seated, tourist. The Canadian seemed no more anxious than any other foreigner in Cuban police custody would be, which meant far from relaxed. Still, Ramirez observed nothing unusual except the crooked scar that ran from the suspect's forehead down to his nose, then twisted at his upper lip, splitting his face unevenly in two.

Sanchez and Ramirez had agreed they would not tell the suspect anything at first. Ellis had no way of knowing the boy's body had been recovered. They would not arrest him, or even let him know he was a suspect. Instead, Sanchez would interview him about his wallet and see what information he volunteered while Ramirez watched from the observation room and waited for Apiro to come down with his preliminary results. Semen, hair, blood: once he knew if they had anything from the items seized at the hotel room, Ramirez would take over the interrogation.

Ramirez hoped Apiro could get laboratory results back to him quickly. He felt his adrenalin pumping, excited to have a suspect already in custody.

Questioning, cross-examining, trapping suspects in their own words: these were his greatest strengths. Like having a strong fish on the line, the pleasure came from playing it out, wearing it down. It was the part of the job he most enjoyed.

This was Ramirez's first case in years involving a child's death, and it was important that the investigation of something so serious be done properly. That he keep thoughts of Edel out of his mind.

Ramirez wondered what kind of animal would rape a boy for his own sexual pleasure, what kind of monster would murder a small child.

The Russian author Leo Tolstoy had a club when he was a boy, Ramirez recalled. Tolstoy's friends could only belong if they could stand in a corner for ten minutes and *not* think of a white bear. Edel was the white bear in the corner. He would have to try not to think about Edel during the interrogation and stay focused on the suspect's responses.

So far, from what Ramirez could see through the two-way mirror, Sanchez had used standard interview techniques. He tried to frighten the Canadian, cajole him, impress him into confessing. Nothing much, except an inconsistency as to when the suspect lost his wallet.

The door creaked open and Hector Apiro entered. The small pathologist was fair-minded and very good at what he did, despite his obvious deficiency. Apiro took a moment to explain his preliminary findings.

"I should have a written report for you in a few hours. But there were some stains on the sheets we seized from Room 612.

Seminal fluid. I examined them under the microscope against the samples taken from the boy's rectum. Both contained motile sperm. We also tested all the underwear in the room. Not the ones he is wearing, of course, he still has those on," the small man joked. "Or at least I hope he does. If not, he will stick to the seat of that plastic chair very soon."

Ramirez smiled. Black humour kept them both sane.

"We found one pair of briefs in the chest of drawers with microscopic amounts of blood that match the boy's blood type," Apiro continued. "The seminal fluid in all the samples appears to be from the same man. Type A blood. I'll do DNA testing to make sure. Of course, I have no way of confirming that the seminal fluid came from *this* man."

"It's his bed; no one else had access to it. It has to be his. That's more than enough," said Ramirez. Sufficient evidence of a crime was all he needed for an arrest. He was pleased he could meet the legal test so quickly. "Anything else, Hector?"

"I found Rohypnol in the child's blood."

"The date-rape drug?"

"Yes," Apiro said. "A powerful tranquillizer that stupefies its victims. Banned in most countries these days. It is hard to find in Cuba, or elsewhere, for that matter. Once it was discontinued in 1986, supplies quickly vanished. But there is still some around, used in veterinary clinics to anaesthetize animals for surgery. Because of this, it should be relatively easy to trace. That is good for you, yes?"

"It certainly helps. I'll get Sanchez to look into it. When was the boy drugged? Can you tell?"

"Assuming he ingested the contents of that one capsule only, early evening sometime. Maybe three or four hours before he died. That's a reasonable assumption, Ricardo. Given his weight, two capsules would have killed him. Rohypnol has a relatively long half-life. I can calculate back from the quantity in the boy's system at the time his body stopped metabolizing the drug — that is, when he died — and come up with a range. But I can't be certain of my results until I sit down with a working calculator. Mine has run out of batteries."

Ramirez shook his head. He could still feel frustrated, even after all these years, at the impediments to a proper investigation. "I'll tell Sanchez to get you some from the exhibit room. So what do you think, Hector? Is he is guilty?"

"Ah, Ricardo, I am merely a scientist. I can only tell you what I have found. But it would be helpful if you could get a blood sample from your suspect so that I could check his DNA against our samples. Even better if you could somehow obtain semen." Apiro laughed. "See if you can get him to spend a few minutes alone with a glossy magazine with big-breasted women and a plastic bag. Although that might be difficult; I have not personally seen such a magazine in Cuba in twenty years."

"Nor I, my friend," Ramirez chuckled, then stated more soberly: "But it is not women that interest him. And we should probably not joke about such things."

"We must, Ricardo. Or we shall lose our minds."

Apiro was right. When they stopped being able to joke about their work, they would no longer be able to do it. They would lack the emotional distance required to conduct an investigation objectively. "Have you determined the exact cause of death?"

"I would rather wait until the autopsy. Are you are still coming?" Apiro looked at his watch. "It's eleven-thirty now. Say two-thirty?"

"I'll be there."

"Well, I should get back to the lab. I will see you later." The doctor peered through the glass. "Interesting scar. I wonder how he got it."

Ramirez was pleased with Apiro's update. Everything was on schedule, ahead of it even. If all went well, he might yet spend some time with his family before Christmas Day was over. Kiss his wife, play with his children, and put the tragic death of this little boy aside for a few hours. And maybe even enjoy some leftover chicken.

He resumed watching Sanchez question the Canadian through the two-way glass while he decided how best to use Apiro's findings.

Ramirez had trained Sanchez himself. He expected that Sanchez would take over his job one day. Likely sooner than Sanchez expected.

Before he joined the Major Crimes Unit, Sanchez spent several years on Patrol, then five years at the Havana International Airport with the Customs section. Ramirez discovered him there and arranged for his transfer. This was another of Ramirez's talents: scavenging not just the supplies his unit needed, but the personnel.

A useful interrogation so far, if not a terribly skilled one. Sanchez needed to learn to be less aggressive, less predictable. Even so, the back and forth of their dialogue was interesting. Not so much for what the suspect said, but how he said it. Watching his body language, Ramirez was sure he was lying. Not that it mattered. Ramirez had enough evidence to arrest him already.

Still, given the political aspects of a case such as this, which involved a foreigner from a friendly country — and a police officer at that — it was always better to have more evidence than needed. Ramirez planned to listen to the entire recorded interview later on, but he was ready to question the man himself and form his own impressions.

He stepped into the bathroom down the hall to change out of his uniform and into his suit and tie. It was time to start the clock.

SEVENTEEN

Mike Ellis looked frantically around the interrogation room, nearly paralyzed with disbelief. The small muscle in his chest began to corkscrew. He took a few deep breaths and tried to relax the tightness above his heart. The boy was *dead*?

"Beaten, raped, and murdered," said Detective Sanchez. "Were you afraid he would tell your wife about your, oh, what is the word in English," he searched for a moment, "your predilection for young children?"

Ellis thought of his missing hours the night before. In his eagerness to be helpful, he had answered questions without a lawyer, had even volunteered information. He might have dug his own grave. His heartbeat throbbed in his ears. *Anxiety.*

"What happened? How did he die?"

Sanchez ignored his questions.

"Your wallet was hidden in the boy's underwear. You were the last person seen with him. We know you gave him a great deal of money, as much as some Cubans earn in a month."

"If you are going to accuse me of a crime, I should have a lawyer," Ellis said, but he was finding it hard to form words. It was getting harder to breathe, and the room seemed much smaller than when he first sat down.

"Do you need one?"

"I've done absolutely nothing wrong here." It was an answer nuanced enough to fail a polygraph, as Ellis well knew.

"If you are innocent, you have no need of procedural protections. Which is good," Sanchez twisted his face into something approximating a smile, "because we have very few of them. You have no right to a lawyer until you are indicted. Once indicted, you can have assistance for your defence, provided you pay for it yourself." The detective paused. "Those are your rights. Now tell us why you killed the boy."

Ellis realized someone else was watching. He tried to see who was on the other side of the mirrored glass but glimpsed only shadows.

"I have no idea what happened to the boy after I saw him," he repeated, careful to speak into the tiny machine, catching his breath between each word. "But before I say anything else, I want a lawyer."

"I have already told you, Señor Ellis, you have no right to one."

Sanchez sat silently, waiting. Ellis wondered if he had taken the right tack. These people were bureaucrats. He wasn't a Cuban, he was a Canadian citizen, a foreign national. Surely they couldn't just detain him indefinitely.

So he had been seen with the boy, so what? The bartender at El Bar would remember him. The woman who had sat with him might be a regular there, someone easy to track down. She knew the bartender; she had called him by name. He reconsidered.

"Detective Sanchez, believe me, I didn't do anything to that boy. You have no reason to keep me here. Am I under arrest or not?" He tried to ignore the muscle turning in his chest, tightening its grip around his heart.

Sanchez raised his voice. "Why did you kill him? Had you already paid the boy for sex and he demanded more money? Were you afraid your wife would find out when he began to follow you around? Or maybe she knew, and that is why she decided to leave Cuba so quickly. Is that what happened?"

"I had nothing to do with this. I didn't lay a hand on that boy."

Ellis heard a rap on the glass and Sanchez looked up. A signal from someone. A summons.

Sanchez left Ellis alone in the room. Ellis wondered if he would leave Cuba alive.

EIGHTEEN

Inspector Ramirez rapped on his side of the glass. Moments later, Rodriguez Sanchez entered the anteroom.

"I'll take over now, Rodriguez. Dr. Apiro has made a strong link between the forensic evidence and the suspect," Ramirez announced. "Your question about how he paid for his drinks was particularly clever. Perhaps you can stay for a while and watch, in case you pick up something I miss?"

"Of course, Inspector. I had no plans."

As far as Ramirez knew, Sanchez had no girlfriend, no wife, and he never spoke of a family. He appeared as relieved as Ramirez that they had the killer in custody this early in their investigation.

"I may turn the tape off and on. To make him uncomfortable," said Ramirez.

Señor Ellis would wonder why Ramirez had stopped the tape, whether it meant Ramirez planned to beat him up. Insecurity was good, so was confusion. They permitted Ramirez to build a rapport with the suspect, to offer him assurances, comfort. Physical force was no substitute for a relationship. But he would be a challenge, this one. A trained policeman would be familiar with his tricks, and the Canadian had a face that was hard to read.

"I'll run a second tape recorder on this side."

"Good."

The anteroom had been designed so that conversations in the interrogation room could be easily taped, and the small recorders, although Chinese, had an incredible range.

Ramirez walked the short distance to the interrogation room and entered. The heavy metal door clanged shut.

"Detective Sanchez," Ramirez said to the mirrored glass. "Can you get Señor Ellis a nice strong Cuban coffee? And one for me? Señor Ellis, we have no cream. Or milk. Rationing, I'm afraid, is a fact of life in Cuba. But we always have sugar. Would you like some in your coffee?"

Michael Ellis shook his head.

Ramirez swung the empty chair in the room around and sat down casually, informally. He spoke to Ellis courteously, like someone who could do business with him.

"Forgive me, Señor Ellis. Let me introduce myself. My name is Inspector Ricardo Ramirez. I am in charge of the Havana Major Crimes Unit. I know you are an off-duty police officer on vacation. I am sure you agree that a child's death is a serious matter? I hope you don't mind giving us a few hours of your time to help us determine the child's whereabouts yesterday."

"I've been here all afternoon and I've told your partner everything I know, Inspector. I only saw the boy briefly. He was begging. I gave him some money. That was it."

The dead man leaned against the wall in the corner, his arms folded. He watched the back and forth of their conversation, his head turning from side to side as if observing a Chinese table tennis match. Ramirez sensed he was being evaluated. He tried not to look at his hallucination.

Sanchez re-entered the room and put two cracked mugs of

coffee on the table, one in front of Ramirez, the other in front of Ellis. Ellis's lacked a handle.

Ramirez reached into his side pocket and pulled out a small bottle of *añejo*. The rum helped calm the tremors in his fingers. He turned off the tape recorder. Sanchez left, pulling the door closed.

"It is excellent, this rum," Ramirez said. "Detective Sanchez and I seized it from an illegal exporter last year. We could have just thrown it away when it was no longer useful as evidence, but that would have been a tragic waste. Most Cubans cannot afford to buy rum as old as this, only tourists. It is a matter of great regret to us — the cost of rum, that is — not our inability to purchase tourists. Are you sure you would not like a taste? As a professional courtesy?"

"No thanks."

Ramirez poured some *añejo* into his own coffee. A few sips and the trembling in his fingers disappeared. He curved his lips at the rare pleasure of rum so aged it tasted like syrup. He put the mug down. The suspect's remained untouched.

"As you know, as a fellow policeman, when one deals with witnesses, there are often small details that one thinks unimportant, only to find out that they are very important. Yes?"

This was how police work went, building details and pursuing leads in the most logical direction. The direction changed with the information one gathered. One investigation could easily turn into something very different. Ellis nodded.

"Perhaps you can indulge me then. You told my colleague that you were very drunk last night."

"Yes," Ellis said. "That's not a crime here, is it?"

"Not for tourists, Senior Ellis, not at all. Or we would have thousands of foreigners in our already overcrowded jails." Ramirez paused, took another sip. "Ah ... nothing tastes as good as Cuban coffee. Did you go to any of our coffee plantations on your tours?"

Ellis shook his head. "My wife didn't like to leave the hotel. We went to a rum factory, that's about it."

"Too bad," Ramirez sympathized. "The tours are something we do rather well. That, I think, and cigars."

Ramirez pulled a cigar from his inside pocket and offered it to Ellis, but the Canadian declined. The dead man looked at Ellis sadly, a foreigner who appreciated neither new cigars nor old rum.

"We have just received a laboratory report concerning the blood tests Dr. Apiro, our pathologist, conducted on the boy's body. There was Rohypnol in his blood."

"Rohypnol? You mean the date-rape drug?"

"Technically, a medication. Like others, not easily obtained here."

The Canadian's brow rippled. It seemed to be the only part of his face that moved naturally.

"Just a moment … you're saying that boy was *drugged*? He looked fine when I saw him. He was running around like a rabbit."

"That is what others have said," Ramirez acknowledged. "Shall we carry on from where Detective Sanchez left off, then? May I ask where you were yesterday afternoon and evening? The tape recorder, I should explain, is standard procedure here in Cuba. We often keep a record of our dealings, because foreigners so often falsely allege that we demand bribes."

All lies. Bribery was endemic. And tape recordings were used only in court proceedings involving serious felonies. Like murder.

"I was with my wife until around dinnertime. That's when she left to take a flight home. After that, I was in a bar in Old Havana until quite late. I've told your colleague that already. The bartender can confirm I was there." Ellis stopped for a moment. "His name,

I think, was Fidel. Yes, that was it. There was a woman who sat next to me. I bought her a few drinks. I don't know her name."

Good, thought Ramirez. Ellis was volunteering information. It meant he was dropping his guard. "What time did you leave the bar?"

"I can't remember; I drank at least two bottles of rum last night."

"What then? Where did you go?"

"After that," Ellis swallowed, and Ramirez noted the small shift in his demeanour, "after that, I went back to my hotel room. The doorman, Miguel, should know what time I came back. I'm pretty sure he was there, he usually is. I got up quite early. I went for a run around five-thirty, six."

I didn't ask him when he woke up or what he did this morning, thought Ramirez. He's overcompensating. Either lying about something, or leaving out something important. "Did anyone see you on your run?"

"I doubt it. I used the back stairs to go out. But I noticed there were police cars on the Malecón when I jogged by, maybe twenty minutes later. It looked like a crime scene. Is that where the boy's body was found?"

Ramirez took out the cigar again, tapped it. He bit off a piece of the end and lit a wooden match. He drew on the cigar a few times as the embers turned red. Fragrant smoke circled above his head. He didn't respond to the question, but neither would Ellis in the same circumstances. It was common for perpetrators to return to the scene of their crimes.

Enough of the niceties. "Señor Ellis, when we searched your room, we found an empty Rohypnol capsule on the floor. Can you explain this?"

Ellis jumped to his feet. "And how the hell did that get there? What the hell are you people up to?"

Ramirez gave him the patient look a teacher might give an overexcited student. "Señor Ellis, please sit down." He motioned to Ellis's chair. "We are interested in finding a killer, not inventing one. If we were to wrongly accuse you, then a very bad person will be wandering around Havana savaging our children. This would not be good for our children, or for our reputation as competent investigators."

Ellis sat back down, his hands balled into fists. "You searched my hotel room? You can't do that. You didn't have a search warrant."

"Very kind of you to explain the scope of my duties to me," said Ramirez, "but we do not need warrants in my country to search hotel rooms. Or anywhere else once we suspect a crime has been committed. The reasonable grounds I understand are necessary in your country do not apply in ours."

Ramirez leaned back in his chair. He drained his mug, put it down, and pulled a notebook and pen from his jacket pocket. He turned the tape recorder on again.

"But there is no need to be concerned. Trust me; we rely only on evidence in Cuba, not simply what people tell us. Confessions have no meaning in my country. Cuban juridical panels do not like confessions. The drafters of our Penal Code seemed to fear that they might be beaten out of people. A reflection of our history, I suppose, when force was the only tool. Now, we prefer science to witnesses, given their unreliability. That of witnesses, I mean. Not of our legislative drafters."

Ellis looked skeptical. But then, Ramirez didn't believe him either.

Ramirez began to jump around in his questioning, to see what Ellis would do. Someone who lied usually found it difficult to move between different topics quickly. When pressed, with no time to invent, they tended to repeat themselves, recycling exact words and phrases.

"Now, as I mentioned, Señor Ellis, we found an empty capsule of Rohypnol in your hotel room. Do you have any explanation for how it got there?"

"None," Ellis shook his head. "Unless it was there when we rented the room."

A poor attempt at invention. "You took the room when — a week ago?

"Yes," said Ellis. "We arrived last Saturday."

"How many times have the maids cleaned your room since then?"

Maids vacuumed every day. Besides, Ramirez was sure the wife would have noticed something on the floor. He drew on his cigar again and the smoke floated to the ceiling. The room was becoming hazy, uncomfortable. The dead man fanned his face with his hat.

Ellis didn't answer. Ramirez pressed. "I understand you were alone in your hotel room last night. Did anyone else have a key to your room?"

"No," Ellis admitted. "Just hotel staff."

"Did you let anyone in?"

Ellis hesitated for a moment, then shook his head. That short pause was enough to convince Ramirez he was lying. A slight wrinkle in what should have been the smooth fabric of an unrehearsed answer.

"I don't know anything about that capsule or how it got there," Ellis said. "Where would I have obtained a drug like that? I was with my wife the entire time."

Now Ramirez was certain. The reference to the wife was another unnecessary detail, another attempt to compensate for something untrue. "Until yesterday."

"Until she left, correct. And after that, I have fully accounted for my whereabouts."

"Except for the period in question, when the boy was killed. This is unfortunate, Señor Ellis. I am sure you appreciate the value of a good alibi." Ramirez did not yet know exactly when the boy was murdered, but Ellis didn't ask, which suggested that Ellis did.

"As a matter of interest, Inspector Ramirez, on what basis did you search my hotel room for evidence? All your so-called evidence was obtained during your search."

A mild attempt to deflect his questions. "Señor Ellis, this is Cuba," Ramirez responded firmly. "Witnesses saw you give the child money. A substantial amount of money. We also received a complaint of a man with your description approaching young boys for sex in Parque Ciudad."

"I wasn't involved in this; I keep telling you." Ellis's voice broke as his façade crumbled.

Good. Ramirez could work with stress more easily than resistance. Time to raise the stakes. He reached inside his pocket and pulled out a small flat plastic exhibit bag. He pushed it across the table. Polaroid photographs. The top one of a small boy, his eyes glassy, and a man, but not the man's face.

Ellis averted his eyes.

"We found these under your mattress, Señor Ellis. Take a look. You can see what they reveal. A boy being raped. The boy was Arturo Montenegro."

"What? Those aren't mine." Ellis slammed his hand on the table.

Ramirez pressed harder. "We also found a pair of men's briefs with blood on them in your room. The blood came from the boy."

Ramirez pulled a document from his jacket. A lab report, typed on a manual typewriter. He threw it on the table in front of Ellis, certain Ellis couldn't read Spanish.

"*What*? Then someone put them there. I didn't do anything to that boy. You have to believe me." Ellis put a hand over his chest, breathing heavily.

Ramirez needed him even more frightened, more vulnerable. He needed Ellis trapped, so he could offer him a way out.

Ramirez leaned all the way over the table. He put his face directly in front of the Canadian's. "The semen in your sheets, Señor Ellis, is the same as semen our pathologist found in the boy's rectum. I have more than enough evidence to arrest you right now. A confession is the only way to save your life."

"I didn't do this, I tell you!" Ellis pounded his fist on the table. He jumped to his feet and threw his chair aside. He kicked it across the room. The dead man leaped out of the way. Ellis bent over and took several deep breaths.

The tiny motor of the tape recorder whirred in the silence while Ellis fought to stop shaking. He slowly righted himself, then his chair. His hands were trembling.

You finally understand your life is on the line, don't you? thought Ramirez. You should have taken the *añejo* when I offered it.

"Inspector Ramirez, you have to believe me," Ellis gasped, his arms gripping the back of the plastic chair. "I've been framed."

"Framed by who, Señor Ellis? Who do you think would frame you for such a thing?" Somehow Ramirez managed to keep the sarcasm out of his voice. "Who had access to your room other than your wife? Would your own wife frame you for such a crime? Perhaps the maids?"

"I don't know. The woman from the bar. She must have come back to my room with me last night."

The dead man put his hat back on and nodded at Ramirez, as if to signal that the interview was over. Not quite, thought Ramirez. But close. He's baited. Not yet hooked.

NINETEEN

Hector Apiro and Detective Sanchez sipped coffee as they watched Inspector Ramirez. Apiro enjoyed seeing Ramirez question suspects. It was good sport, like seeing a man wrestle a swordfish into a small boat, but using words instead of brute strength.

"The woman from the bar." Inspector Ramirez sat back, smiling slightly. "*Now* you say you came back to the hotel with a woman you met in the bar. An alibi you failed to mention previously, even after I reminded you of its importance. And why did you not mention this before?"

"I told you how drunk I was. I can barely remember what happened last night," Señor Ellis said weakly. "But if there was any evidence found in my room, she must have put it there. She's the only one who could have."

"Miguel Artez, the doorman at your hotel, says you came back last night by yourself. He signed a statement to that effect."

Very good, Ricardo, thought Apiro. The doorman had no reason to lie. The *dénouement*, as the French would say. Michael Ellis sat down, hard. He looked defeated.

"Señor Ellis, I am trying to save your life," Ramirez said kindly. "Tell me who held the camera when these pictures were taken. Trust me, it is your only chance."

Ramirez waited patiently. He let his lie float in the air like the smoke above their heads. Apiro knew a confession would change nothing. In a case like this, the state would insist on execution. But Ramirez always liked to be certain.

"Where is the weapon? Did you throw it in the ocean?"

"I didn't kill anyone."

Apiro saw the small twitch, the vein that pulsed in the suspect's forehead. The Canadian was lying about something; Apiro was sure of it.

"You are a very angry man, Señor Ellis. Easily provoked. You are a violent man at times, aren't you?"

Ellis said nothing, as if he couldn't answer that question honestly. But then, Apiro thought, who could?

"I can understand how things escalated. How you didn't mean them to. You were enraged yesterday when your wife left you. Understandable. What did she say to upset you so much? Something cruel? Did she say you weren't man enough for her anymore?" Ramirez was probably inventing, but he seemed to hit some kind of nerve. Ellis flinched.

"I admit, I was upset."

Ramirez spoke to the man even more gently. "Is it not possible, then, that you took your anger out on the boy? That you saw him after your wife left, in the market, or perhaps on your way back to the hotel? Blamed him for the argument with your wife? You were very drunk. You didn't mean to strike him so hard. Not intentional at all, was it? Just a terrible accident."

Ellis said nothing. He looked like a man trying to choose the path that would decide his future. If he still had one.

"Say it," Ramirez shouted, and slapped his hand on the table. "Do not insult my intelligence, Señor Ellis. Did you see the boy later that night or not? Yes or no?"

Ellis shook his head. "No."

"Was he bleeding when you saw him earlier that day? When your wife was with you?"

With that question, Apiro realized the Canadian was trapped. If Ellis said yes, Ramirez could prove he was lying; the witnesses who saw the boy with Ellis in the afternoon had said the boy was uninjured. Yet the boy's blood was on his underwear. It got there somehow. If Ellis said no, he had to admit he was with the boy later that evening. Either way, the swordfish was now thrashing around inside the boat.

"No," said Ellis, looking wildly around the room.

"Then there's only one explanation, isn't there? You must have seen him again later that night."

"I must have," Ellis whispered, and for a moment Apiro almost felt sorry for him. "But I could have sworn I didn't." Meaning he could not swear to it anymore. Ramirez had just placed the Canadian with the boy not just in the afternoon but later that same day.

"He's very good, isn't he?" Apiro said to Sanchez.

Sanchez, who rarely showed emotion, formed the closest thing to a smile Apiro had ever seen him produce. "Inspector Ramirez? He's the best."

TWENTY

"Let me summarize what I understand," said Inspector Ramirez sympathetically. "You admit you drank a lot of *añejo* last night. You were extremely drunk. You blacked out. You remember very little. This is what you have told us so far, yes?"

"Yes," Ellis said. "Yes, I blacked out."

"Then you can't be sure you *didn't* kill him, can you?"

Ramirez took his silence as an answer.

Ellis knew that the failure to deny an accusation was as good as an admission. He just couldn't think of what else to say. The boy's blood was on his clothes and he couldn't remember, had no idea how it got there. Christ, Ellis thought, is it even remotely possible I did kill the boy? But how could I? I went right back to my hotel room after I left the bar. With the woman. Maybe.

"Are you willing to provide us with a DNA sample?"

Ellis shook his head. How could he if he might be guilty? He might as well hand the firing squad the bullets.

Ramirez glanced at his watch and stood up.

"I thought not. Señor Ellis, I am arresting you for the rape of Arturo Montenegro. You will most likely be arrested for murder once we complete our investigation. We have until two o'clock on

Wednesday to file the materials necessary to proceed by indictment. You will be kept in the holding cells here for the moment.
Our prisons are full with political dissidents so there is no room
elsewhere, although perhaps that is fortunate, given the nature
of your crimes. I want you to survive until your trial, believe it
or not. But once indicted, you will be transferred to a prison to
await your trial. Do you understand?"

Ellis's legs began to shake. He knew what happened to sex
offenders in jail, what would happen to a police officer once the
other prisoners found out he was one. It wouldn't matter to them
whether he was Canadian or not.

"You have to believe me. Someone put that evidence in my
room. If you won't let me speak to a lawyer, then please, let me
speak to someone in my embassy."

Ramirez thought for a moment, then nodded. He was careful
to speak into the small recorder. "Of course, Señor Ellis. We will
make arrangements for you to contact your embassy as soon as
possible. However, it is closed today, perhaps tomorrow as well,
because of the Christmas holidays. Is there someone else you
would like to call?"

Ellis hesitated, then he leaned forward so that he spoke directly
into the tiny tape recorder as well. He cleared his throat. "Yes. I
want to speak to Chief Miles O'Malley of the Rideau Regional
Police in Ottawa. As soon as possible."

TWENTY-ONE

Inspector Ramirez walked out of the interrogation room and entered the small room where Detective Sanchez waited.

"Dr. Apiro left," Sanchez said. "He is getting things ready for the autopsy."

"Good." Ramirez turned the tape over to Sanchez for initialling. "Have transcripts prepared, will you, Rodriguez? Both tapes, please."

Ramirez wanted to make sure the juridical panel knew the extent to which he had accommodated the prisoner's request. Señor Ellis had no rights in Cuba. Fidel Castro had never signed the Vienna Convention. If he were American instead of Canadian, Ellis might have remembered Guantánamo Bay.

"Right away. Well done, Inspector Ramirez," Sanchez said. He applauded softly. "That was as close to a confession as you can get from a man so highly trained."

The dead man sat at Ramirez's desk. He tipped the brim of his hat, evidently equally impressed.

"Thank you, Rodriguez. Personally, I keep thinking it's a stupid man who would call the police to report a wallet stolen by a boy he had just killed. Although it may have seemed like the smart thing to do," said Ramirez. "Hard for him to claim innocence otherwise. He must not have realized his wallet was missing until after he disposed of the body."

"So the boy *was* a pickpocket. After all, he kept the badge. Only a child would do that."

Any other Cuban would have kept the money and discarded everything else.

"It certainly helped us. Without the wallet, there would have been nothing to connect the foreigner to this murder."

"The anonymous complaint — don't you think that would have been enough?" asked Sanchez.

"Enough to watch him, perhaps, no more than that. We could never have conducted a search based on that information alone."

"Probably not," Sanchez admitted. But Ramirez knew Sanchez would have searched the room in a heartbeat if he had been alone.

"What about the drug capsule? Why not remove that evidence from his room?" asked Sanchez.

The dead man stood behind Sanchez. He pulled the pockets in his own pants inside out, both empty. It made Ramirez think about a dirty joke they used to tell as boys, where the punch line was an elephant. If it was a joke, his subconscious mind's attempt at humour escaped him, and if it was some sort of clue, Ramirez wasn't sure what it meant. The elephant in the room?

"An oversight, most likely. The doorman confirmed how drunk Señor Ellis was last night. Besides, the maids would have cleaned his room before lunch today. He had no reason to think we would search it. All the evidence would have been vacuumed away, his sheets and dirty clothing laundered. He probably thought the boy's body would wash out to sea and take any remaining evidence with it. But something bothers me, Rodriguez. This man could not have taken that body all the way to the Malecón without some kind of vehicle. Where did he get one?"

"There is nothing to suggest he rented a car or a truck," Sanchez conceded.

"We need to find out. I doubt he could have carried a body to the ocean, even such a small one, without drawing attention to himself. He is a foreigner and recognizable, with all those scars."

"True," Sanchez agreed. "And the Malecón is busy at night."

"There must have been a vehicle, then, a car, maybe a cart. You realize this means we can't rule out an accomplice."

Sanchez nodded slowly. "It didn't occur to me to think about how the body was moved. I thought the strength of the other evidence was enough. As always, Inspector, you are one step ahead of me. Perhaps the wife?"

"We'll see what Apiro has to say about timelines. She may have already left Cuba by then. See if Señor Ellis took a taxi that night or if either of them rented a car. Natasha can help you."

"I'll start working on it. By the way, Dr. Apiro asked where you got the lab report you showed the suspect, since his isn't finished yet."

"I used one from another case."

Ramirez thought it gave him more authority to enter an interview with an official-looking piece of paper, as if he had strong evidence already, even if the document had no relevance. He had walked into one interrogation with a recipe. He always put the purported report on the table and pointed to it as if it were important. That was usually enough to convince the unsuspecting suspect to talk, but it only worked with *turistas* who spoke no Spanish.

Ramirez explained Apiro's early findings to his young colleague, which reminded him to check his watch. Two-twenty. Just enough time to get to the morgue. "Can you arrange for the Canadian to make a long-distance call?"

Sanchez raised his eyebrows, but nodded.

Ramirez would not normally allow such access, but there was no reason to create a political controversy by denying the Canadian a call to his employer. Particularly when he worked for a police department in a country with which Cuba had good relations.

The Cuban National Revolutionary Police might need to work with the Canadian police on a future case someday. It was always best to have reciprocity, now that crime had become so global.

TWENTY-TWO

Detective Sanchez took Mike Ellis downstairs to Booking and photographed him. He told Ellis to take off all his clothes and jewellery, then handed him a pair of orange prison overalls. Ellis stripped naked, removed his watch and wedding ring, and handed them to a guard.

After Sanchez itemized and bagged Ellis's clothes, he put metal handcuffs on his wrists. The guard put thick steel manacles around his ankles and chained his feet together. All Ellis had left were his shoes; even his socks were taken away.

Ellis understood, for the first time, how the people he arrested must have felt. Shock mixed with humiliation, anger, a sense of unfairness. Guilt had nothing to do with it.

Sanchez walked him, hobbled, down the hall from the holding cells to a small room with a metal table, a phone, and one wooden chair. He told Ellis to sit down and removed the handcuffs from his right wrist so he could hold the receiver more easily.

Ellis was surprised Sanchez hadn't beaten him or anything. The police back home would have already turned the hoses on. "Washing the cells down," they would say later in response to a complaint. "Didn't realize there was someone there." Sanchez acted instead as if he felt sorry for him, which made Ellis even more afraid of what awaited.

"There will be a short delay while we find an English-speaking operator who can locate your police chief's home phone number."

Ellis prayed silently that O'Malley wasn't off vacationing somewhere exotic himself.

Sanchez dialled the operator and said the call was to be placed person-to-person, collect. He left the room and locked Ellis in.

Ellis waited on the line, fidgeting, while the Cuban operator made the necessary connections with a Canadian operator, who confirmed she had a listing for a Miles O'Malley. The phone rang at least a dozen times before Chief O'Malley finally answered. A tidal wave of relief washed through Ellis as he recognized his Irish brogue. O'Malley had a strong accent, although he had lived in Canada for more than thirty years.

The Cuban operator spoke first: "This is a collect call from Señor Michael Ellis — will you accept the charges?"

Ellis had been afraid that O'Malley might be out; now he had a momentary fragment of fear that he might not accept the charges. But of course O'Malley did. "Michael, my boy!"

"I'm sorry to have to call you at home on Christmas, Chief," Ellis said, trying to keep his voice strong, "but I'm in trouble."

"Michael, my lad, I can't hear you very well. Party going on here. Merry Christmas, son. Where are you?" Ellis could hear people laughing, glasses clinking. Christmas music played in the background. "My wife's family is over for the turkey. I thought you were on holidays somewhere with that beautiful wife of yours."

"I'm in Cuba."

"Well, that's grand, Mikey. So why are you calling me? What can I do for you?"

"Chief, I need your help. I'm at the Havana police station. In custody."

"Custody — under arrest for what? Too much to drink? Speak up, lad." Ellis pictured O'Malley pressing the phone closer to his ear, trying to catch every word over the noise in his living room.

"Be quiet, for a moment, people," the police chief called out, and the chatter subsided. "One of my men is on the phone, in a spot of trouble." He lowered his voice so that the others couldn't hear. "What's going on down there, Michael?"

"I'm under arrest for sexually assaulting a child, Chief. And maybe for murder."

A moment's silence, then O'Malley's outrage. "Murder? What the hell is going on down there? What kind of sexual assault?"

Ellis took a deep breath and described the nightmare he was trapped in. "I'm being held by the Cuban police. There was a young boy who was raped and killed last night. They said I could be charged with murder. Chief, I've been framed. I don't know by who. The police found the body this morning. I lost my wallet last night; they found it in his clothing. He was drugged with some kind of date-rape drug. They found the same drug in my hotel room along with some photographs. Child porn. I didn't put them there and they aren't mine. But it looks pretty bad."

He didn't mention the woman, not sure how O'Malley, who was happily married and thought Ellis was too, would respond.

More silence on the end of the line. Ellis imagined O'Malley's thick black eyebrows knit together, his forehead furrowed with concentration as he tried to understand what Ellis was telling him.

"Jesus Christ, Mikey. You're in a bit of a state, now, aren't you? You're in a fucking dictatorship there. Do they want money? Is that what this is all about?"

"I don't think so. But Chief, they have the death penalty here for crimes like this. They still use firing squads."

"Christ, Michael, forget a firing squad, you'll be lucky if you survive the night. A policeman in jail on a kiddy rape and murder? You didn't do it, of course." A statement.

"Of course not."

"Good. I knew you'd have nothing to do with such a thing. How can I help? What do you want us to do? Have you called the Canadian embassy yet?"

"It's closed today and probably tomorrow. The police won't let me talk to a lawyer; I was surprised they let me call you. This whole thing is insane. I don't have any idea what my rights are here."

"Then let's work on getting you a lawyer. Let me think on that for a moment." O'Malley paused. Ellis could almost hear his brain ticking over.

"Do you trust them with their investigation, Michael? Are they corrupt? Are they the ones that framed you?"

Ellis's hand shook as he held the phone. "I don't think so, but who knows? It's a damn poor country, Chief. Anything is possible. But no one's beaten me or anything, and no one has asked me for money. And they let me call you."

"Ah, Christ, Michael. Alright then. Let me make some calls. We'll get the consular services involved. To make sure that no one tortures you or anything." He laughed lightly, but Ellis knew he wasn't joking.

"I'll send someone down to keep an eye on things. I can't imagine that the Cuban government can say no to us if a departmental representative asks for copies of their reports in a capital case. We'll offer cooperation, approach things that way."

"I really appreciate it, Chief. You have no idea."

"We've helped the Cubans with some of their investigations in the past; they may need us again in the future. And they like us up here in Canada. They won't want a political situation. But we'll have to pull some strings on this. Shit, man, this is a mess you've gotten yourself into, for sure. You understand, Michael, that taking this approach has risks. If I send someone there and it turns out you've done anything wrong, you understand …"

"I didn't do it. I never laid a hand on that boy."

"I believe you. You're not that type."

"Can you get someone down here?"

"Well, it's Christmas Day, Michael, so it's going to be bloody hard to arrange things quickly. But I'll see if I can send Celia out on a flight today or tomorrow if she's willing. Her husband won't be happy about it, but she'll know where to look and she'll figure out quickly how things work there. She's the only person I can think of in the department who speaks Spanish well enough to go. And she's wicked smart."

Celia Jones was the departmental lawyer. She had been a police negotiator with the Royal Canadian Mounted Police for several years before she quit and went to law school. She had worked as a prosecutor for a while, too, before joining the Rideau Police. Ellis didn't know she spoke Spanish.

"Thanks again, Chief." He realized he had been holding his breath, felt his lungs finally release as the muscle in his chest uncoiled.

"You watch your back there, Michael. I'm not joking. And don't worry. We'll get to the bottom of this, I promise you. What hotel are you staying at? Or rather, where were you staying before all this happened?"

Ellis gave him the information.

"I'll tell her to register at the same hotel, see what she can find out, try to get you released. But I don't want any controversy, any allegations of police interference, understand? There's to be no international scandal. And Michael, if you're guilty of anything, I'll tell her to bring the house down on you. You understand me?"

"I swear I didn't do this."

"I'm counting on that, my lad," O'Malley said.

"Tell her to talk to Miguel Artez if she needs anything when she arrives," Ellis suggested. "He's the doorman."

"You trust him?"

"I think so. I don't know anyone else here."

"And what about that wife of yours — she must be frantic with worry."

"She left yesterday, Chief. She doesn't know anything about this."

"Well, thank Christ for that, then. Do you want me to call her, tell her what's happened?"

"No," Ellis said. "I want her left out of it."

"Alright then, man, we'll leave that for now. Chin up. I'm on it. Try to stay alive overnight, will you? Keep your back to the wall."

The phone clicked a second after O'Malley hung up. Oh, Christ, Ellis thought. Someone was listening.

TWENTY-THREE

It was just after two-thirty. The boy's small body was stretched out on the metal gurney. An overhead light swivelled to wherever Apiro needed it. It had a longer than usual gooseneck to compensate for his shorter reach. Opera music played quietly in the background. Apiro loved the opera, a passion he and Ramirez shared. It formed the original basis of their friendship, since Ramirez had proven hopeless at chess.

Apiro had decided to become a plastic surgeon when he was still a child, growing up, to the extent he grew at all, in an orphanage in Santa Clara. He firmly believed his parents had placed him there because of his freakish appearance. He was determined to do what he could to help others correct their physical defects, since there was nothing he could do for his own.

The Cuban government provided free university education to all of its citizens. Apiro attended the University of Havana, where he graduated from medical school at the top of his class, then took post-graduate studies in cosmetic and reconstructive surgery in Moscow.

In Russia, Apiro felt almost at home. "Tsar Peter the Great

collected dwarves," he explained to Ramirez when he returned to Havana. "Imagine, a city with enough of us to have a collection." In Havana, he knew of no others.

But Russian literature, Apiro discovered, was full of dwarves. His books became a respite, a home he could visit when loneliness gripped him, a place where others like him had been betrayed, hunted, mocked, for no fault of their own.

"Just think of Pushkin," he said to Ramirez during an autopsy. "His Ruslan *ripped* the beard from a dwarf to impress Ludmila. Such courage, the big bully. Ouch, that must have hurt! Or Sinyavsky's Tsores, a dwarf abandoned not just by his mother, but by his dog. Now that, my friend, is an ugly dwarf."

Apiro said that while he studied in Moscow, Chernobyl had increased his kind as well. An unintended bomb, this time an implosion. "Democracies are not the only political systems with the power to destroy a country," he said to Ramirez sadly, shaking his large head.

Eventually, Apiro was required to come back to Cuba to put his extensive training to work helping Castro develop a tourist industry in plastic surgery. He brought with him an appreciation for Russian literature, a stoicism about his circumstances, and a facility for circumventing bureaucracy that had proven useful in navigating their investigations.

When Apiro was called to the seawall that morning and saw a boy whose face was so familiar, his heart had almost stopped. Once he got over his shock, he looked at the boy more closely. Not the same boy I operated on, he thought, exhaling slowly. All that happened years ago. Before this child was even born.

Inspector Ramirez hung up his jacket and put on the white lab coat Hector Apiro required observers to wear in his workspace, a precaution against cross-contamination.

There was no sign of the dead man, but Ramirez had discovered that his hallucinations tended to avoid Apiro and the morgue the way other Cubans avoided bureaucrats.

Apiro stood on the bottom rung of his stepladder at the end of the gurney. He cut a fine line around the boy's skull with a bone saw and gingerly removed the brain. He held it in his gloved hands. It glistened in the flickering fluorescent lights as Apiro turned it slowly, delicately, the way a connoisseur might examine a fine glass of claret.

Ramirez was usually uncomfortable when Apiro examined a body, organs particularly, and the smell of decaying flesh was always unpleasant. But he admired the way the doctor knew exactly what he was doing, his uncanny ability to extract secrets from the dead.

Ramirez sometimes wondered if Apiro was one of Eshu's manifestations. Eshu was the god responsible for communications between living and dead. He was said to have a hundred personas. Like Apiro, he was very small and dark, with black hair, although Apiro's was greying. But Eshu carried a staff, not a scalpel. And Apiro was never cruel.

Apiro turned to speak to Ramirez as if they were of equal height, although he was not much larger than the child on the gurney. "There is some swelling on the contrecoup side of the brain, the opposite side from the trauma, where the brain banged against the skull following impact."

"Is that how he died?"

"Patience, Ricardo. Patience. The skull was fractured in several places: a large hematoma marks the spot of the fatal wound. The boy was either struck or fell. Did he fall from a building? Something one or two storeys high?"

Ramirez checked his notebook. "His body was found in the Caleta de San Lázaro, on the same side of the seaway where you

first saw it. Slightly east of Principe. As you know, all the buildings are across the street. So I doubt it."

"He was on the sidewalk when I arrived this morning," said
Apiro. "Soaking wet. I assumed he had been found in the ocean.
No rooftop swimming pools for Cuban boys in Havana, after all.
But was he on the rocks or in the water?"

"Señor Rivero saw the body floating and pulled it up the
rocks. Another man helped him."

"Hmmm." Apiro's deft hands probed the glossy white surface
of the brain. He climbed down from his stepladder and took the
brain to a scale on a filing cabinet on the other side of the room.
After he weighed it, he removed his gloves to make a few notes
and then walked back to the body.

He moved the ladder then clambered up on it again so that
his short body rested against the gurney. He pulled his gloves
back on, and prodded the boy's body in different places. He
turned it towards him and scrutinized the child's hips, his back,
his buttocks, and the palms of his hands. A few minutes passed
as the doctor continued his slow examination, then he offered up
his opinion.

"The seawall is only a metre or two above the rocks all along
the Malecón. It is possible that the boy died of a fall there, but
unlikely. The degree of force — the shattering of the skull — is
greater than one would expect to find. Also, the injury is to the
left side of the skull. Most people fall forward or backward, but
rarely sideways. When they fall, they usually put their arms out
in front of them to break the fall or land on their knees. The
rocks on the shore are sharp, but this child has no abrasions on
his hands or his knees, just scrapes on his side from being hauled
up the rocks."

"A blow, then?"

"Perhaps." Apiro pointed with his gloved index finger to the skull. "There is a coup injury on the left side of the brain. The fracture is discrete. Not caused by a flat surface but by something narrow, with a round circumference. About the width of a piece of rebar. But the contrecoup injury is there as well as the coup injury. You understand what that means?"

Ramirez nodded. A contrecoup injury resulted from the brain bouncing against the opposite side of the skull after an impact. A coup injury was consistent with blunt force; a contrecoup with a fall.

"Could he have been struck with something on the head and fallen afterwards, accounting for both injuries?"

"Possibly," Apiro acknowledged. "Either someone hit the boy on the side of his head and he fell, or he fell sideways from a fairly good height against such an object, and then hit the ground. Was there a metal post anywhere near the body? Something along the wall or nearby, perhaps submerged in the water?"

"No," Ramirez said. "I saw nothing like that."

"I think based on what I've seen so far that you can be sure he was killed elsewhere and that his body was taken to the Malecón. Whether that points to someone's guilt, I leave to you to determine, but usually when there is an accident, people call for an ambulance or the police rather than moving the body and tossing it in the ocean."

"The body was moved?"

"He was dead in the water." Apiro laughed the staccato laugh that increased in frequency, as did his little puns and jokes, the worse the facts of the case. The cackle of a night gull. "Yes, he was already dead. He wasn't moved for a few hours. There is some pooling of blood, see here?"

Apiro pushed the boy's body over. He again showed Ramirez the wide bluish-purple areas on the boy's back that Ramirez had mistaken earlier for bruising.

"Tissues begin to leak fluid soon after death, Ricardo. If a body is lying flat, the fluid collects, thanks to gravity. These marks indicate the body was left in one position on a hard surface for a few hours."

"Will there be any blood at the place where he was actually killed? What are we looking for?"

"Very little. The skull is an amazing thing. Nature designed it to protect the brain. Unless there is a crushing injury — like a compound fracture, for example where a head is squashed by a truck — there often isn't any blood at all. This is a depressed skull fracture. The cranial bone is depressed towards the brain, but there's no wound to the skin. The bleeding was all inside the boy's skull. His left eardrum shattered on impact, but that would leave only small drops of blood, if anything at all."

"If he was killed somewhere else," Ramirez mused, "how did the Rohypnol capsule end up in Señor Ellis's hotel room? I suppose he could have picked it up and put it in his pocket so that he wouldn't leave it behind at the crime scene. Maybe it fell out when he was getting undressed. But I'm still trying to figure out how he smuggled the boy into his room."

"I can't answer that question," Apiro said. "But you're right. The doormen would never let a boy like this, a boy who begged, into that hotel. Not if they saw him, anyway. They normally won't let such a boy even stand near a tourist hotel without threatening to call the police. And then there is the matter of getting the body from the hotel to the Malecón. Based on the forensic evidence, it looks like the boy was raped in the hotel room but died somewhere else and was put in the water much later."

"Cause of death, Hector?"

"Probably a blow to the head with a narrow pipe, post, or club. An inch to an inch and a half in diameter. Perhaps it even was a piece of rebar."

"Did he die instantly?" asked Ramirez. "And how do you know he wasn't alive when he was thrown in the water?"

"Ah, no signs of drowning, look." Apiro climbed on the table, nearly straddling the body. He pushed hard on the boy's chest. Nothing happened.

"You see? In a drowning victim, there is always some foam left in the lungs. The presence of foam doesn't prove drowning; it can be present after electrocution and other types of heart failure as well. The difference is that, in a drowning, if you remove all the foam and then compress the chest, there is always a bit more that comes out. So no drowning. And yes, to answer your other question, the boy died within seconds of his head injury. There was very little swelling in the brain."

The doctor climbed down his stepladder and sat on a nearby stool. He knew Ramirez preferred to sit when he was standing, and appreciated Ramirez's courtesy. But when they both sat, they had an equality that nature denied them.

"Thank God for that, at least," Ramirez remarked. "That he died quickly. How long was the body in the ocean?"

"From the amount of rigour, perhaps five or six hours. No more. That should help you with your timeline."

"Still under the influence of that drug when he died?"

"Yes and no. Rohypnol is relatively short-lived in its acute effects, but as I mentioned, its residual effects linger. For the first four to six hours, the boy would have been almost comatose. After that, awake but clumsy. Later on, still dizzy, but conscious and alert. I would guess he was drugged around 7 P.M. or thereabouts. I think he died sometime between 10 P.M. and midnight on Christmas Eve."

"You found batteries for your calculator?"

"Yes," Apiro smiled. "Sanchez took some from a camera in the exhibit room for me. There was no film for it anyway." Apiro had long ago accepted thievery as a necessary part of his job. "Metabolism stops at the time of death, Ricardo, so the levels of the drug remain static. If he was alive any later than that, the amount of Rohypnol in his blood would have been lower. So I think he probably died towards the end of that two-hour range, closer to midnight. But that's just a guess. I could be off by an hour or more either way."

"Anything else?"

The doctor dipped his head. "Yes. As you saw, the boy's anus had fresh abrasions. But there is also a laceration that has healed. It extends beyond the anal mucosa into the perianal skin. A second injury, perhaps a week old. We find an injury that serious in less than ten percent of the children with positive findings of sexual abuse. The overwhelming majority of those, I am sorry to say, are girls. I have only ever seen one fissure like it on a boy in my career. Perhaps because boys are more likely to fight back."

A terribly sad reality, thought Ramirez. He intended to teach Estella to kick, to gouge, to scream. But also to run.

"What does that mean, Hector? That the boy was raped before?"

"At least once. With sufficient force to tear his rectum. With the first injury, he would have bled immediately and every time he had a bowel movement for several days. That is why it can take so long for such injuries to heal."

"Señor Ellis and his wife arrived in Cuba a week ago. He could have raped the boy before, too. We'll have to question the boy's family and the children he played with to see if any of them noticed Señor Ellis with the child. When will you have a written report for me?"

"I still have combings, oral and perianal swabs, and dry mounts that I need to test. And I want to run DNA tests on the samples we have collected. We are low on the chemicals we need;

I am trying to locate more. But as I said, I'm quite sure that the semen samples in the exhibits all came from the same person. That is about all I can tell you for now."

"That's more than enough for my purposes. This is a bad one, Hector. Vicious." Ramirez shook his head. "That could be my son on your table."

"Yes, it is a very bad one, my friend." Apiro looked at Ramirez. "May I give you some advice?"

"Of course."

"I suspect other boys may have been sexually abused by the same man as well. The men who do such things are pedophiles. They do not prey on just one child. Perhaps that is where you might wish to continue your investigation."

"I'll speak to Ronita and get her advice. But we will have to be discreet," Ramirez said, a sombre expression on his face. If he wasn't careful, there could be serious political repercussions. A pedophile ring in Havana wasn't something the Minister of the Interior would want to hear about. It would not be good for tourism, at least not the kind Castro still hoped to attract.

The rest of the autopsy would be routine, Apiro assured Ramirez. Mostly weighing organs and labelling exhibits. There was no need for him to stay.

That was good. Ramirez had other things to do to meet his filing deadline. As well as the unpleasant task of notifying the Montenegro family of the death of their young son.

TWENTY-FOUR

A line of laundry swayed on a string hung between a post shoring up the balcony and a curved balustrade. Most of the bright-coloured clothing belonged to children. Small socks and shorts stirred like flower petals. Down the street, a woman washed her clothes in a bucket and wrung them out before hanging them carefully on a similar stretch of line.

The Montenegros lived on a numbered *calle* in the heart of the slums, in one of the more decrepit of the three-storey buildings that lined the streets. Ramirez stood on the sidewalk and looked up at the decaying exterior. Different colours of paint had been stripped away by the corrosive effects of the salt air, leaving the walls a mixture of peeling layers of turquoise, yellow, and pink, much like a child's gumball. Entire walls had collapsed on the third floor, which looked like it was held up by little more than hope.

The Americans had developed a bomb that killed people but left buildings standing. Havana must have been the test ground for the failed prototype, thought Ramirez. The Cuban people are still standing, but all our buildings are falling down.

The Montenegros' flat was on the second floor. Ramirez

climbed the single flight of rickety stairs and knocked on their apartment door. The dead man walked close behind.

A woman opened the door with an expectant look that quickly turned to fear. Ramirez could tell she knew instantly who he was. Nonetheless, he showed the trembling woman his badge.

"May I come in?"

She opened the door slowly. The dead man wiped his feet on the floor as if to enter, but Ramirez gave him a look. He walked back down the stairs, dejected.

The apartment Ramirez entered had two rooms. It was very clean, furnished with a bed that doubled as a couch, a table, and some wooden chairs. Sheets were nailed across the windows in place of curtains. There was an icebox, which Ramirez was sure contained neither ice nor food.

"Are you Señora Montenegro?"

"Yes?"

"May I ask if Señor Montenegro is at home?"

"My husband died several years ago. You are here about my son." She began to cry, anticipating the truth. Two small girls pressed against her skirt as Ramirez expressed his deepest sympathies for her loss. "Is he dead, my Arturo?" she demanded, wringing her hands.

"I'm sorry. He was found in the waters off the Malecón by a fisherman early this morning."

As he watched tears stream down her face, Ramirez decided to let her think the boy had drowned. He could explain the misunderstanding later. On this Christmas Day, he did not have the heart to tell her how coldly her son was murdered.

"When did you last see him, Señora?"

"Noon yesterday. Christmas Eve. He didn't come home last night."

"What was he wearing?"

"A yellow shirt and red shorts with white diamonds. An old pair of blue running shoes with white soles. Size two. A little big for him. Is there any chance you have the wrong boy? Perhaps Arturo is staying with a friend. Is it possible you have the wrong child?" She grabbed Ramirez by the shoulders and shook him, weeping. "You must have the wrong boy."

"I am very sorry, Señora, but the boy we found was wearing red shorts with a white diamond pattern."

No question now as to whose son it was. She pulled her hands away, moaning. She rocked softly back and forth, her arms wrapped in front of her, hugging her shoulders.

"Dear God," she sobbed. "When he didn't come home, I worried about him all night."

"I am sorry, Señora Montenegro, but you will need to identify the body later today. I will send a patrol car for you." Ramirez was sure she had no bus fare.

Señora Montenegro dropped to her knees on the floor, keening in her grief. The younger girl, the toddler, began wailing too. The other stood with her thumb in her mouth. She watched Ramirez quietly. He wondered how much they understood.

Ramirez took the woman's hands and lifted her up. He pulled a chair over with his foot. She collapsed into it. He leaned over her, willing her to concentrate. "Do you have a photograph of your son we can use? I promise to return it."

She pulled a hand away and pointed to a framed photograph of a smiling, dimpled boy on the wall. When Ramirez brought it over, she took it from him and ran her fingers over the boy's face, kissed the glass, then slid it gently into his hand. She pointed to another picture, an older version of the same boy. A teenager. Perhaps fourteen or fifteen.

"Arturo's brother. Dead too. He ran away from a country boarding school in the Viñales mountains in 1998, when I was pregnant with Arturo. The priests told us he fell down the mountainside trying to get home. They never found his body. It was too far for him to walk and the roads are so steep. Then my husband drowned. A fisherman. Arturo was the head of our household. How will we survive now without him? Why?" she pleaded. "Why me? Tell me. Why is God punishing me?"

But Ramirez had no answer.

Ramirez showed Señora Montenegro the photocopy of Michael Ellis's passport and asked if she had ever seen the man in the photograph with her son. She shook her head, distracted. She was far too distressed to be questioned further.

The difficult questions could wait. There were no newspapers in Havana to spread any other information; no way for this woman to find out that her son was murdered.

Ramirez would ask her later about the child's sexual history and see if she would agree to allow the other children in her home to be questioned. They were very young and might not be able to provide much information. For now, given the strength of the evidence, there was no urgency. He gave the woman his card. There was no point asking her to call him; she had no phone and likely no access to one. She could identify the child's body later in the day. But not too late, thought Ramirez, recalling Apiro's refrigeration issues.

"I will come back to see you in a few days. It would be very helpful, Señora, if you could think about Arturo's activities over the past few weeks. Please, try to remember if he mentioned any men he met, anything at all."

"Why do you want to know?"

"These are the usual questions we ask, in a death like this," Ramirez lied. "Meanwhile, I will send a counsellor to help meet your needs."

"I need my son." Tears spilled down her cheeks. "Will a counsellor bring him back? I don't think so. Will a counsellor put food on our table?"

"No," Ramirez conceded. These things were beyond a counsellor's skills. "But she may be able to help you with the arrangements." There was, after all, a funeral to plan. "Again, Señora Montenegro, I am so terribly sorry for your loss. My son is almost the same age as Arturo. I cannot begin to imagine your pain."

The two small girls watched him leave, their big brown eyes wide. The oldest, perhaps three, had stopped crying, but now both girls sniffled, frightened by their mother's anguish. Their lives, Ramirez knew, would never be the same.

Ramirez frowned at the way a smiling boy's life had been snuffed out by a sexual predator. No one should spend their Christmas Day involved in such matters. He wanted to go home and keep his children close, keep the ugliness of the world away from them for as long as he could.

The poor, devastated woman he left weeping in her doorway had lost so much already. Ramirez would make some calls, see what he could do to help. This was Cuba, after all. People had to support each other. There was no other way to survive.

Ramirez walked back down the stairs. He got into the small blue car and started the ignition. The dead man climbed into the back.

Ramirez drove slowly back to the police station. When he looked in the side mirror, he saw the dead man examining the framed photograph he had placed on the back seat, touching the boy's face. The man turned his hat upside down in his lap, like a collection plate.

I have no idea what my brain is trying to tell me, thought Ramirez. For the thousandth time, he wished he had inherited his grandmother's second sight instead of the illness that killed her.

As Ramirez drove by the Ferris wheel, the dead man made a large circle in the air with his index finger. Ramirez saw the big wheel spinning slowly, heard the screams of children at the top. But they were just the usual cries of excitement, nothing serious.

The dead man looked out the car window, his brown eyes sad.

TWENTY-FIVE

The phone rang just as Celia Jones sat down with a glass of eggnog. She was enjoying a lazy Christmas Day, hanging around the house in her bathrobe, reading a book. Her husband, Alex, was doing the *New York Times* crossword at the kitchen table, the only person she knew who was brave enough to do it in ink. They tended to play the holidays down since it was just the two of them, their days off a chance to spend time comfortably alone together. Neither had family in Ottawa. Hers lived far north in Manomin Bay. Alex's relatives were still trapped in Cuba.

"I'll get it," she said, and wandered over to the phone. Miles O'Malley's voice surprised her on the other end of the line.

"I'm sorry to disturb you on Christmas Day, Celia, but I need you to get your ass down to Havana before someone shafts Michael Ellis. Literally. If that husband of yours can spare you for a few days, that is. Oh, and Merry Christmas to the two of you, by the way."

"Thanks, Chief. Same to you," she said. "Havana? What's going on?"

Alex raised his eyebrows at her. She shrugged.

The police chief gave her all the information he had. She was shocked to learn that Mike Ellis faced rape charges, maybe murder, too.

"I'm still trying to work out details of official involvement with all the different jurisdictions. I thought about sending a police officer down, but it's complicated. We're in discussions with the RCMP. They may need to step in quickly if there are any issues around extradition. They're standing by."

"Extradition? That's for people who plead guilty or get convicted. Do you really think he did it?"

O'Malley didn't respond to her question. "Right now, I just want to make sure his legal rights are respected and that he's safe. He's not been the same since the accident."

O'Malley always called it the "accident." A police shooting and slashing that cost him one of his best men and might have ruined the other. An accident that left Steve Sloan dead and Mike Ellis mutilated. Some "accident," Jones thought.

"Chief, I can't give him legal advice," Jones protested. "I don't know anything about Cuban laws. What exactly do you want me to do down there?"

Alex had put his pen down now and listened attentively.

"I want you to find out whatever you can. We can't be interfering with a police investigation in a foreign country, but I won't see one of my men shot to death by a firing squad. I don't care what he's done. My men need to know I'm there for them. I want you in Havana so I can show how actively we worked to support the Cuban National Revolutionary Police. It could help us negotiate a transfer. I want him out of their prison before someone kills him. Or worse."

That's how it would be spun, that she was there to help the Cuban police, not Mike. O'Malley wanted a negotiator, not a lawyer. "And what if he *is* guilty?"

"I don't think he is, Celia, but I don't know how reliable their investigations are. And I need to find out. I can't have a man on my department cleared of a crime like this because of some technicality."

In O'Malley's world, there was no such thing as reasonable doubt. But he was right. If Ellis got out of jail on charges like these because of a technical legal argument, his days on the job were numbered anyway. Someday he'd need backup and it wouldn't be there. His career, maybe even his life, was over unless he could conclusively prove his innocence.

Jones hung up and told her husband what was going on.

"Any chance of the media getting hold of this?" she asked.

"I doubt it." Alex shook his head. "News is tightly controlled in Cuba. There is no information published unless it's been vetted by the police and the Ministry of the Interior. Which are really one and the same thing. I doubt the government will report this in *Granma*; it would deter tourists from coming. And attract the ones they don't want."

"Well, that's good, I guess," Jones said, frowning. "It will help us keep a lid on things up here while I try to find out what's going on."

She checked the online airline schedules while Alex hovered unhappily around the computer. She found an almost empty flight on Air Ontario leaving the next day. Apparently, prospective shoppers didn't travel to Cuba much on Boxing Day.

Alex, Alejandro Gonsalves, was an expatriate Cuban. He had fled Cuba with a wave of refugees in 1994. He didn't talk much about how he made it to Florida, but she could imagine. The two-hundred-mile trip took eighteen months. Castro had agreed to let the refugees leave just as President Clinton declared there was no longer sanctuary for them in Miami. They were held at

Guantánamo Bay. Alex was lucky; he managed somehow to get to Montreal, where he finished medical school.

They met in the Plateau just after he completed his residency. A girlfriend trying to get Jones over her depression dragged her to a party she didn't want to go to. There he was: a smiling Cuban man still grateful for his escape, ecstatic to be in Canada. It was impossible to be unhappy around Alex. He brimmed with optimism and hope for the future.

He made her laugh for the first time in months, taught her the salsa, helped her forget why she'd quit the RCMP. He persuaded her to start over, to be a lawyer, if that's what she wanted, apply to McGill. He convinced her she could do anything. When she was accepted into law school, they went out to celebrate. That night, he asked her to marry him.

She was already in her mid-thirties then — never dared to believe she'd fall in love, that she'd find the right man. They had been together nine years and were still best friends. They had no children, which made the sudden trip easier. The only upside to the one disappointment in their marriage. One they had finally, reluctantly, accepted.

He briefed her while she packed. He went over a list of things he was afraid she might not remember from their numerous conversations about Cuba. How much Cubans once adored Fidel Castro and why they supported his dictatorship. How they nonetheless hoped for his death.

"Castro abolished racial discrimination in a country where the majority of the population are descended from African slaves. Then he made education, even graduate studies, free for everyone. He did the same for health care. Cuba has more doctors than cab drivers now. The Cuban medical system would be even better than the one here if they could just get the medical supplies they need. Castro has a healthy, well-educated population, and they're grateful to him for that, but also enraged by the American embargo. Food and fuel are rationed and have been for decades. The average monthly salary is ten American dollars. Doctors might make fifteen. People are poor and enormously frustrated."

"I knew I married you for your money," she teased, but he didn't smile. He wanted her to fully understand the dangers he'd fled. The dangers she could face.

"I'm worried about you going there. If you listen carefully, Celia, you will hear how angry Cubans are. They've had enough. They're hungry and resentful. But Cubans are also resourceful and stubborn. When transportation was paralyzed by oil short-ages, Castro imported a million Chinese bicycles. Cubans love him and hate him at the same time. Below the surface, everything is in turmoil.

"No one challenges Castro's honesty or his personal integrity, but he can't risk any criticism. He can't let any dissent rise to the surface or he could easily be overthrown, just as he overthrew Batista. The Americans have tried to assassinate him at every turn, so his paranoia is justified. You won't be there as a tourist but as someone reporting to the outside world. This will threaten certain people. Be very careful. Trust no one you deal with completely. The Cuban authorities will lie to you. Understand that everyone, everyone, has a second face. And there are *cederistas* everywhere."

"*Cederistas*?"

"Loyal revolutionaries. In Canada, we'd call them snitches; in Germany, they'd be Stasi. You'd be surprised how many tourists get into trouble because of them. I heard of two backpackers who made the mistake of paying a farmer a few pesos to stay in his home one night after they forgot their tent on a tour bus. The Cuban National Revolutionary Police broke down the door in the middle of the night and arrested everyone. It's a crime against the state to rent a private room, even to a foreigner with nowhere else to stay. Even kindness is considered economically destabilizing these days. Please, Celia, be careful."

"I'll be fine, Alex." She stood behind him and wrapped her arms around his shoulders, holding him tight. "You worry too much. I've been trained to kill, remember? The worst thing that will happen to me in Havana is a sunburn."

Alex shook his head, worried. Behind her bravado, Jones was worried too, but for a different reason. She'd arrive in Havana around midnight Tuesday. That gave her just over a day in Cuba to get Mike Ellis out of there alive. There was no way she had enough time.

TWENTY-SIX

Inspector Ramirez dragged his weary body up the stairs to his apartment. He had worked more than fourteen hours. And there was no such thing as paid overtime in Cuba.

He was worried. If his instincts were right, Michael Ellis's accomplice was still at large, and that meant all the children in Havana were at risk, including his own. He wondered how Sanchez had made out concerning car rentals and taxis and made a mental note to discuss it with him in the morning.

Ramirez ran his hands through his short dark hair. He needed some time alone to recharge his batteries. He looked at the dead man, who smiled back, cupped his hat to his heart, and rejoined the shadows. Ramirez opened the front door and walked into the warmth of his family.

Edel, the shy one, poked his head around the corner. He held a worn soccer ball tightly to his small chest, Ramirez's gift to him that Christmas. Ramirez would try to find the time, and energy, later that night to kick the ball around outside with his son. Other boys would run to join them once they heard the *thwack* of a real ball.

"Papi!" Estella squealed and ran into his arms. He scooped her up and gave her a buzzing kiss, rubbing his light beard across her cheeks until she squirmed away. She gripped her new plastic doll by the neck. Once again, Ramirez was grateful for the exhibit room.

His aged father and mother sat together on the couch. His father held a glass of rum; his mother sipped a coffee. She greeted him in Spanish. An American once, now Cuban in every respect. Ramirez kissed both of them on their soft, lined cheeks. They would be devastated when he died. Their only son. A parent's worst nightmare, to outlive a child. Rita Montenegro had outlived two of them.

Ramirez smelled something good cooking. He stopped to inhale the fragrant scent of *sofrito*, the mixture of onions, green peppers, garlic, and bay leaves that Francesca cooked in a hot pan along with the *fricase de pollo*. His relatives crowded the small kitchen. His sister, Conchita; his brother's wife, her teenage daughter. Everyone, it seemed, was helping Francesca with dinner. Conchita stirred something else on the stove. His stomach complained: he realized he hadn't eaten all day.

Francesca walked into the living room, beamed at him, and wiped her hands on a worn tea towel. She hugged him and ran her fingers over the etched lines in his brow. He knew she worried about him, about the nights he couldn't sleep, the times she heard him talking when no one was there, the twitches and tremors in his legs and arms.

How much longer could he deceive her? Francesca was astute. She knew something was wrong, just not what. For now, they pretended things were normal.

"I am so glad you came home to join us for dinner. Let me get you a drink. You have had such a long day. What kind of case took you away from us?"

She walked back into the tiny kitchen and opened a cupboard, took out a glass. Poured him a glass of rum, squeezed a slice of lime into it. "We have no ice," she apologized. The refrigerator was warm; the power had been out until the late afternoon. It was back on now, more or less.

"I will tell you about it later, my love. Not now. But I will say this, today was hard. I am so lucky to have all of you. I am very glad to be home." His voice caught in his throat and he stopped talking, not wanting her to see him this emotional.

"Well, my goodness, you are serious." She slid her arm around her husband and pulled him close. "But you are truly a lucky man. Yes, indeed. We are all lucky. She was a big chicken I found, generous enough to feed all of us already, and she will do so again tonight. We're making your favourite, *yuca con mojo.* Finish your drink and then you can help me to set the table. There are nine of us again tonight."

Yuca con mojo was a popular dish, made with slow-cooked yucca, lemons, onions, olive oil, and lots of garlic. Ramirez smelled the garlic cooking in the kitchen.

"Conchita will fry some plantains and then we should be done. The rice is ready and so are the beans."

"Fantastic," Ramirez said and forced his tired lips into a smile. "I knew there was a reason I married you." He squeezed her close, tried to reassure her with a hug and a kiss.

She dropped her arm and pinched his backside. "I would like to think there were a few," she whispered, but Ramirez heard the undercurrent of strain in her voice.

She was afraid, and he understood completely. He felt exactly the same way.

TWENTY-SEVEN

The damp, filthy cell they put Ellis in had two toilets. One was used for the usual purpose, the other as a sink. The small room reeked of urine and feces.

The authorities planned to transfer him from the holding cell at police headquarters to the Combinado del Este prison later that week. It was the largest prison in Cuba, twenty kilometres east of Havana, but too overcrowded, too stuffed with political prisoners, to hold even one more person at the moment. Ellis wondered who would be released — or worse — to make a space for him.

Two other prisoners sat on the bed in the already cramped space. They examined Ellis closely as the guard pushed him inside. His scars might protect him for a little while: he looked dangerous. He wondered what other killers shared his cell.

One moved over so Ellis could sit down. The man said "*Hola*" to him nervously, then Spanish words he didn't understand.

"I'm Canadian," Ellis said. "I don't speak Spanish." With his fear, it came out as a snarl. The men looked away.

Their evening meal was bread and rice, beans. The beans on his plate floated in murky grey water. He put the plate on the floor, untouched. One of the inmates looked at him and raised his eyebrows, clearly hungry. Ellis nodded and the man took it gratefully. The breaking of bread broke the ice. Both men spoke English, as it turned out.

The older of the two leaned over. "Have you heard this joke, Señor? Castro gives a speech at Revolution Square and says, 'Comrades, God willing, this year we will have eggs for everyone.' An army general says to Castro, worried, 'But Presidente, we are communists; there is no such thing as God.' And Castro says, 'I know. But there are no eggs either.'"

The younger man laughed, slapping his knee.

Victor Chavez was in his sixties. A journalist and self-described political dissident, he'd been sentenced to six months in jail for hoarding. The police had taken away the toys he planned to give to poor children for Christmas, paid for by Cuban exiles in Florida. Chavez was convinced that the children of Cuban policemen were enjoying them now.

"Two hundred used soccer balls," he complained bitterly. "Skipping ropes and a few dolls. For trying to be Santa Claus, I am a criminal in my own country."

"Do people believe in Santa Claus here?"

"Not officially. All saints, even your North American commercial ones, are discouraged. Christmas was illegal for a long time. It was one of Castro's first prohibitions after the revolution. The government newspaper, *Granma*, warned us then that Santa Claus was a symbol of American mercantilism, inappropriate in a socialist state. We were encouraged to spend our Christmas gatherings eating pork and drinking rum and beer. To amuse ourselves by telling jokes. It came close to an edict, but it was unenforceable. There was no pork."

Ellis shook his head. Cuba was madness. The other inmate, Ernesto Zedillo, a slight man with a lisp, was charged with insulting Castro and public drunkenness.

"How can insulting someone be a crime?" asked Ellis, but he was starting to understand that in Cuba anything could be a crime if it served the government's objectives.

"Look what happened to Oscar Biscet," said Zedillo. "He was a Cuban doctor. He was sentenced to three years in jail for hanging a Cuban flag upside down. Insulting officials in public is a crime here. We can make fun of Castro but must be careful. I cannot tell you what I said, or the guards may report me, only that it involved a horse and Castro's mother. I may be charged with two offences, since my comments could be interpreted as applying equally to Raúl Castro as well."

Chavez chimed in. "We actually insult Castro all the time, but only in jest. Have you heard this joke? A drunk man is at one of Havana's main street corners and shouts, 'You bastard, you murderer, you are starving us to death.' A *policía* runs over and beats the shit out of him. The drunk says, 'Why are you punishing me? I could be talking about anyone.' And the police officer says, 'Maybe so, but the description fits only Fidel Castro.'"

Zedillo laughed uneasily but kept his eyes cautiously on the guards.

"It's okay," Chavez said, shrugging. "They don't speak much English. They come here from the country, most of them, for work. Barely literate. Ironic, isn't it, that the well-educated Cubans are in jails and the uneducated ones are guarding them. If you ask me, that's the crime."

"Speaking of crime, what are you charged with?" Zedillo asked Ellis.

"Rape," Ellis said and watched the men back away from him, to the extent they could in the small cell. "But I was framed. The police searched my room illegally. Someone planted evidence there."

They inched back towards him. Rape was bad, they agreed. But the police were much worse.

TWENTY-EIGHT

Ellis didn't tell the other prisoners what he did for a living. He was sure he'd quickly lose their sympathies. There wasn't enough room for them to sleep on the floor or the cot, so they talked through the night about the political situation in Cuba.

"We worry a bit," Victor Chavez joked, "that when Castro dies, someone corrupt will take power and destroy our economy." He laughed viciously. "Here is a good one: a teacher shows her class a billboard on the road with George Bush's face on it. She says, 'Look at him. This is the man who has caused all our problems.' And a student says, 'Oh, I didn't recognize El Comandante without the beard and the camouflage jacket.'"

They chuckled but were careful to keep their voices low. Chavez said jail was the only safe place to talk politics: no *cederistas*.

Ernesto Zedillo seemed less sure. He was worried about his transfer later in the day to another prison. He was convinced he would be beaten there, if not by the other inmates, then by the guards.

"Why?" Ellis asked. "The jails seem safe enough."

"Only here, not in the country. Things are different there. Besides, I am a gay man," said Zedillo. "Aren't you? I assumed everyone in this cell was gay. This is where they hold us before they transfer us elsewhere. They try to keep us apart from the others."

"Is it bad in Cuba? Being gay?" Ellis asked, evading the question. He considered telling them the truth but knew it was unsafe.

"Of course," said Zedillo. "But it's improving. We have a soap opera on television, the most popular one in our country. Last year, a married man, one of the characters, fell in love with another man. And Cuba is soon going to pass laws to recognize legal status for same-sex marriages. Even so, we are often singled out by the police and beaten because of our sexuality. Just not arrested as frequently as before."

"It is because we are socialists," Chavez agreed. "Socialism is not supposed to exclude anyone; it is based on concepts of equality. That means equal mistreatment for all of us. We all starve equally. Which proves that Marxism works."

"One of the strongest advocates for equal rights for gay people is Mariela Castro, Raúl's daughter. That's Fidel Castro's niece," Zedillo explained. "She is even pushing for rights for transgendered people like me. For the state to pay for the cost of our surgery. You want it done now, you have to pay for it. Imagine, they stopped halfway when I ran out of money. They left me stranded: half in, half out. I'm like a mermaid. I never know which washroom I'm supposed to use."

"I guess in this cell, that's not a problem," said Ellis, surprised that he hadn't identified Zedillo as transgendered. Chavez laughed; Zedillo clapped his hands. "Is the surgery painful?"

"Incredibly," Zedillo said. "But if I had the money, I would do it. You have to be true to who you are, to your emotions, or what's the point of living?"

Ellis nodded doubtfully. He'd never been honest about his feelings for Hillary until he was partnered up with Steve Sloan. And look what happened then.

TWENTY-NINE

Celia Jones sat on board an uncomfortable Air Ontario flight, drinking tepid water and eating tasteless sesame pretzel sticks. The airline no longer provided any food, not even on long flights. She leaned back in her seat, using her coat as a pillow. The airline had stopped providing those some years ago as well.

It was her first trip to Cuba and Alex couldn't come with her. He was afraid he'd be arrested for leaving Cuba illegally all those years before. He was terribly worried, but she was sure that the crappy service on the flight would be the worst part of the trip. After all, Havana was a tourist destination for thousands of Canadians every winter.

She tried to remember everything she knew about Mike Ellis.

A shooting incident earlier in the summer. Steve Sloan died. Ellis was hailed as a hero, a badly wounded man who nonetheless managed to kill the bad guy, even though it was too late for Sloan, who bled to death at the scene.

The two had been as close as brothers. Best friends. The guys on Patrol used to tease them about it. After same-sex marriages were recognized, they joked that Ellis had married the wrong person.

The same way Zelda Fitzgerald had accused Ernest Hemingway of being Scott Fitzgerald's lover. Ellis had only recently returned to work, his face mutilated in the attack.

That alone would screw a man up, she thought. Like looking in a broken mirror every day. And Mike had been a good-looking guy before all that happened: he took care of himself. Dressed well, kept fit.

Chief O'Malley told her to assume nothing.

"If the case is strong, do your best to get Michael home," he said. "Try to convince the Cubans to let us take care of things. If it's weak, do whatever it takes to persuade the Cuban police they have the wrong man."

She sighed. The old saw in police work was that people didn't get charged unless they'd done something wrong. But when she was a police negotiator, she didn't care what mistakes people had made, she just wanted to get them out safely. Someone else could deal with their guilt or innocence. Her job had been to protect the hostage *and* the hostage-taker.

O'Malley saw Mike's arrest as a kind of hostage-taking by the Cuban government, she realized. That's why he'd sent her instead of someone else. Even though she'd given all that up years before, after she'd failed to protect either hostage or hostage-taker. When the man on the icy ledge jumped and nearly took her with him.

The pilot announced that the flight had begun its descent into Havana. Jones closed the files she had downloaded and shut off her laptop. She looked out over the ocean, still acutely uncomfortable looking down, despite all the years that had passed.

It was late and only parts of the city were lit up. Whole blocks had no lights at all. Power shortages and brownouts. Alex had warned her the power supply could be iffy.

The Havana International Airport was a pleasant surprise. It was clean and spacious. A sign said it was built in 1998 in cooperation with the Canadian government.

Jones showed her passport. A friendly beagle, escorted by a uniformed policeman, sniffed her baggage and her pant legs. She saw the sign for a currency exchange counter and walked over, but it was closed. *Shit.*

She checked her billfold, worried she had so little money.

Maybe it's a good thing I don't. She had her Visa card and just enough cash to pay for her meals, not enough for a bribe, if one was expected. Alex told her there were still a few honest officials in Cuba, ones who wouldn't ask for money, but poverty had corrupted most of the others.

She had hoped she could change her money at the Havana airport. Canadian banks were closed on Boxing Day. She had managed to find some U.S. dollars tucked away from a recent trip to New York. But Alex thought American money might be illegal again, the currency as on-and-off-again as the power. She didn't want to be arrested for offering someone U.S. funds. O'Malley wouldn't send someone else to get her out, she thought ruefully He considered lawyers interchangeable. And easily replaced.

She wished Alex could be with her. Impossible, of course. She'd take lots of pictures, call him every day, keep her eyes open for gifts he might like. Later on, when she got home, she'd find a way to make up for lost time.

Jones waved down a taxi. She told the driver she wanted to go to the Parque Ciudad Hotel. She hoped he accepted Visa.

It was pitch black and there was only the occasional working street light. The road was lit mostly by headlights from the few cars and buses still in transit. She was surprised at how many people lined the streets this late at night; at how many more stood patiently in the centre of the road.

"There are two bus systems here," her driver explained. "One for tourists and one for Cubans. It is illegal for Cubans to take tourist buses or taxis. They can accept rides from cars that stop for them and pay the drivers a small amount without breaking any rules. Or wait all day for a *camello*." They drove past one of the awkward-looking buses, jammed full of passengers.

Her taxi pulled in front of the Parque Ciudad. A small group of *jineteras* was gathered in the park across from the hotel, calling out to the foreign men who passed by.

A *jinetera*, Alex had explained, was a prostitute, usually a member of the highly educated elite, forced by economic circumstances to have sex with foreigners. The word itself meant "jockey," but translated into something like "gold digger." Slang for a woman who rode a wallet.

Cuba had no pimps, he said, but the women weren't wholly independent either. They were forbidden by law from entering tourist hotels or restaurants. The concierges, doormen, security guards, even police, made sure the women got access to prospective clients by turning a blind eye for a fee.

Jones was surprised they trolled for customers so obviously. A blue-uniformed policeman stood at the corner, his semi-automatic gun hanging loosely from his belt along with a black radio. Doing nothing, at least not yet.

She wondered what would happen if any of the men responded to the women's calls. Alex had said a *jinetera* could be ordered into "re-education," sent off to the country to pluck chickens and clean barns, to dissuade her from prostitution. More often, however, the police confiscated her money and sent her packing.

A woman peered into Jones's taxi and was evidently disappointed to find another woman inside. Jones tried to pay the driver, who looked equally downcast when he saw her U.S. dollars. The currency, he explained, was illegal. But it was all she had; he wouldn't take Visa.

She offered to leave money for him at the hotel reception desk once she got some from her credit card, plus more for his inconvenience. He had little choice, so agreed. He opened the trunk of his car and reluctantly put her bags on the sidewalk. She made a mental note to leave him enough extra pesos to make up for his uncertainty about being paid at all.

A doorman pushed the revolving glass door for her. He was tall, slim, and smiling, his uniform crisp. His grey hat sat perfectly level on his head.

"*Gracias,*" she said, guessing. "*¿Es usted Miguel?*"

"*Sí,*" he said. Then, in English, "How do you know my name?"

"I was told you could be helpful," she smiled.

"Of course, it would be my pleasure," he responded. "Whatever you need, Señora. Here, let me take your bags."

THIRTY

Late at night, two guards came to get Mike Ellis.

"What is it?" he asked. "Where are you taking me?" But they said nothing. They shackled him and walked him silently upstairs to another small damp room that smelled of urine. An interrogation room, Ellis guessed. Stains ran down one wall. A dark grey ceiling added to the feeling of oppression. A light bulb dangled overhead from an exposed wire.

A beefy man with greying hair sat at a small table, writing in a coiled notebook. He looked to be in his late fifties. He wore a loose embroidered Cuban shirt over dress pants. He stood as the larger guard pushed Ellis inside and closed the door. He reached out his hand to shake Ellis's, but hesitated when he saw the handcuffs.

"Please, Mr. Ellis, sit down." He motioned to a plastic chair. "I'm sorry. They usually remove those for a consular visit. My name is Kevin Dunton. I'm with the Canadian embassy. Miles O'Malley got hold of me about an hour ago and told me about your situation. He must be very persuasive. Foreign Affairs isn't supposed to give out our home numbers. Almost everyone's on holidays until the New Year, including me." Dunton smiled but looked unhappy.

"I can't tell you how glad I am to see you."

"You may not be in a few minutes, Mr. Ellis. But we can talk about the merits of your situation in a moment. My first priority is to make sure you're physically alright. Have you been beaten?"

Dunton turned his notebook towards Ellis. He had written in a neat schoolboy script: *Assume the guards are listening. Don't tell anyone what you're charged with. Or that you're a cop.* He turned the notebook around again and waited expectantly, his eyebrows raised, his pen at the ready.

Ellis nodded slowly. "I guess it depends on what you mean by alright." He held up his wrists, showing the swollen red marks from the too-tight cuffs. "You should see my ankles."

"I expected worse. Do you want me to contact anyone? Notify any family members that you're here?"

"No." Ellis shook his head, thinking how Hillary would react. And how her divorce lawyer would salivate.

"Alright, then. I'm obliged to tell you what we can and cannot do as Canadian consular officers." He tossed a copy of a brochure on the table. *A Guide for Canadians Imprisoned Abroad.* "It's not much. We can't try to get you preferential treatment. Or secure your release from jail. We won't loan you money for a lawyer or for bail, under any circumstances."

"Then what the hell *can* you people do?" Ellis demanded, pushing himself away from the table.

"We'll see to it that you're treated the same way as any Cuban national in the same circumstances."

Ellis snorted. "You're kidding me. That's it? Have you seen the way that prisoners are treated here? We don't even have proper beds."

Dunton shrugged. "That's all you're entitled to, Mr. Ellis. We can't interfere in the Cuban criminal justice system. Someone will make prison visits from time to time to check on your welfare. And the embassy will try to ensure that the people dealing with you keep in mind that, as a Canadian, you have certain rights. But you have to understand that Cuba never signed the Vienna Convention. Your rights in this country are extremely limited."

"So I've heard," said Ellis, frustrated.

Dunton leaned back, narrowing his eyes.

"Do you understand what the situation is here in Cuba right now, Mr. Ellis? Or just how much trouble you're in? Fidel Castro doesn't want Havana to be a sex tourism destination, the way it was when President Batista was in power. Even if our embassy had more power to intervene, we wouldn't get too far trying to exercise it on charges like these, believe me. Frankly, from my discussions with the Ministry of the Interior, I'm afraid the Cuban government may want to set an example. They haven't executed anyone in the last two or three years, but that doesn't mean they won't make an exception."

Ellis let out a deep breath. "Isn't Raúl Castro supposed to be more moderate?"

The diplomat smiled slightly. "A lot of Batista's supporters were executed summarily after the revolution. Is Raúl more moderate? Rumour has it he pulled the trigger himself. Sure, as acting president, he may loosen up some things that annoy people currently. Like letting them have more access to the internet. He may even free a few political prisoners. But don't kid yourself, Fidel Castro's still in charge."

"I can't believe they would execute a foreigner. There would be an immediate international backlash, wouldn't there?" Ellis lowered his voice to a whisper. "I'm a policeman, for God's sake."

"I don't think so." Dunton shook his head. "Remember, the death penalty is on the books in Texas and God knows how many other American states. No one's boycotting the United States as far as I know. It used to be that a foreigner charged here could pay a hefty bribe and be sent home with a wink and a nudge. Not in the situation you're facing. The penalties for charges like this have been drastically increased. A few weeks ago, some Cubans were jailed for thirty years for having sex with schoolgirls. Thirty years in conditions you can't begin to imagine. Some of the prisoners are in extremely poor health. They aren't likely to live long enough to do their time. Castro's response, anecdotally, was that they should do their best."

"But Canada's a friend to Cuba, isn't it? Won't Cuba want to avoid upsetting that relationship?"

"Look, Castro executed one of his own political supporters for drug trafficking. A general. A former hero of the revolution. I don't honestly think he'd hesitate to execute a Canadian if it served his objectives. But, honestly, that's not your biggest problem. The guards might decide to handle things themselves. Or the other prisoners, particularly if they find out what you do for a living. You'll be in jail for a year, maybe two, before you ever get in front of a court."

Ellis blanched. "So you're telling me I'm on my own. That you won't do anything to help me."

"We have a relatively new minority Conservative government at home. It won't be anxious to jump to your defence. These charges don't fit their law-and-order agenda."

"What about getting me extradited back to Canada?"

"There is no formal extradition treaty between Cuba and Canada. But to be extradited, you'd have to agree to plead guilty to all the charges." He scribbled in the notebook and slid it across the table.

How long do you think you'd last in a Canadian jail as a convicted child rapist/murderer and *a cop?*

Ellis looked frantically around the small room. It was getting hot, claustrophobic. He ran his finger inside his collar, trying to breathe normally. The muscle at the top of his chest gripped like barbed wire.

"Jesus Christ."

"It isn't what you want to hear, I'm sure. But part of my job is giving people a reality check. There's no point sugar-coating things: Cuba is what it is. If you'd asked me where to go for a Cuban holiday experience, I would have told you to go to Miami and eat a jerked pork sandwich. I wish people would inform themselves a bit more before they come here. It really would make things easier. They see sand beaches and blue skies with fluffy white clouds: I see *cederistas*."

"So what the hell am I supposed to do?" Ellis demanded, his breath ragged.

Dunton shrugged. "Do what Castro said. Do your best."

The older man stood up. As he leaned over to pick up his notebook, he lowered his voice to a bare whisper.

"Someone always eavesdrops on these meetings. That's why I've given you the hard, cold, party line. My advice, Mr. Ellis, is to do whatever it takes. Bribe an official or two along the way. Believe me, evidence goes missing here all the time. And for God's sake, be careful. This building is full of extremely dangerous men. And I'm not talking about the prisoners."

THIRTY-ONE

The sun was beginning its slow rise above the ocean, but Inspector Ramirez was already at work, looking through the piles of missing-person reports to see if anyone had lost a dead man.

Rodriguez Sanchez usually came in around eight, the rest of the unit at nine. Until then, Ramirez was on his own, his hallucination his only company. The imaginary man sat across from Ramirez's desk, twirling his hat on his finger idly until it fell to the ground. When he bent over to get it, Ramirez saw him wipe foam from his lips. But no one had reported a drowning.

The phone rang and Ramirez picked it up. It was a woman. She spoke Spanish well, with a slightly foreign accent.

"Oh, Inspector Ramirez. I didn't expect you to answer your own phone. Sorry. My name is Celia Jones. I'm the lawyer here from Ottawa to advise Mike Ellis. May I see my client this morning?"

"Yes, of course. You can come by whenever it's convenient." He gave her the address.

"Thanks. I'll be there shortly."

About ten minutes later, as Ramirez looked out his office window, he saw a tall woman with shoulder-length dark hair and a brown briefcase walk up the path to his building. She took a digital camera out of her purse and stopped to photograph the police headquarters. With the palm trees in front and a green lawn rimmed with purple wisteria, the building was very beautiful. Too bad that photographing Cuban police institutions was illegal. Ramirez wondered how long it would take before an officer stopped her. He took a quick look at his watch and wagered less than ten seconds.

At the eight-second mark, a *policía* ran over, shouting and waving his arms. He stood over the woman until she deleted the photograph from her camera. That was as close to a real crime as the policeman would see that day, thought Ramirez. Foot patrol was an exercise in managing expectations. At least he didn't confiscate it. Ramirez doubted so nice a camera would ever find its way into the exhibit room.

The woman, appearing shaken, walked through the gates to the sign that directed visitors to a button for the intercom. A few minutes later, the guard at the front door called up to say Ramirez had a visitor. Ramirez asked him to escort the woman upstairs to the Major Crimes Unit on the second floor.

When she came in, Ramirez smiled and shook her hand. He decided to start things off with a little charm.

"I was not expecting them to send such an attractive woman." Which she certainly was. "Welcome to Havana. May I get you some coffee to begin your day?"

"I would love a coffee, thank you."

Ramirez called out to Sanchez, who had just walked in the door. A few minutes later, the younger man brought in two steaming cups of coffee. Real coffee, from the exhibit room, not cut with chickpea flour like the rationed coffee they drank at home.

"Detective Sanchez makes the best coffee in the police force. We prize this quality almost as much as his investigative skills, which are also excellent."

Sanchez made an expression that almost passed for a smile and put the cups down on Ramirez's desk. He closed the door behind him tightly.

"How was your flight?" Ramirez inquired.

"Fine," she replied. "There were quite a few seats, luckily. I don't think too many tourists book flights for Boxing Day."

No, thought Ramirez, we have nothing to sell. "*Su acento es muy bueno,*" he said. Your accent is very good.

"*Gracias. Su inglés es muy bueno también.*" Your English is very good, too.

"My mother was American, Señora Jones. She married my father just after the revolution. I'm sure it was considered scandalous at the time, on both sides. She has almost forgotten that she once knew English. I rarely get to practice it here."

"Well, you've certainly kept it up," Jones said.

"Thank you." Ramirez inclined his head, accepting the compliment. "It's something I have to work at. But you are not here to discuss my linguistic abilities, nor me yours. You are here to provide legal counsel to Señor Ellis."

"Yes," she acknowledged. "But I wanted to speak to you first. I have almost no background information about these charges. Before I meet with my client, can you provide me with some details and the basis for the charges? And may I take notes?"

"Of course," Ramirez assured her, as he brought out his file. He cast his eyes longingly on the pencil she pulled from her briefcase.

"In other words, a slam dunk," Celia Jones said, once Inspector Ramirez finished his summary of the evidence.

"I am sorry? I do not know that phrase."

"My apologies. It's a basketball analogy. It means you have a very strong case."

"Yes, I think we do."

Jones paused for a minute. "Have you found the murder weapon?"

"No," Ramirez admitted. "It was probably thrown into the ocean."

"How was the body moved?"

"We assume by car."

"Did my client rent any vehicles during his stay?"

"Not that we know of, Señora Jones," the inspector conceded. "But we are still looking into that."

"So someone else was involved in this crime?"

"We are entertaining that possibility."

"If my client is convicted, what penalty will you seek?"

"That will be up to the Attorney General, but almost certainly the death penalty. Your client murdered the boy shortly after savagely raping him. A death sentence could be commuted if your client admits his guilt and agrees to identify the other person involved in this matter. But we do not have plea bargaining here, as I understand exists in North America. Señor Ellis must be tried on every charge for which he is indicted."

"I'm sorry," she said, flipping through her notes. "Can you tell me what you mean when you say the boy was 'savagely' raped?"

"He was beaten. His face was badly bruised."

"Any marks on my client's hands when he was arrested? Or swelling?"

"Nothing obvious."

"I don't wish to inconvenience you, but could I possibly get a copy of your police and pathology reports?" She smiled at him. Two could play the charm game.

"Of course."

When Ramirez returned, she was looking at a photograph of his family on his desk. A round-faced woman with olive-brown skin wrapped her arms around two small children with huge brown eyes. "They're lovely," she exclaimed. "Your wife is absolutely stunning. You must be very proud."

"Thank you," said Ramirez warmly. "Life is short. I am always grateful for my good fortune. Here you are. I have made you copies of everything on the file. I assume you read Spanish fluently as well?"

"Yes," she confirmed. She thought of telling him she was married to a Cuban refugee but wasn't sure how Ramirez might respond to the idea of a Cuban that got away.

She put her coffee cup down and got to her feet. "This has been very helpful, thank you. If you don't mind, I'd like to see my client now. As you know, I don't have much time."

THIRTY-TWO

A guard told Mike Ellis that his lawyer was waiting for him. Ellis shuffled down the hall behind him. Hard metal rubbed against his ankles, leaving angry red welts. His back hurt from sitting on the concrete floor. Even without the ankle cuffs, he would have limped.

The guard opened a door for him. Celia Jones sat alone in the room at a wooden table with two metal chairs. Her laptop was open and booted up. She was reading through a pile of documents as he walked in. She wore small square red-framed glasses, the type one could buy back home in any drugstore to magnify print. She'd pushed her brown hair behind her ears.

"Hello, Mike," she said, and stood up. She removed her glasses with one hand and shook his hand with the other. "How are you holding up?"

"Honestly? I've been better."

She sat back down, invited him to sit on the other chair. "I've been reading up on Cuban law, but I've only had time to skim through the police reports Inspector Ramirez gave me a few minutes ago."

"O'Malley told me he would try to get you to come here. I can't tell you how relieved I am to see someone I know."

"Yes, Miles called me right after he spoke to you. He told me to get my ass down here, actually."

Ellis tried to smile and felt his mouth turn down. O'Malley wore his political incorrectness like a badge of honour.

"I have to tell you, Mike, I'm completely shocked by these charges. Are they treating you okay?"

"No one has beaten me or anything. But if they transfer me to a prison, I'm not sure how long I'll last. And are we safe to talk about what happened? I saw someone from the embassy last night." He leaned over and lowered his voice. "Completely useless. But he warned me that people could be listening."

"Solicitor-client privilege," she said, frowning. "We should be covered. It applies in Cuba, too."

"Thank God." Ellis exhaled. "So what exactly are my legal rights here, Celia? I keep hearing I don't have any." He whispered again: "The consular guy, Dunton, thought I might need to bribe someone to get out of this."

Jones shook her head. "Mike, forget all that stuff, okay? I wouldn't even know where to begin. And you don't want to go back to Canada with that kind of cloud over your head, believe me. But I have to admit, what I've read about Cuban law so far isn't encouraging." She pulled out some papers. "It's unlike anything I've ever encountered. It seems to be based mostly on the Soviet system. There are no individual protections, not in criminal matters, anyway."

Canada's Charter of Rights and Freedoms prevented unreasonable arrest, search, and seizure, and allowed suspects to remain silent, among other things. Once detained, a suspect had a clear, constitutional right to counsel; once accused, the right to a fair and impartial trial. Other procedural protections had been developed by the courts.

But Cuban law wasn't remotely similar. The police could

arrest almost anyone, even someone they merely considered "likely" to be dangerous in the future. "Pre-dangerous" charges, they were called. It reminded Ellis of the movie *Minority Report*, where Tom Cruise was part of a futuristic police force that arrested people before they actually committed any crimes. Just for thinking about it.

"Castro has taken a very hardline position on sex crimes," she explained. "He's increased the penalties drastically, particularly where offences involve minors. If there are special circumstances, the rape of a child can be punished by firing squad. And if they charge you with murder, that's almost automatic. But they haven't done that, Mike, so let's focus on the rape charge. After all, it's the one we have to deal with."

"Celia, I didn't rape that boy. I've been charged for something I didn't do."

"Not formally charged yet, Mike. That's what will happen if the indictment is issued tomorrow." She glanced at her watch. "Let's go over these police reports together, shall we?"

She translated parts from Spanish into English for him. The police evidence seemed overwhelming. It was an inquisitorial system. It was up to Ellis to rebut the facts, and the onus was on him to establish his innocence. The opposite of the Canadian criminal justice system.

"I think they'll have problems getting an indictment on murder," she commented, as if that was good news. "They don't have a murder weapon. They don't even know where the boy was killed. Their pathologist says the body was moved. Coroner, pathologist, lab technician, and everything else: it looks like all this forensic work was done by one expert." She flipped open the report again. "A doctor. Hector Apiro."

"We never had a car," Ellis pointed out. "Hillary and I never rented one."

"Inspector Ramirez has admitted as much. His theory is that you had an accomplice. We need to find evidence to support your alibi. And we need to show who might have framed you and why. It's going to be tough," she cautioned. "You understand, Mike, that even if the murder charge doesn't proceed, the sexual assault of this child was accompanied by force. A court can't — won't — ignore the fact the child was killed a few hours later. If they convict you of this, the prosecutor is going to ask for the death penalty anyway."

Ellis nodded. He knew the stakes.

"This really is a life-or-death situation. I need to know everything. Everything. Don't hold anything back. I hope you don't mind, I'm going to type while you speak. Start by telling me about the boy."

"He was just a little kid who followed us around on Saturday. Begging for money. There are hundreds, thousands, of them here. Hillary wanted him to leave us alone; she said I shouldn't give him anything. We had quite an argument about it. And then she told me she was leaving Cuba. Leaving me."

But Jones wanted to know the details, so he went through what he remembered. The argument, how he ended up in El Bar, the near-fight with the British tourist. And then the woman.

"What happened in the bar, after the man who threatened this woman left? You were alone with her then, right?"

"Yes. But that's where it gets blurry. I'm sure she walked me back to the hotel. I could have sworn she came inside, but Miguel, the doorman, says she wasn't with me."

"Forget what he says. Tell me what *you* remember."

He thought back, grasped at shadows. "Someone held my arm to keep me upright when I got into the elevator. I thought it was Miguel. I couldn't find my room key. I remember fumbling through my pants and shirt pockets before I realized I'd lost it somewhere."

He'd had to get another one at the front counter where a disapproving receptionist frowned at his companion. "The woman, I remember her standing outside my hotel room door while I tried to put the key in. She was laughing at me because I was so clumsy. I couldn't make the key work."

She finally took the plastic card from him and slid it in the slot until the green light blinked. The door clicked open. He lurched into his room, took a few steps, and fell heavily on his back on the freshly made-up bed. The ceiling spun madly above him like a top. After that, he had just the smallest fleeting memory of sinking into the pillows and then nothing, not even blackness.

"Did you have sex with her, Mike?" Celia Jones asked.

"I don't remember. I don't even know if she came inside. Maybe. Probably. Is it important?"

"It could be," Jones said. "They seized your sheets. If you did, there could be evidence on them that proves she was with you that night."

"I don't know," Ellis shook his head. "I just have impressions of what happened, and they could be wrong. I know for sure that someone helped me walk into my hotel room. I could hardly stand up. I thought it was her. But the rest of the night — nothing. It's like I was sleepwalking."

"Well, her being with you may not help you either way, now that I think about it. She could be your alibi. Or she could be a possible accomplice, if you look at it the way the Cuban police are. Do you know if she had a car? Did she say?"

"I wouldn't know. But I remember walking, not driving." He concentrated, tried to clarify the cockeyed images of that night, images as skewed as the Crazy Kitchen at the Museum of Science and Technology back home. That was exactly what it felt like, he thought. As if the ceiling switched places with the floor. He shook his head. "No, that's all I remember."

"Miguel Artez gave a statement saying you came back to the hotel alone."

"He may be right. That's what's so confusing. Cuban women aren't allowed in the hotels. Neither are Cuban men. They have security all over the place to keep locals out except the ones who work there. Big guys, with walkie-talkies. I've seen them tell women who hang around the park across the street to stay away from the front door."

"So Cubans can't come in even if they're with a foreigner, as a guest?"

"No, it's illegal. Like a lot of things here."

Jones flipped through the pages of the file until she found Miguel Artez's statement. "He says you came back to the hotel sometime before midnight, towards the end of his shift. Maybe eleven or eleven-thirty. But definitely before midnight. Does that sound right?"

"I don't know. Maybe," Ellis said. "I heard car horns. Bells. That could make it closer to midnight. The celebrations come to a head at midnight here, like New Year's Eve at home."

Jones flipped through her notes. She changed the subject. "Had Artez ever seen Hillary with you?"

"Sure. Several times."

"So he would have known this woman wasn't your wife if he saw the two of together." Jones shook her head, disappointed. "Maybe he's just mistaken. Christmas Eve, busy night. He may have confused it with another night or confused you with someone else. But it means we have to find someone who saw that woman with you on Christmas Eve. Or find *her* somehow. The boy's death, according to this report," she tapped the autopsy report with her index finger, "happened sometime between ten and twelve, likely closer to midnight. The body was moved a few hours later. That fits the time frame when you say you were with her. If she confirms that, it gives you a viable alibi. Do you remember her name?"

He shook his head.

"Well, you think about it. Maybe something will come back to you."

She tapped away on her keyboard for a few minutes, then looked up at him from the screen. Her reading glasses had slipped down on her nose. She took them off and placed them on the table.

"They have a pretty tight time limit to turn their case file over to the prosecution. It has to be filed by tomorrow afternoon at two or they have to let you go. But they also have pretty strong evidence, Mike. I need to know the truth. Did you have sex with that boy?"

"No."

"You're sure of that? Your statement to the police was equivocal, to say the least."

"I don't know what was going on in that interview. I couldn't think straight. I agreed with just about everything they said to me."

Ellis looked out the window. The blue sky over the brown metal turret pointed to a beautiful day, the palm trees swaying lightly in the breeze. A group of tourists stood in front of the iron fencing, taking photographs of each other, mugging for the camera. A *policía* ran over and admonished them. He saw him take their camera away and remove the film, then hand the camera back, still wagging his finger.

"Is there any chance you were drugged in that bar? Or later, at the hotel maybe, by that woman?"

"What are you thinking, Celia?"

"I don't know yet. I'm really just thinking out loud. But let's assume the woman you picked up actually picked *you* up and that she planned to drug you and steal your money from the beginning. I'm willing to start from the assumption that she was with you that night and that Miguel Artez is wrong."

"What difference does it make?"

"It would explain a lot of things: the way you blacked out, your suggestibility during the interview the next day. It would account for the capsule the police found in your room. It might help us get your statement excluded as unreliable if you were still under the influence of a drug when they questioned you. It doesn't explain away the other evidence, like the blood they found, or the stains. But at the moment, this mystery woman is the only person who had access to your room. I don't think we can honestly suggest that one of the maids was involved in setting you up. More likely to be the woman from the bar, right?"

Ellis concurred. "Look, I can't explain how that kid's blood ended up on my clothing. He wasn't bleeding when I saw him. Maybe the forensic guy just got it wrong. It wouldn't be the first time a pathologist screwed up evidence."

There were several notable cases of wrongful murder convictions in Canada where forensic evidence had turned out to be not just mistaken, but concocted.

"I agree. I think we have to approach this the way you eat an elephant: one bite at a time. Let's start by breaking things down. You say you can't remember much of what happened. Have you ever had an alcoholic blackout like this before? I need to eliminate everything else before I suggest to the police or the court that I think you were drugged."

"This is all confidential, right?" Ellis asked.

"Like I said, solicitor-client privilege," said Jones. "Chief

O'Malley told me to help you. For the moment, that makes me your lawyer, not his. I won't disclose anything you tell me without your consent. Agreed?"

Ellis nodded his assent.

"Good. Now, answer the question. Don't make me nag." She smiled, but she was deadly serious. "Blackouts?"

He took a deep breath. "I've been drinking pretty hard for months. Since Hillary lost the baby in June. I've had a few."

"Enough to forget a whole night like this?"

"Parts of it." He exhaled. There. One secret was out. The first step to recovery, he'd heard, was admitting he had a problem.

"As bad as this time?"

Ellis reflected back on what he remembered of the night. "Close, but nothing quite like this. It may sound silly, but it was almost like I was in a trance. Maybe she did drug me so she could steal my wallet. My safe was open the next morning and all the money in it was missing. I thought Hillary took it, but maybe the hooker did. But I don't know how she would have gotten the combination to the hotel safe. We set it ourselves as soon as we got in."

"She could have got it from you. That's the whole point of a drug like Rohypnol, Mike. It makes people compliant; they do whatever they're told. Women pose for pornographic pictures, have sex with complete strangers, then can't remember anything about it. They act like zombies. You realize that if this woman drugged you, though, it raises a whole new set of problems. The police think you had an accomplice. It could have been her."

"What do you mean?"

"She might have told you to rape and kill that boy, Mike. Maybe for a snuff film or hard-core child pornography, who knows? And it could be that you just don't remember the details."

THIRTY-THREE

Inspector Ramirez had thought about putting the female lawyer in the mirrored room, where he or Rodriguez Sanchez could watch her, but decided that might be too obvious. Instead, he posted an English-speaking guard outside the interview room to listen through the door.

The Canadian lawyer was smart, thought Ramirez, reflecting on their earlier meeting. She had, in only a few questions, exposed the only weaknesses in his case: the lack of a crime scene, weapon, transportation. He agreed with her analysis. He suspected, in fact, that Señor Ellis did have an accomplice. One with a car. One who might have killed the boy.

Not that it made any difference. Murder and conspiracy to commit murder carried the same penalties in Cuba. A death sentence was neither long, nor short: it was infinite.

Ramirez had pondered briefly whether to give Celia Jones copies of the police file but could see no harm in it. Hector Apiro's work was solid; so were the interviews.

The lawyer, if she believed his evidence was sufficiently strong, could possibly persuade Señor Ellis to plead guilty and lead them to his co-conspirator. That would please the Ministry of the Interior: a quick resolution to a politically ugly situation. It would please Ramirez too; he wouldn't have to explain to the prosecutor that he still didn't know exactly where the boy was killed or with what.

Celia Jones once again sat in Ramirez's office. Ramirez put the CD in Sanchez's laptop and hit "play." The dead man stood behind him but fled when he saw the photographs.

"There are almost nine hundred images of children. Most are out of focus, but the content is unmistakable. None are of the dead child." That made it worse somehow, the fact that so many other children had been violated brutally too.

They looked at the photos for a while together, until the lawyer said she'd seen enough. "Sadistic bastards."

"Then perhaps you can understand why we are so cautious here about the internet. Castro wants to try to keep material like this out of Cuba."

"I can understand the objective, Inspector. I'm not sure I even disagree with it. But the internet can be a highly useful source of information. More than just for distributing this kind of vile pornography."

Ramirez nodded his head slowly. "Perhaps. But we are finding that more and more of these photographs are making their way into our country. It is a cause of great concern." He sighed. Sanchez was busier all the time monitoring pornography on the internet. "Tell me, Señora Jones, would you like to see your client again before you leave?"

"I'm wondering if it might be possible to call him a bit later. I have some things I need to do at the hotel."

Ramirez considered this for a moment. It was easier for him to eavesdrop on their phone conversations than their visits. "I don't see why not, Señora Jones. You will need to call the cell guards first whenever you would like to speak to him, so that a guard can arrange to take Señor Ellis to a room with a telephone."

"Thank you very much, Inspector. I appreciate all your help."

"Not at all."

Ramirez escorted her to the stairs, told her to show herself out and to make sure she signed the log-out registry when she left.

Then he called in the guard to find out the details of what she and her client had discussed.

THIRTY-FOUR

Inspector Ramirez was surprised when the Minister of the Interior's clerk phoned to summon him to a briefing with the minister about the charges.

The minister, although responsible for the Internal Order and Crime Prevention section of the ministry, including the Cuban National Revolutionary Police, rarely spoke to Ramirez.

Ramirez was a high-ranking police officer, but his position in the food chain of Cuban politics was only slightly above that of an eggplant. At the evolutionary level of perhaps a chicken. Ramirez smiled at the thought.

He drove past El Pasco del Prado, one of the most beautiful avenues in Havana. The bronze statues of lions and cobbled pavement showed its former elegance, a contrast to the destruction of the tenements. He drove past a poster for the Museo del Auto Antiguo, the Old Havana vintage car museum. A redundancy, if there ever was one, thought Ramirez. The entire city was one big car museum.

He parked his small blue car and walked briskly down the cracked path to the government offices at the Plaza de la Revolución, although he expected he would probably have to sit on a hard wooden bench in the hallway for at least an hour until the minister deigned to see him.

"Go in, Inspector," the clerk said, motioning him through immediately. "He's expecting you."

Astonished, Ramirez pulled open the heavy wooden door to the minister's private office.

"Inspector Ramirez." The politician waved his arm expansively. "Please. Come in, come in. Sit down."

Ramirez lowered himself into one of two soft leather armchairs on his side of the massive mahogany desk. It was an office designed for smoking, not working. The minister had a reputation for being one of the most bureaucratic and least efficient of Castro's inner circle, which was quite an achievement, given the competition. Ramirez was surprised at being feted so warmly.

"You have a Canadian policeman in custody."

Ramirez thought the politician looked worried. Or perhaps distracted. There was no mention of Christmas; none of the usual felicitations. It was unusual in his experience for a politician to get so directly to the point.

"Yes. Michael Ellis. I arrested him for the rape of a young boy. I expect to charge him with the child's murder as well."

"Was he beaten?"

"The boy? Yes."

"No, the suspect. I have to deal with his embassy. I approved a prison visit by a Canadian consular official last night."

"No," Ramirez said. "Señor Ellis has been very well treated." He filled in his superior on the details of the investigation.

"I want you to report to me on this matter directly," said the minister. "And I want to review copies of all your reports, understood?"

"Of course. Whatever you wish," said Ramirez, surprised at the minister's interest. The last time he had seen the Minister of the Interior quite this animated was after the ministry had seized a cargo of smuggled rum. The minister had insisted on sampling bottles from several crates personally. To ensure the rum was genuinely old.

"Are there any known co-conspirators?"

"We believe there was at least one."

"Have any of these photographs shown up in your internet monitoring? And what about the other men in those pictures, are they identifiable?"

Ramirez shook his head. "Sometimes the faces were cropped. In others, the pictures were shot out of focus. There is nothing in the frames to identify where they were taken. As for the internet, Detective Sanchez handles that surveillance. I think if any of the pictures had been distributed online, he would know about it."

"Good. It means there is still time to control this situation."

Ramirez wasn't exactly sure what situation the minister was referring to.

"Thousands of sex tourists come here every week," the minister said, frowning. "Fidel Castro does not want Havana to become a sex tourist destination. He is extremely worried about the incidence of AIDS, which at the moment, as you know, is very low. You know the president's commitment to combating this disease."

Ramirez nodded. Castro had recently sent dozens of Cuban physicians to Botswana to help fight AIDS. But he had also sent several thousand doctors to Venezuela in exchange for oil. With the American dollar no longer legal, Cuban doctors were the new currency.

"Speaking of the president, how is his health?" Ramirez inquired.

Castro had missed his eightieth birthday party in early

December. The celebrations were supposed to complement the commemoration of the fiftieth anniversary of the *Granma* boat landing. Rumours were rampant that Castro had pancreatic cancer and was refusing treatment.

But late on Christmas Eve, a Spanish specialist in oncology and intestinal disorders had been rushed to Castro's hospital from the airport along with some sophisticated medical equipment. Perhaps Castro had changed his mind.

"El Comandante should be returning to his duties soon. But he remains actively involved in all important issues. This situation with the Canadian is of considerable concern to him. As you know, we increased the penalties under the Penal Code to deter *extranjeros* from coming here to commit sex crimes. After this Canadian is convicted, I want to assure you, he *will* be executed."

Ramirez nodded. It was a lot trickier executing a prisoner before a conviction.

"A strategic execution will serve our domestic purposes. The people get soft when there are too many commutations of the extreme penalty. They begin to take liberties. Besides, it is in our political interest to draw international attention away from the dissidents for a while. It will send a message to the Damas de Blanco, with their stupid flowers. Counter-revolutionary worms." The minister shook his head in disgust.

Ramirez was surprised to hear that the minister perceived the Ladies in White as a political threat. The middle-aged women protested by walking silently around Havana every Sunday after mass holding pink gladiolas. Their husbands and relatives were political prisoners. Or as Fidel Castro would describe them, "American-controlled mercenaries."

"Canada is a friendly country, Minister. I had planned to ask the Attorney General to consider capital punishment, but I meant to ask: are you at all concerned about the possible diplomatic repercussions if things take that direction? We haven't had an execution here for several years."

The last involved a group of men who had hijacked a ferry in 2003, intending to flee to the United States. A week after their trial began for terrorist activities, three of them were slumped on the ground in front of a firing squad. Come to think of it, Ramirez wasn't sure if they'd ever been formally convicted. Maybe it was easier to execute a prisoner than he remembered.

"What repercussions?" The minister laughed, shaking his head. "There is a new government in Canada that probably wishes it still had capital punishment. All I expect from the Canadians is a congratulatory phone call."

THIRTY-FIVE

An hour or two after his meeting with Celia Jones, Mike Ellis heard steps in the corridor. Three prison officials walked towards him, accompanied by a guard. The oldest of the three poked his fingers through the bars and waggled them at the prisoners as if they were exhibits in a zoo. All wore the green military fatigues and high brown boots of the Ministry of the Interior. A guard pointed to Ellis. The one with the most stars on his lapel spoke to Ellis in fluent English.

"Your lawyer wants to speak to you on the phone. This request has been approved by the Minister of the Interior and Inspector Ramirez. It is a privilege not usually extended to prisoners. You will have access to such calls for the next twenty-four hours only. You will pay for this courtesy: fifteen CUCs."

But when the guard took Ellis to the phone, it was a public pay phone, where his side of the conversation could be easily overheard. To use it, he had to either have money or a prepaid card. He had neither.

"How am I supposed to speak to my lawyer here? There's no privacy."

The guard leaned over, keeping his voice down. "I can take

you to a private room with a telephone. But you will have to pay me."

"You people have all my money; it was in my pants when you booked me in."

"What size are your shoes?"

The guard took Ellis, barefoot, down the hall to the same room where he had spoken to O'Malley two days before, and waited outside the door.

"Oh, good, Mike. I'm glad they let me call you. Inspector Ramirez said it's no problem if I need to get hold of you by phone."

"Then I guess I'll need more shoes."

"Pardon me?"

"They're like cigarettes in jails back home."

Celia Jones sighed. "I was afraid there might be strings attached. Okay, leave it with me. I'll see what I can do. I just wanted to tell you that I listened to the interview tapes and went through the photographs on the CD."

She said the pictures had been violent, as Ramirez had warned her they would be. Ellis knew what she was thinking. If he collected child porn, she wouldn't care if he rotted to death in a Cuban jail. But she was a professional and kept her thoughts to herself.

"Listen, Mike, there isn't much I can complain about in the interview, except it sounds like the tape was turned on and off at least once. When it resumes, Inspector Ramirez refers to something that wasn't discussed in the recording before: the Rohypnol they found in your room. Do you remember why he turned the tape off?"

"Yeah. He stole some rum from the exhibit room. That's good, isn't it, for us? Won't that make the tape inadmissible?"

"In Canada, yes. Here, I don't know. In a country this poor, I have a feeling that lots of things walk out of that exhibit room. I don't know what the law is here on recording statements; you'd need a Cuban lawyer for that. But that's not really why I wanted to speak to you. The more I think about it, the more I think that woman drugged you. But the police didn't do any blood work on you. I don't know why. Maybe Cuban law doesn't permit it. If they had, I could get it tested for Rohypnol. This long after your exposure, it's unlikely there are even trace amounts left in your system."

"Do you want me to volunteer blood samples?" Ellis asked, anticipating her request. "Ramirez asked me for DNA; I said no."

He heard the uncertainty in her voice. "It's risky. It could clear you, but it could also convict you. If you have Type A blood, that supports the police case. Probably clinches it. On the other hand, if you don't, I can prove your innocence."

"Can't you get my blood type from my service records in Ottawa? It should be on my file. That way you won't have to disclose it if you don't want to."

Except if it turned out Ellis had the same blood type as the samples taken from the boy, that would be the end of his legal representation one way or another.

"Great idea," said Jones, sounding genuinely relieved. "I'll get hold of O'Malley and ask him to send your file here somehow. Good thing you signed that release for me today."

Right now, as bad as it looked, she explained, the police had little hard evidence to connect Ellis to the boy's rape. Their case was completely circumstantial. The police and the technicians had collected all their incriminating evidence from a hotel room. Lots of people had stayed there, probably hundreds. The variety of hair samples, no matter how good the cleaning service, would be a dog's breakfast of elimination and comparison. To link Ellis to the boy conclusively, they needed his DNA to compare to the semen on his sheets and the samples recovered from the boy, and as far as she knew, they didn't have any.

"Be careful, okay?" she said. "Suspects in Canada get convicted all the time because of discarded tissues or gum that the police seize and test. Even combs, toothbrushes. It's probably the same here."

There was no toilet paper in the cell, and the idea that Ellis might see a comb or a brush during his incarceration was almost laughable. He didn't even have a toothbrush. The contestants on *Survivor* were better equipped than inmates in a Cuban jail. He thought back to the mug of coffee Ramirez had tried to have him drink.

"They don't have any DNA, I'm pretty sure. What about that Rohypnol? Ramirez said it isn't very common here. Can you trace that somehow? Find out more about it? Find the woman that way? Whoever she got it from may know where she is."

"I was thinking the same thing. I'll try, Mike." He could hear the fatigue in her voice as she added another item to her to-do list. "I'd better get going. I'm running out of time."

THIRTY-SIX

Detective Rodriguez Sanchez walked into Ramirez's office and pulled the door tightly closed. "Any problems with the Canadian lawyer?" he asked.

"Other than the fact that she's here? Nothing unexpected. Señor Ellis continues to claim his innocence but maintains he can't remember what happened. He said nothing inconsistent with our evidence. By the way, I gave her copies of all our reports."

"Was that wise?" asked Sanchez.

"I thought it best to provide her with as much disclosure as possible. We don't want the Canadian government complaining of unfairness in a capital case. And besides, the evidence is strong." He described his meeting with the Minister of the Interior.

Sanchez leaned forward, puzzled. "Isn't it strange for the minister to be this closely involved in a felony investigation?"

It certainly was, thought Ramirez, given the politician's reputation for doing as little as possible. "He must have the Canadian embassy breathing down his neck."

"Do you think so?" said Sanchez. "They don't usually do much except hand out their little pamphlets."

"Well, someone seems to have pushed the minister's buttons.

Maybe it's because Señor Ellis is a policeman. Think about it: when was the last time the Canadian authorities sent a lawyer all the way here to deal with a client in our custody?"

"That man from Alberta is the only one I can think of. The oil worker. But his lawyer was privately retained, not like this. And that didn't work so well for him."

Ramirez nodded. The oil worker was charged with having consensual sex with a fourteen-year-old girl. In Cuba, that was old enough for her to be married with parental permission. Apparently, he failed to propose. The girl complained when she learned he didn't plan to take her back to Alberta as his bride. His first mistake. His second, from what Ramirez understood, was refusing to pay the prosecutor, Luis Perez, a bribe.

The man's lawyer flew all the way from Edmonton to Cuba to watch the trial. He stormed out of the courtroom, angrily calling the proceedings a "kangaroo court" after the panel refused to hear his submissions. But he wasn't a witness or a Cuban lawyer. The panel, under the constitution, had little choice but to ignore his tirade. Except when it came to sentencing. The oil worker was sentenced in November to twenty-five years in prison.

"I'm almost glad to see the minister's interest," said Ramirez, "although it means more work for both of us. Otherwise, the chances of these charges ever getting to court would be slim once the prosecutor gets his hands on the file."

"Perez." Sanchez shook his head with disgust.

Ramirez nodded. He and Sanchez often worked long nights processing indictments for serious cases only to have Luis Perez slip a few thousand pesos in his pocket and make his own visit to the exhibit room to dispose of vital evidence. Without sufficient evidence to pursue charges, the *extranjeros* returned to their countries as free men.

A few years ago, a politician from the Bahamas was arrested

for having sex with young boys. He was released after he paid a hefty bribe to the prosecutor, rumoured to be twenty-five thousand American dollars. Ramirez had laughed out loud when Castro declared the currency illegal the following week. This had happened only one month before Christmas, and afterwards Perez was as poor as the rest of them. Ramirez and Sanchez had taken great pleasure in wishing the glum prosecutor *Feliz Navidad* every time they crossed his path.

Lawyers. Ramirez shook his head. It didn't matter which side they worked on; they were no friends to the police.

THIRTY-SEVEN

Celia Jones checked at the business centre in the hotel. Her laptop was useless. There was no internet access. There had been none for over a week, the young woman explained. And no, they had no idea when service would be restored. Get used to it, the woman's tone implied, although she was smiling. This is Cuba, Señora.

Jones needed to find a secure computer somehow, one that wasn't monitored by whoever was in charge of surveillance. One where she could find information away from peering eyes. The courts in Canada discouraged trial by ambush. In Cuba, ambush was all she had.

She walked into the hotel lobby, past the sweeping Gone-with-the-Wind-style staircase that defined the Parque Ciudad's main floor. Miguel Artez, smart in his grey uniform, hat, and white gloves, stood chatting with the concierge. She walked towards them.

"Miguel, I need a favour." She tried to appear relaxed, not as sure as Mike that Artez could be trusted.

"*Hola*, Señora …?" He waited for her to give her last name.

"Please, just call me Celia." She shook his gloved hand and he gave her another big smile.

"How can I help you, Señora Celia?" Teasing, knowing that wasn't her last name.

"Miguel, is there any way that I can get internet access in Havana? Do you have internet cafés here, for example?"

"I am sorry, Señora, we do have such places, but Cubans can only use them to send messages on the island. Most sites are blocked by government firewalls. There is no access to international websites at all. But you can use the intranet in the *correos*." The Cuban post offices.

"Is there no way to access search engines here?" she asked, disbelieving. "You mean I can't even get email in this country?"

The concierge walked away from them to answer a call at his desk, disengaging from their conversation. Artez bent towards Jones and lowered his voice.

"Some people have special permissions from the government to use private computers. If you need to use one and it is urgent, I might *hypothetically* have a cousin who might know someone with such an authorization. But it would be expensive, because of the risk. Five years in jail for my cousin. For you, probably a large fine."

"I'll take that hypothetical chance." She smiled and slipped him a few pesos.

It was already five o'clock. Artez said he would arrange things after his shift ended at eight and to meet him in the lobby. That left her a few hours to think, to retrace Mike's steps, and to try to discover who might have seen him with a woman on Christmas Eve, when a small Cuban boy was being violated in unimaginable ways.

THIRTY-EIGHT

Inspector Ramirez watched with Ronita Alvarez through a two-way mirrored glass. It seemed to him that Cuba was full of rooms with two-way mirrors. Half the population spent too much time looking inward, while the other half pressed their faces against the glass, desperate for glimpses of the outside world.

They were observing yet another abused child, from an unrelated investigation, being questioned on the other side of the wall.

The little girl, no more than nine, held a stuffed bear tightly in her hands as a counsellor asked her gently what happened. A tiny camera in a corner of the room taped the child. As Alvarez explained, two copies of the tape would be kept, one for use in the trial, the other to respond to any suggestions that the child had been led in her evidence.

"Only the tape will be used in court. This little girl will never have to face the person who abused her," Alvarez assured Ramirez, reading the question in his eyes.

Alvarez had established the Centre for the Protection of Children and Adolescents with Ramirez's help.

"We dealt with over one hundred cases last year, mostly thanks to you," she informed Ramirez. "But we had some drop-in complaints as well, like this one. A fraction of the true number, no doubt."

Ramirez had pushed for a centre to be created for children who had suffered abuse, providing enough statistics from his department to support its creation. He still hoped that other centres like it would be opened elsewhere in Cuba as well.

"How many reports of children being raped have you had since you opened? Of young children, like this little girl?"

"Of actual rape? Just a small number, one or two. It is hard enough for these children to talk about being touched. I would like to think this means that there are only a few victims. But statistically, I'd be dreaming. As in most countries, most child assaults are not reported."

"How many complaints involve boys?"

"As victims? More than three-quarters are girls, mostly between eleven and fifteen."

"The rape of boys below that age, is it unusual?" Ramirez assumed this to be so, but wanted to hear it from the expert.

"I think that reliable figures are hard to find, and we probably only know about a few percent of the abuses that take place. But yes, I would say statistically that it would be highly unusual."

"How many assaults involve tourists?"

She sighed and shook her head. "A much different story. We have heard many stories of children being abused by men who come here thinking that Havana is the same as the Havana of the 1960s. The foreigners who travel to places like Thailand to have sex with young children are now coming here, too. These children are so poor, so hungry. They'll do almost anything for a few pesos."

Five pesos, thought Ramirez. That was how much Michael Ellis had given the boy. Five pesos: the price of a child.

As Ronita Alvarez was talking, the dead boy appeared to the inspector for the first time. A thin boy in red shorts, his face bruised. He walked over to a hamster cage on a bench under the window and bent his knees so he could watch the small brown animal race around in its wheel. He made a circle with his fingers, tracing its path. He looked at Ramirez and smiled.

"Do you think these tourists, the ones who come here to assault our children, are isolated individuals?"

The dead boy walked over to Ramirez. He shook his head from side to side and pulled lightly on Ramirez's jacket.

"I certainly hope so," Alvarez answered. "Why do you ask?"

Ramirez sidestepped her question as he tried to ignore the dead child. "If I had reason to think that there might be two or more men in Old Havana abusing young boys, what would your reaction be?"

"I would be horrified, but not surprised. In many ways, it's only been a matter of time, what with the increase in sex tourism in recent years."

"I am not sure, my friend, but I have reason to believe that such a ring may be operating here, preying on the boys of the market."

"An organized ring?"

"Perhaps. I think I'll be able to identify some possible victims. I don't know for sure if they have been abused. But we need to find out. If my officers bring the boys to you, can you interview them?"

"Yes, of course," she agreed. "But it will be better if we approach them ourselves. They should be with members of their families. We are not supposed to question them alone. Have they complained to anyone?"

"No," Ramirez acknowledged. "But this will be difficult. I don't know for sure that these boys have been molested themselves. I only know that one of their friends was. He was eight years old. He was raped by one or more men, on more than one occasion." He hesitated, not sure how much to tell her, then decided to tell her everything. "We found his body on Christmas Day. Murdered."

Alvarez gasped. "My God. Tell me this isn't true."

"I wish I could," said Ramirez.

The boy tugged on the inspector's hand, trying to pull Ramirez towards the hamster cage. When Ramirez looked at him sternly, the boy stopped. Disappointed, but obedient.

"But I need to know if there were others," he continued. "With the dead boy, drugs were used to sedate him first, and so part of what we need to know is if these boys have been given anything like that, if there are moments that they cannot remember, times when it hurt to sit down and they didn't know why. That kind of information."

She slumped onto a couch. The centre was housed in a residence and it was outfitted to look like a home, to make the traumatized children feel more comfortable. There were tears in her eyes. "How awful. Do his parents know yet?" she asked.

"Not about the rape. There is only the mother, a widow. She didn't recognize the suspect. I would appreciate it if you could speak to the other children in the household in case they were victims of the same sexual abuse. There are two, both little girls. Very young. Perhaps too young to answer your questions. You must keep this situation discreet, as you can imagine."

"Of course," she breathed. He could see her gathering up her internal strength, although she had not physically moved. "Of course we will help you, Ricardo. Do you have a suspect?"

"Just one," Ramirez acknowledged. He handed her a photo-copy of the Canadian's passport picture. "But I am sure that there was someone else involved. He needed help to move the body to where it was found. Plus, there were Polaroids of the child being abused. From the angle of the pictures, someone else took them."

The dead boy walked back to the hamster cage. He watched the wheel spin round and round.

"Very well, then, Ricardo," Alvarez said. "We will carry out inquiries as you have requested. But I can only deal with one child at a time, understand? If you give me the names, I'll have a counsellor speak to the families and see if they will consent to have the children brought here."

"*Gracias*, Ronita. I appreciate this."

"The children can play with the games or with the rabbits and hamsters." She pointed to the pets used in therapy. "We will help them to feel as comfortable as we can. I can't say how long this may take. They may not wish to speak to us. Their parents may not want them to. Particularly if they have been abused. But we will tape all the sessions."

"May I see those tapes once you're done?"

"If we reach that point. You can even watch the interviews if you like. But you cannot ask questions, only communicate with the professional working with the child through headphones. That is the rule here, now. The investigation must be second to the child, understood?"

The dead boy walked back to Ramirez and smiled, revealing his dimples. He likes the animals, thought Ramirez. Is that how Señor Ellis got the boy to come with him? Did he pretend he had a pet he wanted to show him?

"Is that alright, Ricardo?"

Ramirez realized he hadn't answered, distracted by the boy that Ronita couldn't see.

"Agreed," said Ramirez. "And thank you for this, Ronita."

"I wish I could say it was my pleasure."

THIRTY-NINE

Celia Jones called home, but Alex was out. She left a message assuring him that she was safe, that the police were being helpful. She assured her husband that he had no cause for concern. That she loved him, missed him, wished he could be there.

Then she walked down to the lobby and asked Miguel Artez for directions to El Bar mi Media Naranja. "Ah, yes," he said smiling. "Hemingway's favourite bar. You understand the pun in the name, yes?"

"The half orange?"

"It means the place you go to find your sweeter half."

The narrow streets zigged and zagged, but the bar turned out to be only a few blocks away from the Parque Ciudad Hotel. Not nearly as far as Mike had implied, and that made her trust him even less. He was lying about something, she was certain.

She wanted to find Fidel, the bartender, and see if he could recall the woman Mike insisted was with him at the bar. The bartender told the police he couldn't remember seeing a woman with Mike. She wanted to find out what he would tell *her* in exchange for a little financial enticement.

The famous bar was small. Cozy, a real estate ad would say.

There was a lineup for the restaurant, patrons waiting to be seated for an early dinner. She saw an empty stool at the end of the long mahogany bar and sat down.

It was noisy already, a mariachi-style band playing outside the door. She ordered a mojito and grimaced when she saw the price. Mike had told her it was a tourist trap; he hadn't exaggerated. She asked the man behind the counter if Fidel was working.

"Not today, Señora," said the bartender and shrugged his shoulders. "Maybe tonight."

She asked him if he had seen a friend of hers and described the woman Mike said sat beside him.

He smiled, shrugged again. There were many attractive women in Havana with tight skirts, pink nails, and streaked blonde hair. She was wasting her time looking for that one. Just wait, his shrugs suggested, and you will find others you like here just as much, maybe better. She was mildly offended, then amused, by his assumption that she was looking for a *jinetera* for herself.

"It's important that I find her," she insisted, and reached into her purse to find a pencil. She tore a sheet of paper from her notebook, wrote down her hotel and room number, and told him that if Fidel or the woman returned, it was worth ten pesos for him to leave a message at her hotel.

That got his attention.

Jones finished her drink and left a hefty tip with the payment. She wanted the bartender to remember her as being generous.

She still had an hour or two before Miguel Artez and his cousin met her at the hotel to get her online. She got directions to the Malecón and threaded her way through the tables to the still-bright outdoors. The police report had not been specific about where the body was found, only that it was in the water near the seawall across from the medical towers. They must be some kind of a landmark.

She walked up the Calle Obispo to the Plaza de Armas. It was quite incredible: an outdoor market with bookstands that blanketed the entire tree-lined square, like a library without walls. Dozens of vendors displayed thousands of used books for sale. She browsed for a minute, wondering if the sunlight was good for the covers, the pages. The books were all in Spanish and most were either about the revolution or Catholicism, which surprised her. She had thought that Cuba was secular.

En route to the Malecón, she was repeatedly accosted by beggars of all ages. One grey-haired woman stood in front of her, blocking her way, and held out what she guessed were worthless domestic pesos. The woman wanted her to exchange these for her valuable ones.

"You see?" the woman said. "These have Che's head on them. A good souvenir, yes? A peso for a peso, just a trade." Jones shook her head and walked past the woman, but she was beginning to see why Hillary Ellis became so annoyed.

Old Havana was gorgeous. Jones passed the San Carlos y San Ambrosio seminary, a beautiful stone building constructed by Jesuits in the mid-1800s. Behind it, on the other side of the harbour, stood the Castillo, a Spanish fortress built in 1589 to guard the entrance to Havana Bay. It reminded her of Old Quebec, cobblestone lanes, curved balconies made of intricate wrought iron. In this area, Havana had been restored to what it must have been like before the embargo: it was stunningly beautiful.

Between the seminary and the seaway was a market with stands selling art, crocheted women's tops, coral necklaces, African masks, and brown seed bracelets. Some of the vendors sold African wooden figures. She stopped and bought a pair of silver and enamel earrings for a few pesos, a small silkscreen painting of a mermaid superimposed over the Cuban flag for five more. She thought Alex would like it for his office.

Jones crossed from the market to the seawall, the ocean turquoise today, a deeper blue than the sky. She noticed the small park with the Ferris wheel and guessed that was where the ride operator gave his statement. She asked a Cuban couple in Spanish where the medical towers were; they asked her for soap.

They pointed west and told her the towers were a few kilometres down the Malecón, and so she walked beside the seawall, looking across the street at buildings that had fallen down, apartments teetering on the edge of collapse, and the few that had been restored.

The contrasts were extraordinary. A new hotel was under construction next to a building that was little more than rubble. It had only one complete wall left standing, but nonetheless displayed wet laundry strung between the devastated balconies. The new building was all glass and angles and overlooked the water. It would have looked at home on the waterfront in Toronto or Montreal. The sidewalks beside it were cracked; in the entire block, only the new building had unbroken windows.

She walked three or four kilometres until she caught sight of the towers on the other side of the Malecón. It took her a few minutes to find the spot where the body had been discovered. The bright yellow police tape was still in place, tied between two lampposts. A man with a violin played mournfully nearby, a glass bottle at his feet for coins. She dropped in a few centavos.

She walked to the edge of the wall and peered over, felt a surge of vertigo even at that short height. She forced herself to look down the steep wall to the water. Plastic bags and debris were stranded on the rocks at low tide. Kelp floated in an oily slick. It looked the same as every other part of the Malecón; nothing here to indicate that anything untoward had happened. She took a deep breath and straightened up.

None of the tourists who leaned against the stone wall could have any idea that a child's body was dumped here only days ago. But it was unlikely that the boy had just been carried here and thrown into the water without some attempt at concealment. The Malecón would be a popular spot in the evening, when the ocean breeze was cool. Even late at night, she imagined there would be passing cars, taxis, pedestrians, particularly on a busy night like Christmas Eve.

Jones walked slowly back to her hotel, already thinking ahead. She wanted to put together some kind of a brief for the prosecutor and the juridical panel, something formal to file on the record, what Cuban lawyers would call *conclusiones provisonales*. Objections to the police facts, to the specifics of the charges.

She had to think like a lawyer. She needed to protect the chief and herself from liability if Mike ended up shot to death by a firing squad. Or if something terrible happened to him in jail. O'Malley was right, she thought, frowning. Law was a lot like hostage negotiations.

That morning interview with Mike bothered Jones almost more than the evidence Inspector Ramirez had assembled. She sensed Mike had withheld something important from her and the Cuban police, but she couldn't pin down what it was, or why she felt so uncertain of his truthfulness. Was Mike Ellis the kind of man who would take his wife to Havana for a holiday and then search out a child to have sex with? Was it possible he was a pedophile?

She wondered if his terrible injuries, his undoubtedly damaged self-esteem, could have caused him to seek out children for sex. Children were accepting, non-judgmental, everything it seemed Hillary Ellis wasn't. Still, she shuddered to think that a colleague could have sexually assaulted and killed a child.

But I'm not a profiler, she thought, just a lawyer.

And there was no way to tell by appearance alone. She was

always horrified when the police broke yet another internet child porn ring and trotted out the accused in handcuffs. Accountants and lawyers, teachers, coaches, even the occasional judge. A lot of priests, too, these days.

Behind those scars on his face, Mike could be *anything*; no one knew what went on behind closed doors.

She and Alex had tried to have a baby for years, then applied to adopt one. But Canadian children weren't often available for adoption unless they had special needs. She couldn't imagine caring for a child that was disabled, although Alex was open to it. They had decided to stay on the adoption list and see what happened. Years passed and no children were offered to them. Life had moved on. In her forties now, she doubted she would ever be a mother.

But if she had a child, she would kill anyone who touched it sexually. And she meant it; she knew how.

FORTY

Celia Jones changed out of her suit. She put on a pair of shorts, a light top, leather sandals. Alex had left a message on her hotel phone. He was glad to hear her voice, would be in surgery all day, loved her, missed her too, and hoped she was enjoying the sun. She smiled, played it back several times, couldn't bring herself to delete it.

She had a quick bite to eat at the upstairs lounge beside the beautiful rooftop pool. She worked on the brief as she munched, stopping occasionally to admire the spectacular beauty of the view around her, careful to avoid looking down. The terrace overlooked the squalor of Havana but also framed the majestic Capitolio Nacional. It was so close she felt she could almost reach out and touch its gleaming dome.

The Capitolio was a knockoff of the Capitol building in Washington, built to scale, but much smaller. It held the fifty-foot-high Statue of the Republic, reputedly covered in twenty-two-carat gold. The steps of the Capitolio ran the entire width of the building. At the ground level, they were rimmed with 1956 Chevys and lineups of tourists, along with the ubiquitous beggars, stray dogs, cigar women, and young boys. Even the dogs begged.

She walked to the edge of the terrace and tried to look below but felt dizzy almost immediately. She'd been fine before the crazy suicide jumper. She recalled looking down to the parking lot, seeing his body flattened into sharp angles in the snow, like a white origami swan with red wings. Now she suffered from all kinds of phobias: heights, claustrophobia, even chionophobia, a fear of snow. Not good for a Canadian. I should have pushed him myself, she thought. It would have been easier to deal with.

Looking straight ahead, she saw the Gran Teatro, one of the world's largest opera houses. The ocean sparkled on the other side of the flat tops of crumbling buildings that surrounded her hotel. The view was beautiful and ravaged at the same time. She glanced at her watch and realized it was just after eight. It was so much brighter here in the evening than at home; she hadn't marked the passage of time.

Damn. She was late.

Jones ran to the elevator, pushed the "down" button several times, then jogged down the four flights of stairs from the terrace to her room when the elevator didn't arrive quickly enough. She grabbed her laptop and locked the door, flew down the two remaining flights of stairs to the hotel lobby.

Artez was nowhere to be seen. She hoped he hadn't left. She paced around the lobby for a few minutes before she finally asked the concierge if he knew where Miguel was. He shrugged, apologetic, and said Miguel had finished his shift hours ago.

She might have screwed up badly, but there was nothing she could do about it. She sat at the bar and watched for Artez, while a very good three-member band sang together. The men played guitars; the woman shook castanets, swirled her dress, and stamped her feet as she sang. Jones applauded, but her mind was elsewhere.

She needed Artez desperately. She wasn't sure what she was

going to do if he had changed his mind. She was stranded as it was, without any other access to the internet and running out of time. But then he strolled in and casually waved at her as if he weren't twenty minutes late.

"Come with me, Señora Celia," he said. "My hypothetical cousin is waiting outside."

FORTY-ONE

It was late, long past dinner. Another missed meal with his family. Francesca would be irritated, but Inspector Ramirez had little choice. He had two problems to keep an eye on: a foreign lawyer determined to poke holes in his evidence, and a politician pushing for a conviction.

"I wish I knew where he got the drugs," Ramirez remarked to Sanchez as he put down the summary of their evidence. "That part of this case troubles me the most."

It meant Rohypnol could still be out there, that other children could be drugged and abused as easily as the murdered boy. Ramirez had sent Sanchez to the airport to see if the detective could trace the shipment of Rohypnol through Customs, but Sanchez reported that there had been no deliveries to Havana for years.

"I don't think we need to know where the Rohypnol came from, Inspector," said Sanchez. "We have more than enough evidence to charge the Canadian with rape. It doesn't matter if he brought the drug to Cuba or not: the important thing is that we found it in his room."

Perhaps Sanchez was right, but Ramirez didn't like loose ends.

"Well, I am quite sure that the Canadian did not bring any drugs with him. Likely not even prescription ones. I checked the surveillance tapes you picked up for me at the airport. Nothing."

Ramirez had watched the beagle, the best of the sniffing dogs, walk right past the Canadian man as he stood in the Customs lineup without even a second look, tail wagging. The Canadian had no drugs on him when he had arrived, then, not even small amounts. Not in his luggage, not on his clothes.

The Rohypnol capsule had to have come from within Cuba, from someone who already had it. But Sanchez was right. Ramirez was not trying to indict the Canadian on illegal drug charges or the use of a hypnotic. Instead, in his report, Ramirez asked the prosecutor's office to indict Michael Ellis on the charges of rape and murder, and to request the death penalty, given the special circumstances of the crime.

The dead man met the inspector's eyes. He pointed his index finger, thumb up, bent his fingers into the shape of a gun and aimed it at Sanchez. Then he held it to his own head and pulled the trigger.

After Sanchez left for the night, Inspector Ramirez leaned back in his swivel chair. He folded his hands behind his head, thinking back to their conversation.

Sanchez had raised a good point. Why *was* the Minister of the Interior so involved in this particular file? And if he wanted to ensure the Canadian was sentenced to death, why was Luis Perez assigned as prosecutor? There were too many layers of politics in this case for Ramirez to be completely confident of its outcome, despite the strength of the forensic evidence. He shook his head. There were too many secrets.

His own were becoming harder to conceal. With the stresses of the past week, the trembling in his arms and legs was more pronounced. He had hoped to exhaust himself by working late so that he could finally fall asleep. But the visions seemed to be coming more frequently.

The time would come when he would have to tell Francesca the truth. He'd left it for so long, he no longer knew how to. What was he supposed to say to her?

He was afraid Francesca would want him examined by a psychiatrist. That's if she didn't immediately file for divorce. She would almost certainly insist that Ramirez move out of their bedroom and take his ghosts with him.

That's what would drive her crazy, he thought. Not his illness, but the fact there were strangers wandering around their apartment without her knowing about it. She wouldn't care whether they were really there or not. She liked to keep a clean house when visitors came.

And how would Edel react to finding out his father was either dying or insane?

When it came right down to it, Ramirez wasn't completely sure how anyone he cared about would react to his situation. It wasn't something he was particularly anxious to find out.

But he couldn't keep lying to the people he loved. Ramirez shook his head. He had no idea what to do. He held out his hand and watched his fingers tremble like palm fronds in the breeze.

He opened his desk drawer and pulled out the bottle of rum.

FORTY-TWO

The air was cooling with the evening breeze. An old red car was parked beside the taxis, bleeding diesel. Inside, a statue of the Virgin Mary stood on the dashboard, a string of brown beads wrapped around it. The windows were down, the interior open to the night air.

A woman sat in the driver's seat. "Come, Señora," the woman urged nervously. "Get in. Quickly, please."

Miguel Artez introduced them. "This is my cousin, Juanita."

"*Hola*," the woman said and turned the key in the ignition.

The car snaked along the Malecón, then turned left down a side street, then right. The streets were indistinguishable, except the houses, if it was possible, became poorer and more dilapidated.

Jones lost track of their route. She had to trust that they would bring her back safely from wherever they were going. They drove for eight or nine minutes, then Juanita parked the car. They got out and walked up the cracked pavement.

"Where are we going?" Jones asked.

"Not far now," Artez responded, evasive.

They walked through an archway covered with rocks into a

narrow alley unlike anything she'd ever seen. The housing was the typical three-storey stone-and-wood structures of other parts of Havana, but the back of each building was painted with crazy patterns. Crevices in the stone and bricks were inset with dolls' heads, urns, parts of gates, light bulbs, and all kinds of other unlikely decorations.

Even in the dusk, she could make out leopard and zebra prints painted on the backs of some walls, intricate mosaic designs inset in others. Red flags hung from posts. Figures of men and women jumped from shadows, crafted out of rock, wood, and iron. Masks glared everywhere.

They walked past a bucket that held a number of live turtles that clambered slowly over each other in the murky water.

"The followers of Santería drink the water," Artez explained. "They believe the urine will help them to live longer because turtles live a long time."

"Santería?" asked Jones. It didn't look to her as if those turtles had a very long life ahead of them, trapped in one small plastic bucket.

"The descendants of African slaves believe in blood sacrifice. They pray to the orishas here. The *orishas* are the Santería gods. This alley is their temple."

A male drummer with a brilliant white smile thumped African-type rhythms with his hands on a large drum. A small group of Afro-Cuban women sang, swayed, and clapped along. Torches lit the alley.

There was a small open bar and terrace where a few Cubans drank rum in the deepening shade. A white bust of Stalin sat on a red plinth, next to a building painted with bulging eyes. It was completely surreal, the product of either a mad mind or a brilliant one. Maybe both. The women's singing became louder, climbing towards a crescendo. It was riveting, hypnotizing.

"What is this place called?" Jones asked. For a fleeting moment, it crossed her mind that she had been brought here as a sacrifice.

"The Callejón sin salida," Artez replied. Blind Alley.

"It was created by an artist many years ago," his cousin explained in a tone a tour guide might use to lecture a child. "Tobacco workers settled here originally, from Key West. This is where we have carnival, but also religious ceremonies and initiations. It is illegal, Lukumi, everywhere but here."

"I had no idea anything like this existed."

"Oh yes. Originally, the Yoruba had hundreds of *orishas*, but only a few dozen remain. You may have noticed: most baptized Cubans wear bead bracelets or necklaces to show which gods they have adopted. Yellow, blue, and white for Oshun, the Virgen de la Caridad del Cobre, the goddess of sexual love. She was forced to become a prostitute to feed her children, so she is the goddess of prostitutes as well. Red and white beads for Chango, the warrior, who hides behind the face of Santa Barbara. The Catholics who follow Chango believe so long as they confess all their sins, they will never die without first receiving the sacraments. But like the *orishas* and the Catholics, everyone in these streets gets along. Spanish, black, and others, we have no disagreements. This," Juanita smiled, "is where the real cultural revolution took place."

Jones had never seen such a place in her life: a living space that combined murals, African spiritualism, and pop art. They walked past life-size images of playing cards that leaned against giant cactuses. The cobblestones below their feet had been painted in black and white swirls.

A narrow opening carved out of the stone encouraged them down stairs and into a gallery. Posters and art covered the walls. Piles of CDs were scattered everywhere.

Juanita spoke to a very dark man who seemed to be running the store.

The Afro-Cuban man took them down a hall and unlocked a door, then ushered them silently into a back room. It was piled high with parts of mannequins, overstuffed life-size dolls with blackface, spears, stuffed animal heads, and books.

An ancient PC sat on a table. It was an old desktop, the screen resolution set low so that the screen flickered. It would quickly give her a headache, Jones knew. But it displayed a Google site as its home page and Google was what she needed.

"How much?" Jones asked Artez, knowing the price would be high.

"Twenty-five tourist pesos. Ten for Juanita and ten for Carlos, the manager of the gallery. Five for me. And Señora, if anyone asks, you were never here."

"Fine."

She paid the money, almost a month's salary for each of them, aware they were breaking Cuban laws by getting her internet access on a computer not authorized for her use. She had become a Cuban scofflaw. Probably best to leave that out of her report to O'Malley.

Jones sat in front of the computer. "How much time do I have?" She looked at her watch.

"An hour. No more. And maybe not that long," Juanita said, clearly nervous as the singing intensified above. "The police do not come here often. They believe there are spirits here. And they are right, of course. These alleys are full of them; you must not walk here alone. But do not be afraid. Sacrifices are made to Oshosi, the god of traps, to keep the police away. Some believe that Eshu, our god of the crossroads, is also in charge of electronic communications, not just those between living and dead. Either way, you will be protected. Anywhere else on the island, you would be arrested, trust me."

"It is not safe to be on the computer any longer than that,"

Artez insisted. "The police monitor all transmissions off the island. They will notice that kind of activity."

"And even Eshu can only warn, not prevent harm. He is just a messenger. His attentions are focused on the dead, not the living. Understood?" Juanita asked.

Jones nodded. She could imagine how the local police might feel a sense of discomfort in this place, with the drumbeats, the chanting, and the sense of voodoo that permeated every inch.

Upstairs, bloodcurdling screams rose above the sounds of drumming. A woman yelled that she was possessed. Artez and his cousin quickly left and closed the door. Jones heard the lock click.

Oh, that's just great, she thought. Leave a claustrophobe locked in a tiny room surrounded by crazy people. Like in one of those fucking zombie movies. *Shit.* She banged on the door, but no one responded. Artez and his cousin were gone.

Scary. Jones's forehead broke out in sweat. She tried to focus on the monitor, to block out the woman's screams — until they finally stopped, suddenly. Too suddenly. Somehow, Jones managed to complete her searches and send out her emails before her time ran out.

At exactly the one-hour mark, the doorknob rattled and the lock clicked open. Juanita let her out of the small room. Jones took a deep, grateful breath of fresh air.

Artez and his cousin waited in the gallery. They walked out up the narrow stone stairs into the warm night. The screaming woman was gone. The night air was quiet now. Almost unnaturally still, except for the soft murmur of voices from the outside bar.

"Interesting place," said Jones, looking around. In the sense of the Chinese curse: "May you have an interesting life." Her heart was still stammering. The drummers were gone. No sign of the singers either. Only a small red pool on the ground where the man had pounded away on his drum. She hoped like hell it was paint.

"Would you like to have a drink with us?" Artez asked, and Jones knew they expected it. She appreciated the risk they'd exposed themselves to. She bought them a quick round of mojitos at the outdoor stand, along with a CD of Afro-Cuban music for Alex.

She paid almost fifteen times more than the warm, iceless drinks were worth when the man running the bar insisted she pay tourist pesos instead of domestic ones, but she didn't complain. She wanted to make sure they would take her back to the hotel. I don't want to piss them off, she thought. I don't want to be left here alone, that's for sure.

As they drove back to the Parque Ciudad, she discovered they'd been only three blocks from the Malecón. Blind Alley seemed a million miles away, a place intimately connected to the spirit world, yet to the outside world as well, in a way the rest of the island wasn't. Thanks to the internet and a telecommunications god.

But Jones needed to return to Blind Alley the next day to check her emails, to see if the chief and Cliff Wallace, the head of the Drug Squad, had responded to her requests. Until then, she was limited in what she could do.

She made arrangements with Juanita to use the computer again first thing in the morning. The woman seemed thrilled at the easy money, and Jones was relieved she'd be returning during daylight. They agreed to meet at 7:30 A.M. outside the hotel, across the street from the front door.

Juanita dropped them both off. Artez was working the late-night shift, and he excused himself to get changed. Jones thanked him, then realized he was waiting for a tip and pressed another few pesos in his hand.

"Were there any messages for me?" she asked the receptionist at the front desk. The hotel had voice mail, but messages could also be left with the switchboard.

"Just one," the receptionist told her, reaching behind her for a pink slip of paper. There was no name provided. Someone had left a message for Celia Jones at ten minutes after eight. Her female friend was at the bar.

Celia Jones ran all the way to Hemingway's favourite drinking spot, but by the time she arrived, the blonde woman was gone. The apologetic bartender shrugged and put his hand out for the money. Jones slapped the pesos in his palm, angry that she'd missed the woman by so little time.

She ordered another mojito to quell her nerves after her experience in the alley and to compensate for her disappointment at just missing the mystery woman.

She looked at the photographs of Ernest Hemingway hung on the wall as she sipped her drink. As she recalled, Hemingway's mother had dressed him up as a little girl for two whole years, even called him Ernestine. Hemingway's own son was a transvestite: Gregory at birth, Gloria when she died in a women's prison in Florida. Ernest Hemingway had committed suicide. So had his father. Blew his brains out with his favourite gun. Behind the smiles on the wall, there were dark secrets, tangled relationships, and some serious mental issues.

Cuba was making Jones nervous.

She paid the bartender and left feeling desolate. She hoped she had done the right thing by finding a link to the internet instead of waiting for his call.

FORTY-THREE

After another restless night's sleep, Inspector Ramirez swung his legs over the side of his bed, careful not to wake his wife. He looked at the clock. Not even six. He was not only tired but hungry. He arrived home around midnight, then straight to bed. He had eaten almost nothing the day before, only a plantain *croqueta* from a street vendor.

Francesca was still asleep, snoring lightly. He tiptoed into the kitchen and pulled out a plate of leftovers from their small fridge. *Moros y cristianos*. Beans and rice. Literally translated, it meant Moors and Christians. Everything in Cuba is either political or religious, thought Ramirez. Even our food.

He turned to walk into the living room with the plate of food in his hand and almost collided with the dead man. He managed not to drop it; only the fork clattered to the floor. The ghost leaned against the doorway in the darkened room, his arms folded. He looked unhappy.

"You scared me," Ramirez whispered, his heart pounding. "Once this indictment is issued, I'll get to your file. Sanchez and I finished almost all the paperwork last night. We'll go through it again this morning; then we're done. And then, I promise, I *will* find out who you are."

The dead man shook his head, unconvinced.

"Who are you talking to, Ricky?" called Francesca. He heard the rustling sounds of her getting up. "Is someone here? I heard a noise."

"I'm talking to myself, *cariño*," said Ramirez softly as his wife walked into the kitchen, buttoning the front of her robe. "I was hungry; I dropped a fork."

"I hope this ends soon," said Francesca. "You have been working late every night this week. And then back at the office early each day. Last night, you talked to yourself in your dreams, too. I'm worried about you. You haven't had a proper night's sleep for weeks, Ricardo. You're living on air. Look how much weight you've lost: it's as if you are melting. It's not healthy to work so hard."

"I know. But it's almost over, Francesca. The charges will be filed this afternoon. Once this is done, things will get back to normal."

"I hope so," said Francesca, but he wasn't sure she believed him. "They don't pay you enough for this kind of aggravation. They don't pay you enough even without it. Here, let me warm that up for you."

She took the plate out of his hand and opened the cupboard to remove a heavy frying pan.

Ramirez raised his eyebrows at the dead man, signalling he should leave. The ghost looked longingly at the rice and beans, but left, gripping his hat in his hands.

I still don't know your name, thought Ramirez. But like the rest of us, you were hungry. Which doesn't really help me narrow the search to find out who you are.

FORTY-FOUR

The clock alarm buzzed at six-thirty, and Celia Jones dragged herself free of dreams of white swans with broken wings.

She packed up her laptop and put it in her briefcase. She wondered how she'd be able to transfer information from the old computer in the gallery to her new one. Her laptop didn't even accept diskettes, only CDs and memory sticks. She hoped the computer in the gallery had a working printer and a lot of toner if she couldn't crack that nut. She showered and dressed, then walked down the two flights of stairs to the restaurant for a quick breakfast.

A woman, a beggar, pushed her face against the window next to her table, pointed to her mouth. A husky security guard ran along the sidewalk and briskly hustled the woman away.

Juanita was already waiting across the street. Once again, Jones thought how unfair it was that Cuban women were not allowed in hotels. Alex was right. Havana had two faces: the one the tourists saw and the real one.

This time, they travelled to the alley without Miguel. The same dark Afro-Cuban opened the office and provided Jones with a written password to get online. Juanita said she would wait upstairs. Thankfully, no one locked the door.

The office was even more disorganized than before. Jones removed piles of CDs from the chair and sat down. She was happy to see there was a working printer and a stack of copy paper. She booted up the computer, logged on, and checked her emails.

There were messages from Miles O'Malley and Cliff Wallace. The chief had PDF'd everything on Mike's police file for her, encrypting it with her birth date. He must have been up all night, she thought. He's worried about Mike being convicted. Well, so am I.

She opened his attachments quickly and began to print them off while she read Cliff Wallace's email.

According to Wallace, Canada was the only country that allowed Rohypnol to be exported to Cuba. Because of this, it was easy to trace deliveries: shipments had to be approved by both Canadian and Cuban authorities. He had checked the paper trail with the help of a Customs and Immigration official late the night before.

The last shipment of Rohypnol was authorized for delivery to a clinic in Viñales by a Candice Olefson from Ottawa. Olefson filed her itinerary with the request: she left Ottawa on December 18 and would return home on January 2.

Wallace included the clinic's name and address. For privacy reasons, Customs wouldn't release a copy of the manifest itself without a warrant, not even to the Rideau Police. But Wallace had found out that Olefson was registered at the Plaza Martí Hotel. That was just between the Paseo de Martí and the Avenida de las Misiones, not far from the Parque Ciudad Hotel.

Just for interest, Wallace had included a National Crime Information Centre caution about a "Viper Lady," a young woman, or perhaps a man dressed like one, in Costa Rica, who cozied up to men in bars, drugged them with Rohypnol, then stole their money. A caution was like a BOLF, an alert to "be on the lookout for" an offender on the move.

Just as the last pages came off the printer, the lights began to flicker in the room. She lost the dial-up connection and then the power went out.

She called for Carlos, who explained that the telephone line was not always reliable and that power outages in Cuba were frequent. She walked upstairs and told Juanita about the early end to her session. The woman offered to bring her back later that morning if she needed to finish her session, but Jones had run out of time.

She asked Juanita to drop her off at the Parque Ciudad Hotel. She gave her the twenty-five pesos in the car. Her computer time had become expensive: fifty pesos for two hours' access, a small fortune in Cuba. That didn't include the drinks she had purchased, and she had no receipts for any of it. She winced, knowing the costs would come out of her own pocket. Her Scottish ancestors were rolling over in their graves. She couldn't help but notice that Juanita didn't offer a refund even though she didn't get her full hour.

She needed to get to the Plaza Martí Hotel and find Candice Olefson. She hoped the woman hadn't left for a day tour somewhere or, worse, for another part of Cuba.

It was just after nine in the morning. She had less than five hours until Inspector Ramirez filed for his indictment.

FORTY-FIVE

The dead man sat in the front seat of the blue mini-car as Inspector Ramirez drove to work. He pointed to Ramirez's gold wedding ring.

What is my brain trying to tell me? Ramirez looked more closely at the dead man's hand. He narrowly missed a coco-taxi in the heavy morning traffic as his car swerved. The round yellow fibreglass vehicles were mounted to mopeds but worked more like rickshaws and moved just as slowly. He pulled back into the correct lane, ignoring the complaining horns.

He hadn't noticed it before: the faint mark of a missing ring. A white line through the brown skin of the dead man's ring finger where the sun hadn't tanned it. But it wasn't unusual for a fisherman to remove his wedding ring so it wouldn't slide off when he pulled up his heavy nets. The ring itself could be in the dead man's pockets, or it could be at the bottom of the ocean. No way of knowing until someone found the body.

If I ever lost my wedding ring, Ramirez thought, the police wouldn't have to look very far to find my murderer.

"I was wrong to think you were a bachelor. Then why has no one reported you missing? If not your wife, why not a fellow worker?"

The dead man shrugged.

This was Cuba: someone always noticed when someone was missing. Despite its size, once you took away the *turistas*, Havana was really a small town.

"Unless your family thinks you're still alive."

At least three thousand Cubans attempted to make the ninety-mile trek across the Straits of Florida each year. They used pieces of drywall, old tires, dinghies, even wrecked cars they had converted into clumsy boats. Most were stopped by the U.S. Coast Guard and returned to Cuban shores before they ever set foot on American soil. But many others drowned in the rough waters or were attacked by sharks. It was possible that this man had tried to leave the island and drowned on his way to the United States.

But if that was the case, thought Ramirez, why come back?

Inspector Ramirez and Detective Sanchez sat side by side, their documents spread out on Ramirez's desk. They once again went through the exhibits that would be filed in support of the indictment. Ramirez wanted to make certain that nothing was missed.

The dead man looked over the inspector's shoulder as he flipped through the sheaf of papers. As he had throughout the week, Ramirez tried to ignore him. "Have we had any reports of a man drowning?"

"No, Inspector. Why do you ask?"

"No reason," Ramirez said, although he realized it was a strange question. He quickly changed the subject. "Were you and Natasha able to find any car rental records, Rodriguez?"

"No. I'm sure that neither Señor Ellis nor his wife rented a car," said Sanchez. "They might have borrowed one, but I think that's unlikely."

"Good. And are Apiro's DNA tests back now?"

"Yes. I have made a copy for the case file. Dr. Apiro has

established conclusively from DNA that the stains on the sheets came from the same man who raped the boy."

"Excellent. It will be very hard for Señor Ellis to argue that someone else's semen was on his sheets in a room where only he had the key."

"I think we have more than enough evidence to meet the test of probable guilt." Sanchez looked reasonably happy, although his expressions often required interpretation.

"I certainly hope so. I don't want this animal released to wander the streets of Old Havana again. According to the minister, Fidel Castro wants to send a strong message to foreigners that our children are out of bounds."

"That means a conviction for sure. No juridical panel will acquit this man once they hear of Castro's interest."

True enough. The panels were often biased towards guilt even without such high-level encouragement. Ramirez remembered the first time he appeared before one as a young police officer. Instead of asking the accused whether he was ready to plead innocent or guilty, the panel chair, a judge, had simply asked the accused if he was ready to plead guilty.

"My God," the man said, "don't you even give a man a choice?" No one in the court dared to laugh.

There was no need to stack the deck this time, however. Even Sanchez agreed. The evidence against Michael Ellis was overwhelming.

And the Canadian lawyer, in her various telephone discussions with her client, had found nothing to rebut it. She had spoken freely to Señor Ellis, not realizing that in Cuba, where she was not qualified as a lawyer, she enjoyed no privilege in her communications. It would have been negligent of Ramirez not to make arrangements to listen in on conversations that, if useful, were admissible in court.

"Even so, Rodriguez, there could be a great deal of foreign interest in this trial. We need to make sure we do things right," Ramirez cautioned. "The Canadian government knows about the charges. We can expect their reporters to come here and ask questions. No foreigner has been executed by a firing squad in Cuba for decades. The last one was that American, after the Bay of Pigs, remember? The one whose family sued the Cuban government?"

"I saw a story about that case on the internet last week, Inspector. It seems an American court awarded his family four hundred million dollars. Another judgment like that could destroy our economy," Sanchez joked.

Ramirez chuckled. He stacked up the documents he planned to attach to his report to the Attorney General. He hoped there was enough toner to make copies. Transcripts of the interrogation in which Michael Ellis admitted he met the boy and gave him money. The witness statement from the man on the seawall who observed just how angry Ellis was after the boy left. The photographs Sanchez found under the mattress. But not the CD; it was suspicious but not directly relevant.

And then Miguel Artez's statement that Ellis came back to the hotel on Christmas Eve alone. The doorman's statement not only contradicted the Canadian's false alibi, but also established the completely unexpected and sudden departure of the suspect's wife, close to the boy's death. That, in itself, was a powerful piece of evidence.

On top of that, Ramirez had Hector Apiro's opinion as to the cause of death, along with the pathologist's meticulously detailed forensic analysis. And now he had positive DNA results confirming Apiro's earlier tests as well. Circumstantial, yes, but it should be more than enough to persuade the Attorney General to proceed.

Yes, thought Ramirez, it is a "slam dunk."

FORTY-SIX

A terrace with tables and chairs surrounded a dazzling fountain just off the lobby of the Plaza Martí Hotel. Birds trilled in the exotic garden and stained glass flooded the space with refracted colours and light. Celia Jones walked to the reception desk and asked if a Candice Olefson was registered.

The smiling young man confirmed Señora Olefson was a guest and pointed to a beige wall phone. Jones was relieved when Olefson answered. She explained to the surprised woman that she was working on a file for the Rideau Regional Police Force. "Can I take a few minutes of your time?"

"Oh sure, come on up. I could use a break; I've been writing all morning."

There was no elevator in the building, so Jones walked to the second level and knocked on the door. A woman who appeared to be in her thirties let her in.

The room had two double beds, a walnut desk with a laptop, and a carved wooden armoire. It was tastefully decorated, with light peach walls and beige marble-like tile flooring. Luxurious bedding. Olefson pointed to a bentwood rocking chair next to the desk and invited Jones to sit down.

"Can I get you something, a coffee, some orange juice perhaps? I have a very well-stocked mini-bar here with every kind of rum you can imagine. I shouldn't tell you this," she laughed, "but I get it re-stocked every day."

"Orange juice would be great. What a gorgeous hotel."

"You should see the view from the rooftop pool. It's absolutely breathtaking."

"Do you have internet access here?" Jones asked when she saw that the woman's laptop was turned on. "We're supposed to have it in my hotel, but it's been down for days."

"No. Just satellite television. Which so far has amounted to some really dreadful Chinese trivia game shows. They make *Jeopardy* seem like an adrenalin rush."

Olefson cracked open a small bottle of juice and pulled out a glass from a shelf in the armoire.

"I'm almost glad there isn't any," Olefson said. "I'm trying to finish writing a mystery novel. It helps that there aren't any distractions. I'm at that point where I'm trying to work out the twists and turns. Nothing worse than too much foreshadowing. I set it in Cuba; that's why I'm here. My agent told me if he saw one more book about vampires, he'd stake his own heart."

"I'd love to hear about your book, Candice, but I'm afraid I don't have a lot of time."

Olefson smiled and sat on the edge of the bed. "Sorry. Writers. We should get paid by the word, the way lawyers used to bill. We'd all be rich. You mentioned something about the Rideau Police. So why *are* you here? And how can I help?"

"I can't discuss specifics, but I understand you volunteer sometimes to bring veterinary supplies into Cuba? I need to know about a shipment you brought in last week." Jones reached for a notepad in her purse and pulled out a pencil.

"Yes, I come here quite often. I've always been shocked at the terrible poverty, but it's the dogs that break my heart. Maybe you've seen them? They look like terriers, with short ears and a curled tail?"

Jones nodded. The stray dogs were all over the city. Sickly looking animals, starving, most of them. But she hoped that Olefson would get to the point.

"I'm a crazy dog-lover, but I can't take them all home with me. So I decided to help. Drugs for Dogs is an NGO in Toronto. I live in Ottawa, but I deliver veterinary supplies for them whenever I'm here. It wouldn't surprise me if some of them make their way into the human population, but that's okay with me. The people here are so pleasant and easygoing that you tend to forget how much they struggle to survive every day."

"You brought supplies on this trip?"

"Sorry, yes. For a clinic in Viñales. That's a couple of hours from Havana. There was a bus tour last Tuesday; I delivered them then. I prefer not to rent a car; I think they're held together with chewing gum and wire. Amazing, really, that they're still running. In most countries, it's the doctors who are highly prized. Here, it's the mechanics."

"Was there Rohypnol in the package?"

"Yes, there was," the woman said, worried. "Am I in some kind of trouble?"

"Not at all. I just need to find out if any of it went missing."

"It's interesting that you ask, because apparently there was a problem this time. And you're right, it was the Rohypnol. I think they use it on the animals to get them ready for surgery. Anyway, it wasn't in the box."

"How did you find out?"

"The clinic called me the next day to ask about it. I told them I gave them everything I had. They asked if I could double-check with the folks in Toronto to see whether it was in the original package or not."

"Were you able to find out?" Jones asked.

"Not yet, because of the holidays. I left a message on their answering machine. I think the staff at the Viñales clinic were worried it went missing on their end. It wouldn't surprise me if it was stolen. I've had coffee and rum taken from my luggage at the airport. Even tampons, believe it or not."

"I guess it would be awkward to run out." Jones cringed at the notion.

"Run out? They haven't had any for years. It's easy to understand why people steal things once you've spent some time here. I usually bring extras of stuff like that to give away. People will follow you for miles asking for hand soap or pencils. It's hard to believe the things people will beg for. I guess you can't know how important something is to you until you've lost it. Or think you will."

Jones glanced at her pencil. She thought about how casually she had waved it around in front of Inspector Ramirez. "Was the package sealed when you took it to Viñales?"

"The Customs officers here opened it to check the contents at the airport. They closed it up after that."

"Do you have anything that lists the contents?"

"Yes. There's a manifest that travels with the package. I have to produce it at Customs. They stamp it. I imagine they keep a copy. I don't keep the stamped copy, that goes to the clinic. But I always make a few copies of the original in case I have any difficulties at Customs here. Usually, people are just grateful I'm trying to help."

Olefson walked over to the desk and reached for a stack of papers. She shuffled through them until she found the one she was looking for. "Here."

Jones scanned the list quickly. Penicillin, gauze, sutures, Bactrim, Polysporin, and Rohypnol. The quantities were listed as well.

"Terrific, thanks. Did anyone else have access to the package before you turned it over to the clinic? I know I'm sounding a bit like one of those check-in attendants at the airport, but did you leave your bags with anyone, unattended? Even for a moment?"

"No, I don't think so." Olefson paused. "Now wait a minute. Come to think of it, I did ask Nasim to hold it for a minute when I took photographs."

"Nasim?"

"A guy I met on the tour to Viñales on Tuesday. A Brit."

"Do you know his last name?"

"You know, I don't. I wish I did. But I have a picture of him on my laptop, if that helps. I used to have it on my digital camera, but he took off with my camera on Christmas Eve and I never saw him again. Thank God I had already downloaded most of my photographs; I need them for details when I'm writing. Let me see if I can find it for you." She sat down at the desk and opened a file on her computer.

"He stole your camera?"

"We had arranged to have a drink here on Saturday on the rooftop terrace, to celebrate Christmas Eve," Olefson said. "I asked him if he could go through my photographs with me to see if there was anything he thought I should put in my book. He asked me about one of them, and then he literally ran off. He still had my camera in his hand. I called after him, but he kept right on going. Even stiffed me for the drinks."

"Did you call the police to report the theft?" If she had, there might be some follow-up: a name, birthdate, something to identify this Nasim person further.

"No, I kept hoping I'd run into him or that he'd bring it back. I assumed he was staying here, at the hotel, but the receptionist couldn't find anyone registered with that name." Olefson scrolled through her files until she found the picture. A small dark man in a navy shirt, wearing white sandals and a straw hat. He smiled for the camera.

"Can I get a copy of this?"

"Sure," Olefson said. "I can loan you a memory stick if you promise to return it."

"I have my laptop with me, thanks. Do you remember which photograph it was that interested him so much?"

"I do, actually. I took it on the Malecón. It was a picture of a couple of tourists with one of those young boys that hustle tourists for money. It looked like a Diane Arbus photograph. You know, where everyone's pretending to smile but you can cut the tension in the air with a knife."

"Do you still have it?"

"No, I took it on my way back to meet him at the hotel. My only copy was on the camera."

"What time did you take it?"

Olefson thought. "I was meeting Nasim at six, so I dunno. Maybe five? Five-thirty?"

"And that was on Christmas Eve?"

The woman nodded.

"Can you remember anything else about the people in the picture? It could be important."

"Really? Well, the woman had her head turned, so I couldn't see her very well, but she was gorgeous, I could tell. The man was bending over the boy. I was across the street, but even then I could see there was something wrong with his face. The man's, I mean."

Too bad Olefson didn't have a copy. Jones wondered why a British tourist so badly wanted a picture of Hillary and Mike Ellis that he stole a stranger's camera. Or was it the boy that caught his eye?

"Can I ask why you're so interested in Nasim? And the veterinary supplies?" said Olefson.

"I can't tell you much, Candice. I'm just fishing around for information for now." Jones smiled reassuringly. "But I really appreciate all your help."

Olefson downloaded the photograph for her and Jones headed back to her hotel, trying to piece things together. Alex could solve this puzzle, she thought. It's not like there aren't enough clues. But Alex wasn't here. She wasn't as quick as he was, as agile in connecting dots. That's why she worked in pencil.

She stopped at the reception desk when she got back to the hotel, but there were no messages. By the time she got back to her room, it was noon. There was no blinking light on her phone to indicate any voice mail messages: Alex must still be in surgery.

Jones called the police station and left a message for Mike to call her, then sat on the bed and waited. She checked the time nervously. Two more hours.

FORTY-SEVEN

The guard took Mike Ellis to the phone to speak to his lawyer for what Ellis guessed was the last time.

"Do you know someone named Nasim?" Celia Jones asked immediately.

"No," he said, but he heard a change in the tone of her voice. She hadn't even said hello.

Jones filled him in on what she'd discovered. "I have red flags going up all over the place."

"No kidding. Do you think this Nasim guy is involved in this?"

"It's worth checking out. I'm going to call the clinic myself and follow this up a bit more before I accuse a British citizen of anything — the chief made me promise to avoid any international scandals — but it's a pretty good lead. I also found out quite a bit about Rohypnol online, Mike. It's easily slipped into someone's drink. Completely tasteless. It causes dizziness, hot flashes, and amnesia. Within minutes. All the symptoms you experienced."

"So you were right. I *was* drugged."

"I think so. And by that hooker, most likely. I just missed her at El Bar last night."

"Too bad," Ellis said, disappointed. They needed that woman. Even so, Celia had accomplished a lot in little more than one day.

"I've been doing some thinking," she said. "That boy's body had to be covered up or wrapped up in something to disguise it before it was thrown in the water. I walked to where the body was found. It's a very busy spot. So it's not just a weapon they're missing, but a weapon *and* a vehicle *and* a tarp or a sheet of some type."

The only sheets missing from Ellis's room were the ones the technicians seized for forensic testing. Another crack in the wall of Ramirez's case.

"Those photographs under the mattress are a problem. Do you know if the maids check under the mattresses when they change the linens?"

"I doubt it." Then he understood why she'd asked. "You think those photographs were there before."

"That's crossed my mind. In which case you might not have been framed at all. Whoever stayed in that room before you did might be someone the police should look at."

"Celia, that could be our best argument." Ellis's mind raced through the facts. "The pathologist said that boy was abused once before, right? I was with Hillary every minute from when we arrived in Havana right up until she flew out. She can confirm that. That proves someone else raped that boy. Maybe we can argue that all those photographs are connected to *that* person, that it only makes sense that whoever abused the boy the first time, raped and killed him on Christmas Eve. Similar fact."

In Canada, similar fact evidence created an inference of guilt, even in the absence of other evidence. If the modus operandi in two crimes was similar enough, the legal inference was that the person who committed one crime committed the other.

"I agree, Mike. But there's just over an hour left. I don't have enough time to stop Inspector Ramirez from filing his evidence today. I'll have to get Hillary to swear an affidavit in Canada and get it here somehow. That could take days. I'm going to talk to O'Malley and see if I can stay here a while longer. We're on to something; I just need more time to follow up on it, to file a proper set of objections. I have to make sure I can pull things together in a way that's persuasive. We only have one shot at this."

Ellis felt his hopes sink like a lead lure. "They're going to transfer me to a prison in a couple of hours. You know what my chances are there, Celia. I'll be dead within a week."

FORTY-EIGHT

Celia Jones hung up, frustrated. Mike was right. Guilty or not, he wasn't likely to survive the Cuban prison system long enough for it to make a difference. And so far, she hadn't found anything concrete enough to seriously challenge Inspector Ramirez's case. Just speculation so far; no hard evidence. But her instincts told her that the police were wrong.

Then she remembered the other reports she had printed in Blind Alley that morning. She'd forgotten all about them. They could have Mike's blood work in them. If his blood type is different from the forensic evidence, she thought, I may still have time to get him out of there.

She yanked the papers out of her briefcase, scattering them on the bed, and quickly searched in her purse for her reading glasses. She rifled through the pages, looking for a medical report.

Thank God. There was a lab report in the file. She scanned through it. Mike was Type A blood group. She began rooting around in her papers for the laboratory reports that Ramirez had copied. What blood type were the stains on the sheets? Type A or AB?

She finally found Dr. Apiro's report, glanced quickly at her watch. Less than an hour now. *Shit*. The samples he'd taken were Type A, too. That just made Ramirez's case stronger.

She sat down heavily on the soft bed, heard the springs creak. Maybe she'd been right in the first place and Mike was guilty after all. Her instincts had been wrong before. Too bad; she was starting to like him. But if he raped and killed that little boy, he deserved whatever he got.

She looked at her watch again. There was really nothing else she could do with the small amount of time she had left. Ramirez was probably already on his way to the prosecutor's office, or would be shortly.

She picked up the other unread documents and began to pore through them. Mike Ellis's service record was on the top of the pile.

He was thirty-eight, six years younger than she was. He joined the force at twenty-six, spent the next twelve years on Patrol. No disciplinary charges. Quite a few commendations.

Almost six months ago, on June 2, 2006, he had been dispatched to a "trouble with man" call with Steve Sloan. The call came from a rough part of Ottawa. Something went wrong when they got there. According to the report prepared later by the Special Investigations Unit, the suspect had a knife. He slashed Mike in the face before he could unholster his gun. Sloan had his gun drawn but there was a scuffle and it discharged. The bullet hit Sloan. He died at the scene. Despite his injuries, Mike managed to pull out his own gun and kill the suspect. He was in line for a medal of bravery.

It happened. Civilians were surprised when someone armed with a knife managed to hurt or kill a policeman with a gun, but it was like rock, paper, scissors. Sometimes paper won.

Mike went on medical leave while he recovered, then disability leave after he developed recurring anxiety attacks. He returned to the job in November, but was taken off Patrol and promoted to the rank of detective in the Child Abuse and Sex Crimes Unit.

O'Malley must have wanted to put him somewhere where he wasn't likely to be threatened by men with knives or guns, Jones thought. Mike was a hero. O'Malley wanted to give him a chance to recover. Some recovery. Locked in a Cuban prison, slowly starving to death.

After a shooting, members were required to take counselling. Jones skimmed through the stack of papers, looking for the psych report. *Good.* O'Malley had sent the doctor's interview notes as well. Mike met with the departmental psychiatrist, Dr. Richard Mann, on six separate occasions. Hillary attended the third session with him, at Dr. Mann's request. Mann diagnosed Mike with chronic post-traumatic stress disorder, PTSD, because of his chronic depression, anxiety, flashbacks.

Mike told the psychiatrist about his trouble sleeping after the incident. He talked about his overriding sense of guilt at Steve Sloan's death.

"How do you feel about the fact you killed a man?" the doctor had asked, according to his notes. Mike's answer was, "It should have been me instead of Steve."

Before the shooting, Hillary wanted her husband tested to find out why she couldn't get pregnant, but he was reluctant. It seemed to be a source of strife between them. Then Steve Sloan died, only a day after Hillary announced her unexpected pregnancy. She miscarried the following week.

The psychiatrist noted how devastated Mike was by the baby's loss, that whatever ambivalence he'd felt about fatherhood had disappeared. "He displays a range of contradictory emotions with respect to his wife's pregnancy. His ambivalence is not fully conscious but presents in an extreme form."

Meaning what? That Mike didn't want to have children until he lost one? Whereas Hillary seemed to lose her enthusiasm for motherhood altogether, according to Apiro's detailed report of the contents of Room 612. A woman who wants children doesn't usually take birth control pills, thought Jones. There was a backstory to that relationship, for sure.

She read the rest of the psychiatric report, but nothing in it helped. Too late anyway. Less than thirty minutes left.

She flipped idly through laboratory and medical results that Dr. Mann asked Mike to provide. She stopped when some baseline tests for Mike's medications caught her eye. She read the tests again more carefully, then reread Mann's notes and the lab report with Mike's blood type. Then she read all of them together once more, to make sure she fully understood what they said.

Heart pounding, Celia Jones raced out the door to the hallway and ran down the stairs to the lobby, holding a single piece of paper.

She prayed the hotel had a working fax machine, that Ramirez hadn't left the building, that she could get to him in time, before he indicted an innocent man.

FORTY-NINE

The prosecutor's office was across the street from the police station. Inspector Ramirez was on his way down the stairs, exhibit binder and case file in hand, when an officer called him back.

"The Canadian lawyer is on the phone. She says she needs to speak to you urgently."

Ramirez contemplated telling the officer to take a message, but decided fairness compelled him to accept the call. He would have to make it short. He jogged back up the stairs and strode down the hall to his office. He pushed down the flashing button, and picked up the phone.

"I have a deadline, Señora Jones," Ramirez said curtly, looking at his watch. "I am truly sorry, but I have to go. I need to get this information to the Attorney General's Office in less than half an hour."

"Please. I have a medical report that proves my client didn't rape the boy, he couldn't have. Your forensic evidence points to someone else. Please look at what I've found before you do this. I'm in the business centre at my hotel. As soon as I hang up, I'll fax you the report. It's only one page. I'm begging you. Please."

Ramirez hesitated a moment. "I can wait for a few minutes, no more."

He gave her the fax number and hung up the phone, irritated. If this was a delaying tactic, he would have her arrested. He walked over to the unit's fax machine, but kept his eye on the clock.

The fax rang within seconds and a page curled through. He pulled it off, scanned its contents. A blood test. Michael Ellis had Type A blood. Why was this woman so insistent that he read information that actually strengthened his case?

Annoyed, Ramirez made a quick call to Apiro, but the doctor was out. He left a message on the doctor's answering machine to say he was heading over to the Attorney General's Office with his case file but would leave a report on the desk in his office for Apiro to examine. The Canadian lawyer seemed to think it was important. It could be added to the other reports and statements later. But Ramirez confirmed he was leaving to file materials for the indictment *now*.

The dead boy sat in Ramirez's office, swinging his legs back and forth on the wooden chair. He's already bored being dead, thought Ramirez. He wants to play.

Ramirez quick-stepped back down the hallway, then jogged down the stairs taking two at a time. He pushed through the iron gates and sprinted to the Attorney General's Office. He pulled open the heavy wooden door, nodded at the security guard, and ran up the stairs to the prosecutor's office on the third floor. Breathing hard, he was just about to hand the documents to Luis Perez for formal registration when Perez's phone rang.

"It is for you, Ricardo," the prosecutor said. "Hector Apiro."

Perez handed Ramirez the phone, raising his eyebrows quizzically. It was 1:51 P.M.

"What is it, Hector?" Ramirez asked. He gripped the receiver tightly and turned away so Perez couldn't see that his hand was shaking. He tried to catch his breath.

"I looked at the report that the Canadian lawyer sent you and it is very interesting," said Apiro. "Señor Ellis was treated with anxiolytic drugs last June. But before he took the drugs, he was given a pre-treatment hematological baseline test. To establish his baseline for liver function before he started treatment so that possible damage to his liver could be monitored. The drugs are very hard on the liver."

"Hector, I'm afraid I don't understand what it is you are trying to tell me," Ramirez interrupted, his breath still ragged. He had only minutes left and no time for lengthy explanations.

"Sorry, I am getting to it. These tests establish that Ellis has a Lewis blood antigen and that he is a Type A non-secretor. That is important."

"Hector, you're losing me. What does all this mean?"

"It means that Señor Ellis does not secrete his blood type antigens into his bodily fluids the way other people do. So his seminal fluid, even his saliva, cannot reveal his blood type. Only his blood can do so. If the semen samples on his sheets and in the boy were his, we would not have found any blood group in them. That is what being a non-secretor means."

"But you *did* find a blood group. Type A," Ramirez protested. He was confused.

"Exactly, Ricardo. Which means that those samples came from someone else."

Ramirez felt his rape charge collapsing, along with the air in his lungs. "You mean he's innocent?"

"I cannot say he was not involved. But the seminal fluid I found in this boy's body came from an assailant who was, by definition, a secretor. So, yes, someone else raped the boy."

"But who?"

"Ah, Ricardo, we do not yet have the science for me to look at a DNA sample and tell you whether it belongs to a dark man, or a short man, or a hairy one. I can only compare other samples to the ones I have. But if you can provide me with such comparatives, I can quickly tell you if they are from the same man. Within 99.999 percent probability. Provided, of course, I have the supplies I need."

One minute left. Ramirez was far from convinced that the Canadian was uninvolved. What about those photographs from the hotel room? The empty capsule? And Sanchez, whose instincts were solid even if his methods weren't always, was as convinced of the man's guilt as Ramirez.

Did he still have enough evidence to file? Apiro's expert opinion had changed. If Ramirez tried to keep the Canadian in custody while he searched for more evidence, he needed a plan for the juridical panel. But he had no plan and no time to develop one.

The photographs did not show the man's face. Ramirez could not prove that Señor Ellis was the man in them, or that Ellis concealed them under the mattress himself. The Rohypnol capsule was empty; it could not be directly traced to the boy. As for the murder, Ramirez had no place of death, no weapon, not even motive with this new evidence. It would be hard to explain to a juridical panel why someone would kill a child that someone else had raped.

Should he file his materials anyway and hope to fill in the holes in his investigation later, try to come up with some excuse as to why he needed more time? Would the prosecutor accept them, having just overheard his side of the conversation with Apiro? Luis Perez was corrupt, but not stupid.

Or should he let his only suspect go? Less than ten seconds to make up his mind.

Luis Perez waited patiently, also eyeing the clock. "Are you going to file those papers, Ricardo?" he asked. "You are almost out of time."

Maybe Sanchez is right, thought Ramirez. Maybe it *is* easier to frame the guilty. He handed his papers to the prosecutor.

"Thank you for letting me use your phone, Luis."

"Problems with the case?"

"A misunderstanding with Dr. Apiro. I'll straighten it out."

Ramirez left the building. He walked past the guard at police headquarters and up the stairs, too distracted to return the guard's salute.

The Canadian authorities would be furious. But he had made the only choice he could; he just hoped it was the right one. If Señor Ellis was proven innocent, he could always be released later. *If* he survived jail.

Ramirez would keep him in the holding cells and delay his transfer to prison by another day. That would force the Canadian lawyer to move quickly. It might even help her client beat the odds.

FIFTY

Celia Jones hung up the phone, disconnecting her long-distance call. *Shit. Shit. Shit.* O'Malley was livid. Mike was going to be transferred later that night to a prison. And after that? She didn't know.

She could almost see Inspector Ramirez's argument: that Mike's involvement couldn't be negated just because he hadn't raped the boy himself. There was still that capsule, those photographs. As for the argument that the CD and the Polaroids could have been put there by a previous hotel guest, well, Ramirez wasn't buying it.

Jones showered. She tried to scrub the smell of failure from her skin before she put on fresh clothes.

She went back over her notes, the file, the transcripts. It was almost six o'clock when she finished rereading everything. She ordered a salad from room service and went over the outline of her lawyer's brief. Something in this file nagged at her, but she couldn't put her finger on it. Something didn't fit.

She had to find the woman from the bar. That was all she had left. If Mike Ellis was convicted of something he didn't do, if he was executed and he was innocent ... she imagined the soldiers lined up with rifles, the shots. Mike collapsing, blindfolded, bloodied. Dead. She thought again of the man who had jumped, who had died, broken, in the snow.

She would never forgive herself.

Jones passed Miguel Artez in the lobby with a brief nod and made her way through the revolving door without his help. She walked quickly to El Bar, planning to leave more money with the bartender to secure his interest.

When she got there, she was astonished to find a blonde woman who looked a lot like Hillary Ellis sitting primly at the counter.

The woman's hand rested lightly on the knee of a tourist. Sunglasses with pink frames shaped like hearts were pushed on top of her streaked hair. The man beside her was large and sweaty and seemed pleased with her attention. He wore a Toronto Maple Leafs T-shirt and mopped his damp forehead with a paper napkin.

The bartender caught the woman's eye and nodded towards Celia Jones. The woman withdrew her hand from the man's knee.

Jones sat beside the heavy man and said quietly, under her breath, "This woman is involved in a police investigation. I suggest you leave quietly, while you still can."

"Christ," the man said. He threw a few pesos on the bar, disgusted, and fled. He didn't look back.

The woman was annoyed rather than angry. "Why did you do that? What did you say to him?"

Jones ignored her question. "My name is Celia Jones. I'm Mike Ellis's lawyer."

"I do not know who Mike Ellis is. I am very sorry, Señora. I think you have the wrong person." The woman turned away.

Jones leaned in but kept her voice low. "Listen to me. I know who you are, and I know what you are. I'm no threat to you. You have to trust me. I'm not with the police." Not a complete lie. She didn't work for the *Cuban* police. "I'm trying to find out how to get Rohypnol around here. I heard you had some with you on Christmas Eve when you met my client."

"I do not know what you are talking about."

"Rohypnol. A date-rape drug."

"And you think I would have such a thing? I do not use such drugs," the woman stated indignantly. "I have no need to. You can check my bag if you like. I keep very little in it, except a few condoms. They are hard to find here — do you have any by chance?" She smiled, teasing. Trying to use her charm, but it wasn't working. Jones shook her head.

"My loss," the woman said.

"What about this drink?" Jones pointed to the fat man's abandoned mojito. "If I have someone check this, will they find Rohypnol in it? You'd better tell me. Because the police are looking for you. Right now, I'm the only thing keeping you out of jail."

"I truly do not know what you are talking about, Señora Jones."

"Let's not be clever," Jones said. "Mike Ellis has spent three long, uncomfortable days in a jail cell at police headquarters for something he didn't do."

"In jail? For what?" the woman asked, shocked.

Jones lowered her voice. *Jinetera* or not, the bartender was watching them closely, and she wasn't sure exactly who else he was taking money from. "For the death of a little boy who was connected to you somehow."

The woman sat up straight then. "A little boy? Which little boy? Tell me quickly. Which boy? Was it Arturo?"

"You knew him? Who was he to you?"

The woman didn't answer. Tears welled in her eyes. Jones threw some money on the bar to cover her drink. "Let's find somewhere else to talk. I need to know what happened here on Christmas Eve."

The woman got clumsily to her feet and reached for her tote bag. She put her hand on Jones's shoulder to help stabilize herself as she climbed off the high stool, almost collapsing as she did. She was almost six feet tall in her high heels, and bottle-thin. She fumbled to put on her sunglasses. "What's your name?" asked Jones.

"Maria. Where do you want to go?" the woman asked, choking back tears.

"Somewhere safe. Where we won't be overheard."

FIFTY-ONE

"So, Inspector, did Luis Perez accept the file? Will he issue the indictment?" asked Detective Sanchez.

"Yes, but we have a problem." Ramirez quickly explained the new evidence. "I have to meet with the minister in a few minutes to make sure that our acting president understands the situation. There could be a problem if anything happens to Señor Ellis in jail before his conviction. Disruption of our trading relationship with Canada."

Why did Señor Ellis have to be a police detective? thought Ramirez. And why did they send a good lawyer when there were so many poor ones? This woman, Celia Jones, was complicating his life.

"I want you to put Señora Jones under surveillance. We have to find Señor Ellis's accomplice, and the source of those drugs. I think she will lead us to one or the other. She'll act quickly; she knows she has very little time. I let her think her client is being transferred to a prison tonight."

"And he isn't?"

"Tomorrow. I don't want him harmed before we can prove his guilt. Too risky. Perez accepted the indictment only because he thinks there will be something in it for him; he overheard my end of the conversation with Apiro. He knows there's something wrong with the case, just not what. He doesn't have the report Señora Jones gave me; Apiro still has it. But he will probably ask her for money once he goes through our materials and puts it together with what he heard."

"He'll withdraw the charges," said Sanchez, clearly unhappy.

"For a price? Of course. It all comes down to those drugs, Rodriguez. If Señor Ellis did not bring Rohypnol into Cuba himself, then the capsule we found in his room links him to the person who did. That drug is the key. We need to find out where it came from. So does Señora Jones. To save her client's life. She doesn't yet know that Luis Perez takes bribes."

"She'll find out soon enough." Sanchez stomped off, frustrated.

The dead boy stopped spinning in his chair and looked at Ramirez. He held out his empty palms.

FIFTY-TWO

They walked out into the late afternoon sun, through the semi-shade of the square, then up the Paseo de Martí to Trocadero and west to the Avenue de Italia, another wide, tree-lined boulevard. Celia Jones looked around. No one followed them except a few stray dogs.

"Here," the woman said and pointed to a wrought-iron bench surrounded by palm trees and flowering bushes. "It is usually private here. I sometimes bring my clients here. Sometimes they only wish to talk, too."

She took her sunglasses off and wiped her eyes with the back of her hand, leaving a trail of mascara across her lovely face. "The man in the bar just now. You knew he was my client?"

"Yes, I gathered as much."

"It's a shame," Maria said. "I hate to lose a paying customer." She wiped her eyes again. "Are you sure it was Arturo who died?"

"Yes."

"How?"

"He was beaten. Sexually assaulted. They found his body in the ocean."

"Oh my God," Maria cried out. "That poor child." She bent her head down and wept. After a few minutes, Maria lifted her head and searched Jones's eyes. "When was he killed? On Christmas Eve?"

"How did you know?"

Once again, the woman sobbed quietly. Then she put her pink sunglasses on and Jones could see the effort it took for her to compose herself.

"Tell me about the boy. How do you know him?"

"How can I be sure you are not working with the Cuban police?"

"They arrested Mike Ellis. They think he was connected to this."

"Was he?"

"No."

"Why should I believe you when you say that?"

"Because he says he was with you. If he was, he couldn't have done this."

The woman nodded. "Can I trust you?" she asked uncertainly.

"You have to."

Maria considered this for a moment. "Alright. I will tell you everything I know."

"Let me write this down, okay? Maria, what's your last name?" She pulled out her notebook and pencil.

"My real name is known only to me and my mother. By now, she has likely forgotten it as well. But I go by the name Maria Vasquez. Before I answer your questions, I need to know this: did he suffer, little Arturo?"

"No. I don't think so. He died quickly. Around midnight, the pathologist said."

"Thank God for that. He should have gone straight home. He was supposed to go straight home."

"You knew this boy well enough to care about him. Who was he?"

"A boy I tried to protect. A good boy. One who deserved better."

Maria put her head down and wept again, her shoulders shaking. "Why did they arrest him?" she asked. "Señor Ellis was with *me* on Christmas Eve. Arturo was alive after I left the hotel. Señor Ellis had passed out when I left. He could not have done this terrible thing."

"Someone planted evidence in his room. I need to find out who. And I need you to tell the police that you were with Mike that night so that I can get him out of jail before someone kills him. You're his only chance."

"You understand that if I admit to that, I can be locked away for being a prostitute? I could spend years in jail."

"Do *you* understand that he could be executed by a firing squad for murder? I need to know exactly when you were in his room. What time did you leave?"

The woman sighed and slowly bobbed her head in assent. "I was not there for long. From around eleven to eleven-thirty, perhaps a little earlier. Just long enough to put him to bed. He fell asleep almost immediately. He could not have moved for hours, I am sure."

Maria wiped her eyes. "I still can't believe Arturo is dead. He was a delightful boy, full of fun. A real boy, you know? Full of mischief. One who liked to play."

"How did you know him?"

Maria hesitated. Jones sensed she was holding something back.

"I saw him on the Plaza de Armas one day, being harassed by the police. I felt sorry for him. I told the police officer I was his mother. A lie, but it kept him from harm. He was such a good, happy little boy. After that, I gave him food sometimes, when he was hungry. And I knew he was getting into trouble, serious trouble, with the boys he was begging with."

"What kind of trouble?"

"About a week ago, Arturo told me a man named Nasim was giving the boys money to take their pictures. There was always another man with him, a Cuban. Arturo didn't know his name. Señor Ellis met him. The foreigner, that is. Nasim. Nasim was at the bar on Christmas Eve at the same time we were. Until Señor Ellis told him to go away."

"The man with the straw hat? The British guy? That was Nasim?" Another word completed in the crossword puzzle.

"Yes, how did you know? He used to take the boys to an abandoned building on Campanario. He asked them to pose for pictures, but I could tell from the way Arturo talked about it that the poses were sexual. Arturo would not tell me much more than that. He was very ashamed. I was certain he was being abused."

"What did you do?"

"I could not stop them from going. They are so desperate, these children. They will do anything to support their families. Nasim had told them to come back to the same building on Christmas Eve for more money, and candy, too. The other boys wanted Arturo to go. But I could see the risks. I had to stop those men. And so I went to the building on Campanario with Arturo. Only Nasim was there. I told him to leave the boys alone, that I was reporting him to the police. And I did. I thought Arturo would be safe."

"You called the police?"

"Yes. I did not give my name, but I told the officer what I knew. I even gave him the address of the building. But no one arrested him. I realized that as soon as I saw him in the bar."

"Why did Nasim come to El Bar that night?"

"To threaten me. He knew I had reported him to the police. He was very angry. He said I was nothing but a stupid *puta* and that he had a powerful friend who would hurt me if I opened my mouth again. He drew his finger like this." She mimicked slitting her throat. "He told me to keep my nose out of things that did not involve me. It frightened me, that Nasim knew I made the call."

"You were afraid that someone in the police department had tipped him off."

"How else could he know? The fact that he was out on the street and not in jail meant I was in great danger."

"In danger of what?" asked Jones.

"Of disappearing, Señora. It happens here. More often than you would think."

"Why didn't you say anything to Mike about this?"

"What could I say? We were going to spend the night together, so I knew I would be safe for at least that night. I assumed Nasim would leave Arturo alone if he thought my client was a policeman from another country."

"Mike was your client?"

"Yes, of course. We had agreed to meet there, at the bar. At seven. We made arrangements over the internet."

"Mike says he never saw you before that night."

"Not in person, but he emailed me in the afternoon."

"He used his name?" Jones asked.

"No. Of course not. Men never give me their real names online. And I never, ever, give them mine."

Jones thought back to her interview with Mike. Then she shook her head. "This doesn't make any sense, Maria. Mike was with his wife pretty much all afternoon right up to dinnertime on Christmas Eve. And there is no email access from his hotel: the server's been down for days. I don't see how it could have been Mike who contacted you. It had to be someone else. "

"But he sat on the third stool. That is where I always meet my clients. The third bar stool, at El Bar, at exactly seven o'clock."

"When were these arrangements made?"

"Late that afternoon. Maybe five-thirty or so. Why?"

"Then it couldn't have been Mike. There were witnesses who saw him on the Malecón around then. With his wife."

Jones hesitated, not wanting to scare Maria unnecessarily. On the other hand, the boy had been murdered. The woman had reason to be frightened.

"I think you were set up. I think the person who contacted you is involved in all of this somehow. In Arturo's death."

"Why would you think that?" Maria asked, shocked.

"Because if Mike wasn't the person who contacted you, no one else showed up at El Bar that night at seven except Nasim. Was he ever a client of yours?"

"No, of course not." Maria bristled. "I am very particular."

"Well, you tell me how he knew exactly where to find you, and when. I don't believe that was an accident."

"I had not considered this before. So you think he found me on the internet, and how do you say, 'lured' me to El Bar? My God, I could be dead. That must be it." Maria wiped her eyes again. "It is ironic, you know. If I tell the police, they will care more about the fact that I had an internet transaction than about the sex. I could go to jail just for going online. Five years for unauthorized internet transactions."

This country *was* insane. "Why El Bar?" asked Jones. "Why not some other bar?"

"The bartender, Fidel, protects me. I am not supposed to be inside the bar. He takes a small commission for turning his attention the other way. He warns me if he sees the police."

"How did you connect with this man over the internet in the first place?"

"I have a webpage."

"I thought Cubans didn't have access to the internet."

"It is not easy, Señora. But nothing is impossible. See?" Maria brought a cellphone out of her tote. "I am not supposed to have this, either. But I do. I must be very careful not to be accused of prostitution. I could be jailed for years. And so, like the other girls, I use computers to find my clients."

"Your clients, are they always foreign tourists?"

"Yes," she nodded. "They come here from all over the world. Even some Americans still visit Havana, although it is illegal. But we must be careful; we can all be jailed. So it is best to go somewhere where others will lie for us, like El Bar."

"Tell me about the man you were supposed to meet. What else can you remember about him?"

"Not very much. He wrote his emails in English. There was some urgency, as I remember. He wanted to meet me that afternoon."

"What can you remember from the bar? Can you remember anything else about Nasim?"

Maria took a moment to think. "Not really, no. Only that after Nasim showed up, Señor Ellis became very drunk. So quickly that I was worried about him. I thought I should get him back to his hotel. I had to almost carry him there."

"Did Miguel Artez see you come into the hotel?"

"The doorman? Yes, of course. Miguel knows all the girls. He takes money to let us in when we have a customer. He even helped Señor Ellis to the elevator. By then, Señor Ellis could hardly stand up."

"He lied to the police. He said Mike was alone, that you were never there."

"Of course he did. That doesn't surprise me at all. Miguel is not stupid. He is not going to go to jail to protect someone like me. He would never admit he allowed a Cuban woman into his hotel with a drunk *turista*. He would be fired first, then arrested."

"There was no security guard there that night?"

"On Christmas Eve? All the hotels have a reduced staff. Everyone wants to be at mass or at home with their families."

"Did you and Mike have sex?" Thinking of the sheets, the hard evidence the police might want before they'd believe Maria Vasquez's story.

"Nothing happened, Señora. He passed out and I left. I was very worried about Arturo because of Nasim's threats."

"Did you take money from Mike's hotel safe?" Jones asked. Then she realized where Mike's wallet had gone.

FIFTY-THREE

The Canadian lawyer was unhappy with the turn of events. So was Detective Sanchez. And so, it seemed, was the Minister of the Interior.

The medical report, Ramirez assured the politician, didn't mean that Ellis was innocent. It simply meant that someone else was in the hotel room that night, left his seed on Ellis's sheets, his underwear in Ellis's drawer.

"We will find him, Minister, trust me. The killer has to be someone that Señor Ellis knows. The new evidence eliminates a woman."

"Then it must be a man."

Ah, yes, Ramirez thought. The minister's famed powers of deduction. "Most likely another foreigner. I've never, in my entire career, heard of a child killed in a sex crime by a Cuban."

"A homosexual?"

Ramirez shook his head. "Unlikely. The man, or men, who drugged this boy and then disposed of him so casually brutally violated this child for their own selfish needs. This is a different kind of man than those who take pleasure in the company of consenting adults."

Yes, there were men who preferred to have sex with men in Cuba, but they were gay men, not pedophiles. Lonely men, forced to hide their true nature. Despised by policemen not just in Cuba, but as he had seen, in Russia, too. A threat to *machismo*, Latin and Slavic, it seemed.

The only thing Ramirez had noticed about homosexuals over the years was that they were prone to dramatic displays of violence in their domestic disputes. Like the man he had in custody now, who had stabbed his lover forty-three times with a piece of glass because he wrongly suspected him of having an affair. Jealousies, it seemed, ran deep in the gay community. The men could be just as vicious as any woman.

Here, the police harassed them and sometimes beat them. Ramirez came down hard on men in his department who behaved with such cruelty. He had demoted one of his detectives who acted that way and put him back on the street to lean on lampposts.

We are all Cubans, thought Ramirez. We are lucky enough to have a common enemy in the Americans; it keeps our minds off our difficulties. We must not turn on each because of something we cannot control, like who we love.

"This is exactly what we were afraid of," said the minister. "This boy's murderer came to Cuba precisely because there are children like this to exploit. Even small sums of money will entice hungry children to do things they would never consider doing if their stomachs were full. The Americans and their embargo, this is all their fault." He shook his head. "You have Detective Sanchez following the Canadian lawyer now?"

"If her client knows who raped that boy, then she does, too. And if she doesn't, she'll find out soon enough. It's just a matter of time before she contacts the suspect or he finds her."

Señora Jones would lead them straight to the accomplice,

Ramirez was sure of it. To the man who had raped, and most likely murdered, Arturo Montenegro.

"You'd better hope so, Ramirez."

After his meeting with his superior, Ramirez drove back to Old Havana, unhappy himself. He was tired and grumpy. His solid case had crumbled with one piece of paper: the only evidence the female lawyer had produced.

He parked his small blue car and walked up the concrete path to the police station. The dead boy walked beside him, skipping a little. Avoiding the cracks.

Ramirez walked up the stairs to his office. No sign of Rodriguez Sanchez, which was good: it meant the lawyer was on the move. He called the switchboard and asked her to hold his calls for a few minutes. He needed to consider his future, professional and otherwise.

"Put no one through except my wife or Detective Sanchez. And the minister's clerk if she calls, of course. *Gracias*." Although the minister was unlikely to contact Ramirez, he'd left his implied threat hanging in the air like the smoke from his cigar.

Ramirez opened his drawer and pulled out the bottle of *añejo*. He poured himself a drink, then another. He watched his fluttering fingers settle down, lose their independence. For the first time in almost a week, he let himself think about his illness.

The New Year was around the corner. It was almost 2007, a new start for the world, and possibly for Cuba.

Despite the minister's assurances about Castro's health — in fact, because of them — Ramirez believed that Fidel Castro was seriously ill. Change was in the air. Ramirez didn't want to waste what remained of his life by worrying about the future. There was too little time for remorse. This was the only way he could manage, he decided. After all, no one ever knew how much time they had left. The dead man who followed Ramirez all week probably expected to catch many more fish before he drowned.

Ah, well. The Christmas holidays were almost over. Ramirez still hoped he could find time to make love to his wife, to convince her that things were fine, even if they weren't. The only form of sexual and social intercourse left, he thought wryly, that was not yet regulated by the Cuban government.

The dead boy looked away, embarrassed.

FIFTY-FOUR

"It was you, wasn't it? You took Mike's wallet."

Maria Vasquez shrugged. "He owed me money for the night. It was not my fault he became so drunk. Christmas Eve is one of the best nights of the year: we all charge extra. I could not afford to lose that income. Yes, I took his wallet. I hoped he would think he had lost it. But I took nothing else, I swear. Only what he owed me."

"Why take the whole thing? Why not just the money in it?"

"He was so drunk, I was not sure he would remember our arrangement the next morning. I was afraid if only the money was missing, he would think someone had stolen it. And if he called the police to report it stolen, people had seen us together. I could have been arrested. Better if he believed he had lost it."

That made sense. Celia Jones hesitated to think what the penalty for prostitution *and* theft might be.

"Besides, credit cards can be replaced, as can passports. Tourists lose them all the time. Much harder for me to replace a lost client on Christmas Eve. I took nothing more than that to which I was entitled."

Jones could see her point. "And then you went looking for Arturo."

"Yes. I knew I could not trust the police to protect him if they were protecting Nasim. I went down the back stairs, and ran all the way back to the Plaza de Armas. The boys there told me Arturo was at the Plaza de Marzo, that he was hurt. I ran all the way there. When I saw him, I realized my worst fears. His face was badly bruised. He said a man had dragged him into a car. The other man, not Nasim. The man made him drink something; after that he could remember nothing."

She put her head down again and cried softly. Jones patted her hand.

"I gave him the wallet. It was something to cheer him up, to play with, maybe sell for a peso or two. It was Christmas, after all. It was all I had. There are no toys in Cuba, Señora. Besides, I could not keep it. If the police stopped me and I had a foreigner's identification on me, I would have been arrested for that, too."

Maria smiled a little, remembering. "He really liked the gold badge. But he was still so dizzy and confused. I told him to go straight home to bed, and if anyone asked about the wallet, to say he found it. His apartment was just around the corner. I should have kept him with me," she said, choking up again. "If I had, he would still be alive."

"Why didn't you?"

Maria shook her head, and Jones dropped it; the woman clearly felt guilty enough as it was. "It seems pretty clear, then," she said. "Nasim must have found Arturo and killed him after you left."

Maria nodded, sniffling.

"How did he get into Mike's room?" Jones wondered out loud.

"Who?"

"Nasim. He was the only person who could have framed Mike.

He had photographs of Arturo and the other boys. Someone put photographs of Arturo under Mike's mattress."

"Señor Ellis lost his room key that night. We had to get another one from the receptionist."

Jones paused to think. "Maybe he didn't lose it. Maybe Nasim stole it from him at the bar."

"I remember that Señor Ellis's jacket was on Nasim's bar stool, but it fell to the floor. He could have taken it then. He must have gone to the Parque Ciudad before we arrived there. He could have tried the key in all the doors until one opened. Those plastic keys are only used in the new wing of the hotel."

"So he drugged Mike at the bar," Jones said. "I assumed it was you. But he would have known that Rohypnol would slow Mike down and give him time to plant the evidence."

"Do you think he drugged and assaulted Arturo before he came to El Bar?" asked Maria.

Jones nodded. "Probably. That fits the timeline. Then killed him afterwards to shut him up."

"I remember wondering what happened to make Señor Ellis so drunk. He was too drunk to make love. And that is the first time that has happened to me, ever."

"How many drinks did you have that night?" Jones was unsure how reliable a witness Maria Vasquez would be if she was drunk.

"Me? Just one. I had a mojito and then Señor Ellis poured me a glass of rum. But I don't usually drink rum, except at celebrations. He drank it himself." Her eyes widened. "He drank *my* drink. Do you think perhaps Nasim meant to drug me instead?"

"I don't know. Maybe."

"Thank God I did not drink it. I would be dead now." The *jinetera* made the sign of the cross in front of her chest. "But why did Nasim frame Señor Ellis for a murder that hadn't yet happened?"

Jones thought for a minute. "He didn't frame Mike for murder, but for rape. He knew Mike was a foreign policeman. He must have been worried you would tell Mike he'd been luring children to Campanario and that Mike would follow up on your complaint."

"Then it makes sense. Once Nasim put that evidence in the hotel room, he could do whatever he wanted to Arturo and implicate Señor Ellis. And if he had someone on the inside of the police force, he had a way to lead the police right to Señor Ellis as well."

The anonymous complaint that had so conveniently resulted in the search of Mike's room the next morning had undoubtedly come from Nasim, thought Jones. Nasim likely had a cellphone. Mike Ellis had been set up very neatly indeed. "There was other evidence in his room, though, Maria. Stains on the sheets that matched semen found on the boy."

"Nasim had photographs with which to arouse himself. That would not have taken him long. Besides, we were at the bar for at least another hour after he left. He had time."

"Then it's Nasim we need to find," said Jones. "Do you have any idea where he could be?"

"No," said Maria. "But if he hears of your interest in this investigation through his police contact, he may go back to the address where he took the boys. To remove the evidence of his crimes. I would do this, if I were him."

Jones nodded. Maria might be a hooker, but she was smart. That was exactly what someone like Nasim would do. Cover his ass.

"Come, we can go there together," Maria urged. "We should go before he has a chance to clean up. I know exactly where it is."

Jones borrowed the woman's cellphone and tried to reach

Ramirez. He wasn't in. Neither was Sanchez. But according to Maria, Campanario was only a few blocks away.

Maria was wearing four-inch heels, but that didn't seem to slow her down. On the way, Jones asked, "How much was your client supposed to pay you for the night?"

"Around one hundred American dollars. Worthless now, but not for long. Although I will deny these arrangements later. Trust me, I do not want to go to jail for prostitution. Or be re-educated." Maria frowned. "Being educated once was bad enough."

"Is that where you learned to speak such good English?" Jones asked.

"Thank you. Of course, like all Cubans, I learned my English at school. And then, I had a very good tutor for a year. A doctor. He enjoyed literature and used to read to me. I hope someday to get a university degree. I only do this because I need the money. And because sometimes, I mean someday, I hope to meet a nice man who will accept me for who I am."

They turned right on San Miguel and left onto Campanario. Maria pointed across the street to a boarded-up three-storey apartment building.

"There it is." Maria started to walk towards it.

"Maria, we should wait for the police," said Jones, and grabbed her arm. "We don't have any weapons if there's anyone in there."

"Speak for yourself," Maria said, and pulled off her stilettos.

FIFTY-FIVE

The building was pitch black inside. Celia Jones took a moment to let her eyes adjust to the darkness. "What floor is it on?" she whispered, gripping a rock she had picked up from the crumbling walls.

"Third," Maria Vasquez whispered back. She stood so closely behind that Jones could feel her breath on the back of her neck.

Jones hoped her police martial-arts training would come back to her if she needed it. She was rusty, but in pretty good shape from years of salsa dancing.

They edged their way up the creaking wooden staircase. Some streaks of light peeked from the boards nailed over what had once been windows.

The building was completely abandoned. Most of the apartment doors had been removed, probably for reuse elsewhere. There were no lights; all the fixtures were broken. There was no electricity. "Don't put any weight on the railing," Jones whispered. "It's loose."

They finally reached the third floor. Maria pointed to a room at the end of the hallway, to the right. Jones followed her to the end of the hall, stepping as lightly as she could. The floor groaned beneath her feet. Maria was still barefoot, clutching her shoes. Jones could hear her rapid breaths. Her own heart pounded in her ears.

They stopped, waited to see if they'd been heard, if there was anyone else in the building, but it was quiet. Not even the sound of birds scrabbling on the ledges.

Jones motioned to Maria and they took the last couple of steps to the apartment. It was one of the few in the building that still had a door, left slightly ajar. Jones pushed it open just a little more.

The boards over the windows inside had been removed so the room had light. She swung the wooden door as slowly as she could. It creaked.

There was a soiled mattress on the floor and marks in the dust. Empty plastic water bottles. A child's yellow shirt, discarded. But there was no one there.

She pushed the door all the way open and took a few steps inside. Dust motes swirled through the broken window as the sun scattered its dying rays.

"This is it," Jones said. "I'm sure of it. Be very careful not to touch anything. Arturo was probably killed here."

"What do we do now?" Maria asked.

"We call Inspector Ramirez, and then we wait until he gets here. In case Nasim comes back."

Jones took another step forward, careful to avoid the marks on the floor, and looked more closely at the small yellow shirt. There were blood spots on the mattress and a pair of small blue running shoes beside it, no laces.

"Those are Arturo's shoes," said Maria. "But he was not wearing them when I saw him on Christmas Eve. What a terrible place this is. What an awful place to die."

Jones heard the door open below and footsteps on the stairs.

"Quiet," she whispered. When she poked her head out the door, she saw the top of a straw hat.

"It's Nasim," she shouted, and she ran down the hall to the wobbly staircase.

Nasim turned and fled down the stairs. He missed several steps. He landed hard on his feet, then ran out the front door and up the cracked asphalt of Campanario, pumping his legs hard, headed towards the Malecón. The straw hat flew off, rolled crazily down the sidewalk.

He was quick, but Jones managed to catch up to him. She jumped on his back and they both went down. Nasim fell face-first, throwing his arms out in front to break his fall, and Jones landed hard on top. Maria was right behind them, swinging one shoe around in the air like a club.

The two of them managed to pull Nasim's arms out from under him and yank them back behind him. Jones put all her weight on Nasim's back to keep him down, but he was struggling hard to break free. "We need to tie him up somehow."

Maria pulled a scarf out of her bag. "Here. Use this."

Somehow they managed to tie his hands together. But when they turned him over, it wasn't Nasim that Jones had tackled. It was Miguel Artez.

FIFTY-SIX

What the hell? "What are you doing here? Why did you run away?" Celia Jones demanded.

She propped the hotel doorman up against the wall of a building. Miguel Artez sat, with his hands tied behind him, on the dirt and weeds. He began to laugh.

"You tell me, you bastard," said Maria Vasquez. She held the stiletto heel of her shoe like a knife to his throat. "You tell me what happened to Arturo."

But Artez didn't answer. As Jones looked at him, she wasn't as surprised as she might have been. She had never been as sure of him as Mike was; he was a little too helpful, a little too eager to insert himself into any problem that presented itself.

"The police are on their way," Jones said. "They'll make you talk."

"The police?" Artez said, quietly laughing again. "You have no idea what you are involved in, Señora."

"Oh, yes I do. The police are going to do a lot to you for raping and killing that little boy."

"What are you talking about?" The doorman sat up straight,

the smile wiped from his face. "I know nothing about a boy being killed."

"Arturo Montenegro," Maria said, and she bent over and slapped his face, hard. "You know exactly who she is talking about. Just eight years old."

"Ouch," Artez winced, his cheek reddening. "There's no need to hit me. I don't know what you are talking about, trust me."

"You do know what happened to him, you cockroach," Maria said, and she slapped him hard again. "You and Nasim killed Arturo and you tried to frame Señor Ellis. You told the police I was not with him on Christmas Eve when you knew I was. You bastard. You lied and Señor Ellis ended up in jail. He could have been killed."

A small trickle of blood ran from the doorman's nose. "Stop hitting me," he begged. "I didn't kill anyone. I only put the pictures on the internet. I uploaded them for Nasim so that he could share them with others. Men who like such things."

"Liar," Maria spat. She was going to slap him again, but Jones stopped her.

"Say that again? You did what?"

"Photographs. Nasim took photographs of the boys. I have access to the internet. It is rare to have that access here; you know that, Señora. I post photographs for clients sometimes. That is all I have ever done. A small business of sorts." He gave Jones a pleading look, shrugging his shoulders. "I am an entrepreneur, that is all."

"You mean a *bisnero*," said Maria. "A hustler."

"Why are you here now?" asked Jones.

"Nasim emailed me this afternoon. He told me to meet him here to get more photographs from him."

"Don't play games," said Maria. "Admit it, you raped Arturo. You were the *Habanero* that Arturo told me about. You were in

the room the day those photographs were taken. Filthy pictures."
She clenched her hand into a fist.

"No, I was not." Artez looked up at her, pleading, then Jones.
"I swear. This is the first time I have been here. Usually Nasim
brings me a memory card and we meet at his hotel. I know
nothing about Señor Ellis being framed. I never knew he was
charged with anything, or that he might be. No one said anything
to me. All I did was process Nasim's photographs, I swear."

"Wrong answer," Maria said. And this time she hit Artez with
her fist. Jones heard the cartilage snap in his nose.

"Please, Señora, do not let her hit me again," Artez pleaded. "I
told you the truth."

Maria had her hand clenched to punch him a second time, but
Jones stopped her. "He couldn't have raped Arturo on Christmas
Eve, Maria. He was working the front door of the hotel all night.
It had to be Nasim."

Maria dropped her fist, but her fingers were still curled tightly
together. "Too bad about your nose," she said. "But we have very
good plastic surgeons here. Besides, it will add character to your
face."

They heard the sound of an engine. All three turned their
heads as a police car drove slowly along Campanario.

FIFTY-SEVEN

Detective Rodriguez Sanchez parked the patrol car and got out. He looked at them quizzically, and then at the blood streaming from Miguel Artez's nose.

"What is going on here?"

"She hit me," said Artez, tipping his head back to stop the bleeding. "Maria. She was going to hit me again."

"You be quiet," Sanchez said firmly. "I will take a statement from you later. I want to hear what happened from them before I talk to you. For the second time, what is going on here?"

Celia Jones answered. "You should be looking for a British tourist named Nasim. That's his first name. He raped and killed Arturo Montenegro. Miguel was supposed to meet him here today. Miguel claims he was just the webmaster for some pornographic photos of Arturo and some other children that Nasim took. But Nasim had someone with him during those assaults. A Cuban man. It had to be Miguel. I think he helped Nasim get rid of the body. His cousin has a car. A woman named Juanita."

"Not me," Artez moaned. "I swear. I just uploaded his photographs."

"You," Sanchez said, "be quiet."

He turned back to Jones. "Ramirez was right about you. He was sure you would lead us to Señor Ellis's accomplice."

"Señor Ellis had nothing to do with this," said Maria. "It was Nasim who killed Arturo. I was with Señor Ellis that night. He is completely innocent. And I would like my scarf back, please. It's one of my favourites."

Sanchez pulled a pair of handcuffs from his back pocket and untied the scarf around Miguel Artez's hands. He handcuffed Artez properly and handed the scarf back to Maria. Then he pulled Artez up hard by the metal cuffs and walked him over to the police car. He pushed him roughly into the back seat and slammed the door.

Maria rubbed her knuckles. They were already swelling.

"I am glad I did not have to use these." She picked up her stilettos and looked at them fondly, then slipped them on. She grinned at Jones. "These shoes were expensive. Hard to find here. But I'm like a blind squirrel; I always find a nut."

"Everything's upstairs, in an apartment on the third floor," Jones told Sanchez, pointing to the building. "I'm sure Forensics will have a field day with all the evidence they find in that room. We thought we'd better head over here in case he planned to come back to clean it up."

"It all ties together," Sanchez acknowledged. "I will call this in and get Dr. Apiro and our laboratory technicians over here right away. Meanwhile, you're right: this Nasim character could show up at any moment. He may be dangerous. It is better if you're not here. We can get written statements from you later." He took out his notebook and wrote down Maria's name. "Your address?" he asked.

"It varies," she said.

He raised his eyebrows but didn't inquire further. "Señor Ellis will be released within a few hours, Señora. Trust me, we will have Nasim in custody in no time. Even if he does not arrive for his meeting with that scum." He directed his eyes to Artez in the back of his car. "We have eyes and ears all over Havana, do not worry. All over Cuba, for that matter. Thank you again for your help. If I do not see you before you leave, Señora Jones," he added, as he got back into his police car, "have a safe trip home."

The two women walked back towards the Parque Ciudad Hotel. Jones was tired and hungry, but elated. She had closed the case for the Cuban police and she had firmly established Mike's innocence. She was already imagining how happy Miles O'Malley would be to hear the news.

Without Miguel Artez overseeing the front door, Maria couldn't come into the hotel, so Jones offered to take her to the Ambos Lados for dinner later that evening. It was supposed to be yet another of Hemingway's favourite restaurants, with a wonderful view of the city from its rooftop terrace.

Maria declined, explaining she wasn't allowed to eat there with a foreigner. She didn't seem that upset.

Jones asked if she'd like to join her somewhere else for a bite to eat, but Maria said there was someone she wanted to find, an old friend she hadn't seen in years.

She gave Jones a quick hug. And then she was gone.

FIFTY-EIGHT

Hector Apiro was quite surprised to be called by reception. He was in the morgue, in the midst of a procedure on one of his cadavers. It was a time, as always, when he had asked not to be disturbed so he could sculpt in deepest silence. Annoyed, he hopped from his stepladder and answered the phone.

"There is a young woman at the front desk asking for you," the receptionist said. "She says it is personal. Shall I tell her to go away?"

There was a tone of disapproval in Consuela Gomez's voice that intrigued Apiro. It wasn't often that a woman came calling for him, particularly one that Consuela disapproved of so overtly. "Of course not," he said. "I shall be right down."

Apiro was even more surprised when he saw who it was. He recognized her immediately.

"My goodness," the surgeon said, delighted, "it has been a long time." He embraced the tall woman with his short arms, which surprised Gomez, who had never seen him show physical affection, even so awkwardly. "Come, I'll make some coffee."

Gomez frowned as she watched them walk to the elevator.

Jineteras were not allowed in the building. Apiro called back to her. "Everything's fine," he assured her. "She's an old friend."

The elevator door creaked open. Apiro admired the woman's looks as the door closed behind them. The elevator buzzed at the thirteenth floor and the door opened.

"You see," Apiro said. "I am not afraid of bad luck. Most buildings pretend their thirteenth floor is their fourteenth floor, as if an entire floor has disappeared. And people believe the illusion." He laughed his staccato laugh, amused at the notion that so much of life was illusion, that so much of his work had been to make the thirteenth floor, at least in other people's lives, disappear.

"What name are you going by these days?" he asked. "Still Maria Vasquez?"

"Yes," she nodded.

"Ah, Maria. The Virgin. I always thought it was a good choice."

"I think you will be disappointed to know what I have become. It is hardly the occupation you would have wished for me."

"As I remember, you used to say that when you grew up, you wanted to be a foreigner," Apiro chuckled. "Here, let me see your face."

She leaned over, towering over his four-foot figure, and he traced his fingers gently over her cheekbones. "Extraordinary," he said. "Beautiful."

"*Gracias*. Thanks to you."

"Not at all," he said. "I simply enhanced what was inside."

Maria followed him. Her high heels clacked down the somewhat dingy corridor until they reached his office. It was small, with a large window that overlooked the ocean.

There were books piled on books. There was a child-height swivel chair that might have been covered in fabric once, the upholstery worn through to the batting beneath. A stool was buried under papers. He pulled it out for her and reached underneath the books for a coffee mug as well.

"Here, sit, please. Let me make you some coffee. It's not too late at night for you?"

She shook her head.

Apiro located a glass coffee pot. He excused himself to get some water, leaving her to look around his office. He came back with an electric kettle, which he plugged in. When it whistled, he filled his glass pot with fresh grounds and water and let the coffee steep. He pushed down on the metal perforated top, so that the coffee grounds stayed at the bottom.

"They call it a French press," he explained. "Who would have guessed the French would know anything about making coffee?" He poured them each a mug of the rich brew. "Real beans," he said. "From the black market."

Maria sat quietly for a moment as she sipped. "Are you angry with me?" she asked. "That I left without saying goodbye?"

"Of course not. I never expected you to stay," he lied.

"I never even thanked you for paying for my surgery."

"You knew?" At the time, he'd considered it as good an investment of his small savings as any other. As for the rest of the medical supplies he'd needed, he had begged, borrowed, and even stolen some of them.

"Yes, of course," she said, tears welling in her eyes. "It is still the kindest thing anyone has ever done for me."

He handed her a handkerchief from his pocket. She wiped her eyes with it, then folded it neatly and gave it back. "I missed you, Hector. I'm happy to see you looking so well."

"You missed me?" he said, surprised. "Really?"

"Of course," she said. She looked at his walls. "I assumed you would be married by now. But I see no photographs of a family, only your degrees and certificates. You're not married?"

"Me? Of course not," Apiro scoffed. "I mean, seriously, what woman would want me?" He looked at his short legs as if the answer was self-evident.

She reached out and touched his arm lightly. "Any intelligent woman would be lucky to have you. I think women are more thoughtful than you give us credit for."

"Speaking hypothetically, that may be true, Maria. My reality has always been a little different."

"Mine, too," Maria agreed. "But you, of all people, ought to know better than to judge someone by their appearance. You transform people's looks all the time."

"I used to," Apiro said slowly. That much was true. Or at least had been, before she ran away from the hospital in the middle of the night and broke his heart.

"If you don't have any plans, Hector, I wondered if we could perhaps have dinner together," she said tentatively. "I have a friend who owns a *paladar* where we could go. It is intimate and quite romantic and the food is wonderful. He accepts American dollars; I have some to spend. I want to explain to you why I left so suddenly, but I would rather do it over a glass of wine. I am afraid I may become emotional, talking about it."

"A *paladar*? You and me?" he said, afraid he'd misheard her. "You mean on a date?"

He stiffened, waited for her to laugh at the word that had escaped his lips, for the hot wave of shame to pass through him when she did. A ridiculous idea. *Romantic*? He must have misunderstood her.

"Yes," she said, smiling. "Just the two of us, Hector. That's exactly what I had in mind."

"But you were my patient," he protested, hardly able to believe what she was saying. That she was attracted to him, too. "There are rules."

"I was your patient almost nine years ago. I think the ethical issues are behind us now, don't you?"

Apiro saw the warmth in her eyes. His face creased into a smile as he realized that whatever she'd fled all those years ago, it wasn't him.

"Maria, of course we can go out for dinner, a hundred of them, if that's what you'd like. But you need to understand that I've never had a date with a woman before. I am not exactly sure what I'm supposed to do."

"I am sure you will figure it out," she said, laughing. "As long as *you* understand that you won't be my first."

"I would feel proud to be among the first hundred," said Apiro, smiling.

"You see, Hector? That was entirely the right answer, even if your numbers are a little low."

A moment later, Hector Apiro became the first man Maria Vasquez had ever kissed.

FIFTY-NINE

Mike Ellis wasn't sure of the time, but he knew what was coming. His legs began to shake when he heard the footsteps in the corridor. The guards opened the heavy iron door. One watched him cautiously, his hand placed on his baton protectively.

Ellis said goodbye to his cellmates. Victor Chavez wished him a happy capitalist New Year; Ernest Zedillo wished him a full stomach. They shook hands, then Ellis was led into the corridor.

The guard wearing Ellis's shoes took his leg shackles off and Ellis rubbed his swollen ankles. He followed the men down the hall, dragging his feet.

He was going to die in a Cuban jail, he was sure of it. The other prisoners would find out what he was. He would never see trial. He was terrified but tried hard not to show it. Ellis had never expected to die in jail. He always considered suicide more likely.

Detective Rodriguez Sanchez stood in the hallway, holding a pair of running shoes. "Your lawyer wanted you to have these. You're free to leave."

"You're letting me go?" Ellis didn't believe it. He suspected a trick. Sanchez could shoot him in the back as he walked away and claim he had tried to escape.

"Yes," Sanchez confirmed. "As of this moment, you are not under arrest. Your lawyer will explain why. You will receive back all of your property." Sanchez glanced at the guard and said something to him in Spanish. "Except your shoes. I understand you gave them away."

Sanchez handed Ellis his wallet and ring and the other items taken from his pockets.

"Inspector Ramirez has your passport. He has asked that you stop by his office to retrieve it tomorrow. By the way, I put the money we found in your pants in your wallet, all of it. There will be no charges deducted by the Ministry of the Interior for your stay with us, at Inspector Ramirez's request."

Ellis's tailbone was sore, and he was stiff from days of sitting and sleeping on the hard cell floor. He was confused, trying to process the fact of his release. "That's it? How will I get back to my hotel? Will someone take me there?"

"Your hotel is within walking distance, but yes, we can find you a taxi if you wish."

"I'm really not under arrest anymore?"

"No. A foreigner, a man named Nasim, killed the boy with the help of a doorman at your hotel. Miguel Artez. The doorman probably put the evidence in your room, although he denies it. Or let Nasim in to do so."

Ellis nodded, at once shocked and relieved.

"It looks as if I was mistaken about you, Detective Ellis." Sanchez shook Ellis's hand. "I apologize, sincerely. It is quite an ordeal we put you through." Ellis couldn't help but notice that Sanchez had used his title for the first time.

"Accepted," said Ellis. "No real harm done. I needed new shoes anyway. I'm just glad you found the people responsible."

"You must be anxious to get back to Canada. It seems Havana has not been much of a holiday for you."

"I am. I have some things I need to attend to."

"You may want to leave Havana sooner than originally planned, then." The implication was clear: before Detective Sanchez changed his mind.

"I was thinking the same thing," said Ellis.

"Enjoy the rest of your vacation, Señor. But don't stay too long."

Detective Sanchez left and the guards returned Ellis's clothes. Ellis changed out of his prison overalls in a nearby bathroom. He put his watch back on. He held his wedding ring in the palm of his hand for a long time, but finally put it back on his ring finger. He slid his wallet into his back pocket and tied up his running shoes.

He walked out of the police station. He expected someone to run after him, tell him it was a mistake, and slap handcuffs on him again.

But it was as Sanchez had agreed: a taxi waited. It was just after 7:30 P.M. He opened the car door and got in, asked the driver to take him to his hotel. There, still bewildered at the turn of events, he paid the cab driver from the money in his wallet and walked up the sidewalk to the grand revolving doors of the Parque Ciudad Hotel.

The concierge pushed the doors open for him. Miguel Artez, Ellis realized, was likely in jail.

"Did you find your wallet, Señor Ellis? I haven't seen you for a while."

"Yes," Ellis acknowledged. He realized the concierge had no idea what had happened or where he'd been for the last three days. "Yes, I did get it back. Thanks." There was no point in explaining.

The first thing he did when he got to his hotel room was to call Hillary, but if she was at home, she wasn't answering. Her parents' number was unlisted and he couldn't remember what it was, but he wasn't sure they'd accept his call anyway. He called Celia Jones, but there was no answer there, either. He left a message on her voice mail to say he would try again later.

Ellis ate in the hotel restaurant, his first decent meal in days. *Ropa vieja*, a kind of shredded steak. Black beans and yellow rice. He didn't even order an alcoholic drink, just water. He realized he'd made it through two whole days without a single panic attack.

When he got back to his room, he tried to call Jones, but once again there was no answer. That night, with a real mattress beneath him, he slept like the proverbial lamb.

Mike Ellis was still dead to the world on Friday morning when the phone rang. It was Jones.

"I'm sorry for not calling you back before now, Mike. I had to report to O'Malley last night. And catch up with my husband." She quickly went over the details of Miguel Artez's arrest. "You must be thrilled to be out of that jail."

"You can't imagine how good it feels. I plan to wander around Old Havana today and enjoy myself for the first time in months. Maybe longer."

"I'm going to take a tour bus to Viñales myself," Jones said. "It's leaving in half an hour. I want to see the countryside and visit the people I dealt with at that veterinary clinic. The clinic manager just called me and confirmed what we suspected. They've been losing Rohypnol from their deliveries for years. I'm going to call Inspector Ramirez's office when I get off the phone with you and let him know what I found out. I'd like to do some fundraising for the clinic when I get back home. That woman went well out of her way to help us."

"I'm sure they'll appreciate it. Count on me for a big donation. When do you leave for Canada?"

"Tomorrow. I really want to be home for New Year's Eve. Plus, I have to prepare a lengthy report to O'Malley about this whole experience. And figure out my expenses. Just trying to explain them to Accounting will be a challenge, given these two blasted currencies and the fact that I don't have proper receipts for anything."

"You *are* from Ottawa, aren't you?" Ellis said. Ottawa was one of the most bureaucratic cities in the world. Or at least he'd thought so, until he came to Cuba.

"I guess I am," she laughed, but he could tell she had already moved on, was already thinking about something else.

"Thanks again, Celia, for all your help. I mean that. If you hadn't come to Cuba, I'd still be in custody, maybe even dead. I feel like I owe you my life."

Ellis was changed by the events that had taken place. He had been given a second chance at a new life and he wasn't about to lose it.

"Let's not do that whole Chinese thing where I'm responsible for the rest of your life now, too, okay?" she said, laughing. "When are you going home?"

"Tomorrow too, I think, if I can change my flight. I have some things to work out with my wife. About the divorce. It's time I faced up to some things."

"Well, I hope it all works out the way you want it to. Listen, if I don't see you before you leave Cuba, the best of luck. And Happy New Year."

"You, too. But I'll see you at work."

"Of course," she quickly agreed. But he noticed that she said "goodbye" when she hung up, as if she wasn't sure. As if she feared that she might not.

SIXTY

Inspector Ramirez was at an autopsy, the switchboard informed Celia Jones. The inspector would be tied up for hours. Jones left a message and asked if Detective Sanchez was in. The operator put her through, and he picked up the phone.

"Nasim Rubinder committed suicide yesterday," Sanchez told her. "He never showed up at the Campanario address, although we kept it under surveillance. Artez told us he was registered in a room in the Plaza Martí Hotel under the name Daljit Pradesh. We went there to interview him, but there was no answer at his door. We found him lying on the floor inside. An overdose of Rohypnol, it appears. Dr. Apiro says he died sometime in the afternoon. We matched his fingerprints through Interpol. He was wanted in England on over a dozen rape and child pornography charges from 2005."

Rubinder had owned a modelling business in London, Sanchez explained, but his models were teenage girls. He used date-rape drugs on at least fourteen of them that the British authorities knew of. He made pornographic tapes of himself having sex with them, then posted these on the internet. Following an international sting operation, he and a number of others in the child pornography ring were arrested. He was released from custody on a high cash bail but managed to flee the country.

"Where he went after that is not clear," Sanchez said. "He arrived in Cuba only two weeks ago. We have informed the British authorities. Needless to say, they are quite happy: his death closes a number of files. And soon our own file can be closed on the death of Arturo Montenegro, once we tidy up some loose ends."

"You must be very pleased, Detective Sanchez."

"That Nasim Rubinder killed himself, instead of being killed by the state? Less paperwork, certainly. But I think Inspector Ramirez would have liked to see him stand trial. I am happy, however, that we finally found the right man."

"What will happen to Miguel Artez?"

"I have arrested him for illegal use of the internet, allowing Cuban nationals into a state-run hotel, procuring, and child pornography. Those are very serious charges. Others will follow as our investigation proceeds. We are still looking for the car that transported the child's body to the Malecón. Miguel Artez's cousin has also been questioned, but so far she appears to be unconnected. At the moment, it looks like the boy's death involved just those two men, Rubinder and Artez. Artez denies it, of course. But the prosecutors will file their indictment against him on Saturday. Unfortunately for them, but good for us, Saturday is a working day in Cuba for the prosecutors as well."

"Your charges sound pretty solid to me."

"I am sure Artez will be convicted," Sanchez agreed. "As long as he has no Canadian lawyer helping him." Jones wasn't sure if he was complimenting her or not.

"Now, can I help you with something, Señora? Is there a reason you wanted to speak to Inspector Ramirez?"

"Perhaps you can let him know I received a call from the Viñales veterinary clinic earlier this morning. The manager says there have been thefts of Rohypnol going back several years. I'm going to take a bus tour to Viñales today, to pick up the manifests for the deliveries."

The clinic had no working fax machine, but Teresa Diaz, the office manager, had promised to make Jones copies, provided their copier had enough toner.

"There is no need for you to travel to Viñales, Señora. We can follow up on that information ourselves. But we appreciate your efforts. Truly. A very bad man is dead; another is in police custody. There is time, now, for us to write up our reports. No urgency at all."

"I've already paid for the ticket," she said. "I'll be leaving in about a half-hour. I'm looking forward to it. It's my day to be a tourist. I really would like to meet these people at the clinic, too, you know — they've been lovely to me. I want to see if I can do something to help them when I get back to Canada. At the very least, I'll take them some soap from the hotel. But thank you for everything. I'll make sure I drop the copies off at your office before I leave for the airport tomorrow morning. And thank you for letting me know about Nasim and the charges. I'm so glad Mike is out of jail. I can't imagine what would have happened to him if he'd been transferred to a prison."

"Señor Ellis was lucky, Señora. Because believe me, I can "

SIXTY-ONE

Inspector Ramirez wanted to see Nasim Rubinder's autopsy with his own eyes. The file was technically closed. Even so, Ramirez wanted to make sure the man was actually dead, see it for himself.

He was still shaken by the images Sanchez had found hidden in Rubinder's hotel room. There were five CDs concealed under the mattress, thousands of images of prepubescent girls being assaulted, most in their early teens.

Ramirez thought of his own young daughter and shook his head in disgust. He would feel more comfortable, for a change, once he saw Hector Apiro actually slice the brain from this monster as well as his other organs. He wanted no chance of Rubinder's return in any form.

Once again, the dead man followed him patiently, but only as far as the door. Ramirez had made no progress on the man's death, given the events of the week. He still had no idea of his identity.

Ramirez entered the small morgue, hung up his jacket, and put on a white lab coat. As always, autopsies made him feel uneasy. He coughed lightly to keep his stomach contents down. The room was warm. He ran his finger around his collar to loosen it.

By contrast, the surgeon seemed completely comfortable in the heat. In fact, he looked happier than Ramirez had seen him for some time. He was humming as he worked. Ramirez tried to put his finger on it. The pathologist seemed *taller* somehow.

The first thing Inspector Ramirez noticed about the body stretched out on the metal gurney was the coarse dark fur that covered the man's chest, arms, and legs. Rubinder had been a very hairy man.

"You know, Hector," Ramirez said, as he pulled up a stool, "I am almost sorry Rubinder killed himself. He would have had an unpleasant time in custody once we arrested him. A quick death was in many ways too good for him. I can say that out loud, now that I am no longer required to be dispassionate about the evidence."

"I would not give up your professional objectivity quite yet, my friend," Apiro cautioned. He lit a pipe and drew on it. The smell in the morgue was notably worse, the refrigeration unit still out of order.

Ramirez walked back to his jacket and pulled out his cigar. "And why is that, my friend?"

"Like you," the doctor said, reaching for his stepladder, "I do not care much for loose ends. But loose hairs are important. That was something that bothered me, once I saw this man's body. As you can see, he had a lot of hair. He should have shed everywhere. But the one thing we did not find in Señor Ellis's room, or on the boy's body, were any hairs matching his. I would have expected some hair to be transferred to the boy or his clothing in the course of an attack. So I took the liberty of checking Nasim Rubinder's blood type against the semen samples we had taken."

"And?"

"Rubinder was Type B."

"But the semen samples we took from the boy and those sheets were Type A, were they not?"

"Exactly. There is no match. And Miguel Artez is Type AB. I confirmed that from blood samples on the shirt he was wearing at the time of his arrest. Apparently, he had a bloody nose when he was brought in. Some kind of street justice?"

"There was some of that, yes. The woman who hit him had quite a right hook," said Ramirez. "So that rules out Miguel Artez as well?"

"I'm afraid so. Someone else raped the child."

"*Dios mio*, I have run out of suspects," Ramirez exclaimed. If it wasn't Ellis, or Rubinder or Artez, then who was it?

"Perhaps the maids did it after all," Apiro said, chuckling.

Ramirez took a moment to digest this new information. "Were there other men in this child sex ring, then, that we don't know about, Hector?"

"All I can tell you for sure is that neither Nasim Rubinder nor Miguel Artez raped the boy. Their blood types are different from the semen found on the hotel room sheets and in the boy's body. The science is clear, Ricardo. Where it leads you, I cannot say."

"You are absolutely certain someone else raped the child?"

"Yes." Apiro looked up at him. "Beyond any doubt."

Ramirez pondered this for a minute and then nodded. "Then I have to set aside my previous assumptions. When I think back, Rubinder took photographs, but his attraction for children seems to have involved adolescent girls. There was not a single photograph in his CD collection of any young boys. And it could not have been Artez, in any event. He was working at the hotel until just after midnight, and the boy was drugged and raped before then. My two-person theory was based on an assumption that Señor Ellis was guilty but had no car. But the entire crime could have been the act of one man. Someone with a vehicle."

Apiro inclined his head. "You have assumed that everything Miguel Artez told you is a lie. Perhaps you should instead assume that he was truthful. Maybe that will help?"

Ramirez nodded. "Good idea, Hector. He gave us a written statement. He insists he never met the boy and that he didn't know the boy was dead. If that is true, then someone else abused the child. Along with a car, that person also had to have access to Michael Ellis's room. But who? What connections have I missed in the evidence?"

Apiro pulled over his stepladder and sat on the second rung.

"I have a theory," Apiro suggested. "I told you, I have only seen injuries such as the ones Arturo Montenegro suffered once before. It is the only time in my career that I have seen a boy of that age, of any age, beaten so badly.

"It was a long time ago, almost fifteen years. A case involving another eight-year-old boy, when I was still a surgeon at the children's hospital. I alluded to it the other day. I have to be careful about what I tell you; there are certain things I cannot disclose. Doctor-patient privilege is very strict. I gave an oath when I became a doctor to protect it. For example, I cannot give you the name of the child. But some of the information you need may be in your own records and who knows, perhaps it will help point you in a new direction."

It was January 1992, just after Christmas, Hector Apiro explained. The boy was attacked at a boarding school in the Viñales mountains run by the Catholic Church.

"Father James O'Brien, the principal, brought him to the children's hospital," said Apiro. "Accompanied by a policeman. There were no ambulances in Viñales at the time and only the church vehicle had sufficient fuel to make the trip. He had been raped, with enough force to suffer internal bleeding. He refused to say who attacked him.

"He would not even speak to us when he first arrived," Apiro recalled sadly. "His face was swollen purple like an eggplant. The surgery was complicated because the bleeding was intense. But the operation went well and the boy survived. His body began to heal. He spent more than a month in the children's hospital while he recovered from his injuries."

"Did he ever tell you what happened?" Inspector Ramirez asked.

Apiro shook his head. "I tried to find out. I spent most of my free time reading to the boy, hoping he would eventually open up to me. But he was severely traumatized. Small wonder. His ribs, even his cheekbones, were broken. The policeman eventually told me it was another boy at the school. The offender was a minor himself, a fifteen-year-old boy, too young to be charged, and so there was nothing that could be done." In Cuba, children under the age of sixteen could not be charged with a criminal offence.

"I never knew the attacker's name. And so," Apiro explained, "I was powerless to do anything. It was not my job to get involved in police matters — not then, anyway — but to offer care. I checked on the injured child several times a day, and then as the weeks passed and the boy improved I became increasingly busy with my other patients and left his care to the ward nurses."

"What happened to him?" Ramirez asked. "After he recovered, I mean."

"They sent him back to the same school."

SIXTY-TWO

Celia Jones waited outside the hotel for the lemon-coloured bus to pull up. It was a glorious, sunny day.

She climbed into the bus with twenty or so other tourists, Europeans, mostly. It was about a three-hour drive to Viñales, the guide explained, with all the stops.

The bus drove past the Gran Teatro de La Habana, and then turned onto Calle San Martín. The tour guide pointed out a collapsed ruin with trees growing on the roof, all that was left of the original theatre. It was sad to see the devastation of what was once a cultural icon in Havana. She took a photograph to show Alex, but realized how heartbroken he would be to see it. She deleted it from her camera.

The bus drove down the Avenida Simón Bolivar and the Avenida Salvador Allende. They passed the Memorial José Martí, a giant tower with a statue of the hero, poet, and author, founder of the original Cuban Revolutionary Party.

They stopped for a few minutes at the Necrópolis Colón. It was a forty-acre cemetery, filled with over two million graves, the guide explained. There were gravestones and monuments of every conceivable shape and size. It was a lush green area, blanketed with mariposa lilies — the Cuban national flower — as well as vibrant hibiscus, pale orchids, and bright bougainvillea.

It was the first cemetery Jones had ever been in that didn't make her uncomfortable. Most of them were silent, with only the birds singing. This was a place of laughter, colour, scent. If there were spirits wandering around here, unlike the ones in Blind Alley, they didn't frighten her. She had only a few minutes to take photographs before the tour guide said it was time to get back onboard.

The landscape changed once they left Havana. Flat farmlands mutated into small bright green hills shaped like pincushions. *Mogotes.* Then high, jagged cliffs. She hadn't realized they would be travelling into the mountains. She felt queasy every time the bus lurched close to the edge of the road.

About two hours into their tour, they stopped for lunch at a town called Soroa. They were taken to a waterfall and an extraordinary orchid garden, fragrant with perfume. Jones had never seen orchids growing in the wild, or so many different ones. She took pictures of every variety. After lunch, a splendid buffet of bright green avocadoes, mangoes, yams, pineapples, and almost unbearably fresh papayas, they got back in the bus.

The yellow bus chugged along the twisting road. Jones saw the occasional pedestrian doubled over, straining to walk up the steep incline. In the valley below, workers moved like small insects, droning away in tobacco fields.

She wondered what the altitude was and shivered as the air cooled. The bus climbed higher and higher up the winding road, her stomach churning with the turns. She managed somehow to keep her lunch where it belonged, but she was starting to feel decidedly unwell.

It was a relief to see the sign for Viñales. The tour guide said it was a friendly place and to expect a warm welcome, despite the colder temperatures. The bus finally stopped on the main street, allowing her to escape.

They were given a few hours to wander around town and told to meet back at the bus no later than four. Some of her tour mates rented bikes. Chinese ones. Heavy, awkward bicycles that looked as if they were made out of one piece of bent metal.

Jones asked a man for directions to the veterinary clinic. On the way, she stopped to look at children playing in the yard of an orphanage. One small girl, little more than a toddler, sat in a dilapidated wheelchair. The others pushed her around and around in circles as she squealed with delight. A boy swung the ends of two long skipping ropes tied to a tree while another girl jumped through them, kicking up dust.

Double dutch. Jones had played it herself as a child. She loved watching them, hearing their peals of laughter. Her heart ached, once more, at the fact that she and Alex had no children.

The veterinary clinic was located on the second floor of a building on the main street. Celia Jones introduced herself to the woman at the reception desk and was pleased to discover it was the same woman she had spoken with earlier. Teresa Diaz greeted Jones warmly.

"I pulled out all our forms for Rohypnol shipments we received, going back almost five years. I made copies for you. As recently as last week, four capsules were missing."

Jones saw that the last few pages were hard to read, the toner low, and was immensely grateful that the woman had used the clinic's scarce supplies to assist with her request. There was great kindness in this country.

"May I contact you after I return to Canada? Please let me know what supplies you need most urgently; I'd like to help. I'm married to a Cuban doctor. I'm sure we have friends who would make donations as well."

"That would be wonderful," Diaz exclaimed. She thanked Jones profusely and gave her a card with the number and address of the clinic handwritten on it.

The veterinarian, Dr. Vincent, would contact Señora Jones through the Drugs for Dogs agency. Diaz shook Jones's hand enthusiastically and thanked her again for her kind offer of assistance. Jones thanked her for her own, and handed the woman a bar of soap before she left. As she walked down the stairs, she scanned through the forms, examining the signatures at the bottom of each page.

As she reached the bottom step, she looked up. When she saw who was waiting for her on the street, her blood ran cold.

SIXTY-THREE

"They sent him back to the same boarding school where he was assaulted?" Inspector Ramirez exclaimed. "The child must have been terrified. And what of his attacker, the older boy? What happened to him?"

"I don't know, Ricardo. I often wondered whether he received counselling for his psychological problems, but I had no way to follow up. As a minor, his identity was protected. Reluctantly, I let the matter go."

"And you think that boy, the older one, might be involved in this?"

"He would be a man now, but I think it merits checking into."

Ramirez reflected. It was possible Apiro was right. That kind of aggression was unusual. Ramirez had never seen such violence in the hundreds of sexual abuse cases he had investigated, and Apiro had only seen it once before, despite his thousands of patients. The victims were roughly the same age; the attacks took place at the same time of year and displayed a similar type of violence. Perhaps there were other attacks over the intervening years, children too frightened to report their assaults. A common modus operandi could not be excluded simply due to the passage of time.

"Sanchez searched for similar offences on our databases," Ramirez said, "but nothing showed up."

"The boy had no record," said Apiro. "He was never charged. And remember, this was years ago."

That explained it, thought Ramirez. The reason Sanchez had not been able to track it down. It would never have occurred to Sanchez to check for old files involving young offenders so long ago.

"We should have the police report in our archives. I'll call the clerk and ask her to look for it, now that we have some dates to work with." Ramirez did some quick calculations. "If the young offender was fifteen in 1992, he would have been born in 1977, or thereabouts. That would make him twenty-nine or thirty years old now. It should be easy enough to check for a birth date between, say, 1976 and 1978, and a sexual assault case in our youth offender records for Viñales. What hospital was it that you worked at then?"

"The Hospital Pediatrico y Cardiocentro Infantil. The children's hospital."

"And the date, you said, was just after Christmas?"

"Yes. January."

Ramirez walked over to the wall phone and called the police archives. He gave the clerk the information. It took only a few minutes before the phone on the wall rang; he grabbed it. The clerk had found the file easily with the information he had provided.

Ramirez asked her to send a patrol car to the morgue with the file. About twenty minutes later, he held a dusty folder in his hands. Apiro watched closely as Ramirez opened and flipped through it, searching for the name of the assailant.

And there it was, on the police investigation report, a reference to the fact that the boy's attacker was a young offender with a date of birth of April 16, 1976, and then, a few pages later, his name.

"My God," Ramirez said, astonished. "It was Rodriguez Sanchez."

SIXTY-FOUR

Detective Sanchez stood on the street, his police car parked at the side of the road.

"What a surprise to find you here," said Celia Jones as casually as she could. When she saw he was alone, she considered running back up the stairs. But she wasn't sure how dangerous he might be, and she didn't want anyone in the clinic to get hurt.

"I wanted to make sure I got copies of those records," he said. "We want to wrap things up today with our investigation."

But he'd said it wasn't urgent. "That's a long trip for you to make; it must have taken you hours," she said, feigning ignorance. "It really wasn't necessary." She looked around. Hoped she might see another police car she could wave down. But there was no traffic, not even a bicycle.

Teresa Diaz looked out the window and waved at them. Jones had no choice but to wave back.

"I am afraid it was, Señora." Sanchez stepped towards her and she felt the hard round edge of a gun barrel press into her side. "Please get into the passenger seat of the car quietly. I am sorry it has to be this way."

She did as she was told. He started the car and drove slowly through town until they left the outskirts of Viñales. He held the steering wheel with his left hand and the gun in his right, its muzzle pointed at her. They passed a few cars but there was nothing she could do. She was trapped.

They drove several miles outside of town before the car left the main road. Sanchez steered it through a gap in the trees and down an overgrown road, the ruts dotted with small shrubs. The car bumped along. There were no houses for miles.

Sanchez finally parked in front of what looked like an abandoned school. The main building was overgrown with weeds and moss. A second, smaller brick building behind it appeared to have once been a residence of some type.

He told her to get out. She opened the door and stepped into the shade. She wondered how long she had left before he killed her. She began to shiver. She felt as if she was watching a scene unfold from a distance, was almost surprised at her feeling of detachment. She recognized the early stages of shock.

"I truly am sorry, Señora Jones," said Sanchez. "I did not want things to come to this. I told you not to come here."

"It wasn't Nasim who stole the drugs, was it?" she said. "It was you. I thought it might be."

"How did you know?"

"I wasn't completely sure until this moment. But the thefts from the drugs listed on these forms took place over a period of years, which ruled out Nasim Rubinder. And it's your signature on those forms."

He inclined his head, without releasing his grip on the gun.

"Very good. You make connections almost as quickly as Ramirez. But that is the problem, unfortunately. Before I joined Ramirez's office, I worked in Customs. I was the officer who approved the contents of all drug shipments at the International Airport. If Ramirez goes into those records, he will discover that each time I checked a delivery of Rohypnol, some went missing."

"And the one last week?"

"I was at the airport doing something else. The officers in Customs were busy. I offered to take over their duties so that they could have a coffee break. They were delighted."

"Did you bring me here to kill me?"

Jones wondered just who said there was no such thing as a stupid question.

Sanchez stepped forward. He pointed the gun at her forehead and took the forms from her hands. He folded them and put them in his jacket pocket. "Thank you, Señora, for helping me to find a paper trail that could have convicted me. I will make sure these are destroyed. I've already gotten rid of the ones at the Customs Office."

"My disappearance will be a little hard to explain, won't it?"

"Oh, I do not think so, Señora. You took a bus tour. You left the group and wandered away from town. No one saw where you went. You did not return to the group when you were supposed to. Perhaps you took a walk to explore the mountains. It is very steep at parts of the road. There have been accidents. They will assume you were struck by a car or a bus. There will be a search; I may even insist on one. But trust me, I will make sure no one finds your body."

No one knew she was here, and even the tour guide wouldn't think to look for her this far from town. It was too far to get to by foot and she hadn't rented a bike. Besides, it was only around three and no one would miss her at the bus for at least another hour. She would die here, then, most likely within minutes.

She took a deep breath, savouring the mountain air, thinking the unimaginable. At any second, Sanchez would tire of talking to her. He would pull the trigger, and Celia Jones would cease to exist.

SIXTY-FIVE

Rodriguez Sanchez, Inspector Ramirez thought in disbelief. Images from the investigation flashed through his mind.

Sanchez had access to the Canadian's hotel room; they had searched it together. It was Sanchez who suggested the search and Ramirez had agreed, despite the weak grounds.

The reference to the anonymous complaint on Christmas Day about a scarred man approaching boys in the Parque Ciudad had originated with Sanchez. Ramirez had never checked with the dispatcher to validate the complaint. He had trusted Rodriguez, his protégé. His friend.

Sanchez found virtually all the evidence located in the Canadian's hotel room. Sanchez must have slipped the photographs and CD under the mattress while Ramirez searched the bathroom. Ramirez had left him alone outside the locked hotel room while he talked to Hector Apiro in the lobby. It was Sanchez who planted his own semen on the sheets, knowing it would match the semen in the boy's body. He probably exchanged his underwear with a pair from Ellis's dresser.

Sanchez framed Ellis.

He must have killed the boy and used his police car to

transport the body. He claimed he was out of gas on Christmas Day after Ramirez told him the boy's body had been found, probably to give himself enough time to clean up the car. It was Sanchez all along.

Sanchez showed up at the address on Campanario a good ten minutes *after* Jones and Vasquez had arrived. He wasn't following them, despite Ramirez's orders to keep the Canadian lawyer under surveillance. Because he knew there was no need to. Because he knew Señor Ellis was innocent.

Sanchez knew about the address on Campanario because he had been there before, was on his way there again for some unknown reason. He must have been surprised to find Celia Jones and Maria Vasquez there already but played along.

Ramirez concentrated. Why would Sanchez go to Campanario?

Probably to dispose of Miguel Artez, to remove any remaining link to his own crimes. The arrival of the lawyer and the *jinetera* had thrown off those plans, but Sanchez had recovered. He always was quick-witted.

If Miguel Artez was telling the truth, Artez had no way of knowing who Sanchez was, had never seen him, could not possibly have known that the man who arrested him had lured him to Campanario, pretending to be Nasim so he could kill him. Sanchez had probably killed Rubinder too. Which meant Rodriguez Sanchez was the link to the drugs.

"Hector, you must have Sanchez's blood type on record."

All the police officers, even the detectives, gave the department blood samples and fingerprints to use for elimination purposes and in case of an emergency, when blood transfusions might be needed urgently.

"Let me check." Apiro went to a filing cabinet in the corner, rifled through some files, and pulled out the one he wanted. He flipped through it. "Yes. Sanchez is Type A. And a secretor."

"We need to find him right away," said Ramirez. "I think he killed Nasim Rubinder. And covered up his involvement by making sure he went back to Rubinder's hotel room on official business last night, so that his fingerprints and hair could be explained away."

He called his office and asked if Sanchez was there. But the detective he spoke to said no, Detective Sanchez had left an hour before, for Viñales.

"Viñales?" Ramirez wondered out loud, still holding the phone. "Why would Sanchez drive all the way to Viñales?" Then he turned to Apiro. "I think I know the answer. My office says I have a message from Celia Jones. She went to Viñales today as well."

SIXTY-SIX

Mike Ellis had just returned from his run and was planning what to do on his last day in Cuba when the phone rang. Inspector Ramirez was on the other end.

"I am sorry to bother you, Señor Ellis, but this is an urgent situation. Do you know why Señora Jones has gone to Viñales today?"

"She planned to visit a veterinary clinic there. Didn't she call you?"

"She only left a brief message. I was at Nasim Rubinder's autopsy. When did you speak to her?"

"This morning. Around nine, I think. She said the tour bus was leaving around a half-hour later. She was supposed to call you right after she got off the phone with me."

"She must have spoken to Sanchez."

Ramirez quickly explained to Ellis what he had learned. "Sanchez has left for Viñales. She must have found evidence to tie him to these crimes. Please, Detective Ellis, think carefully. Can you remember what she said about this clinic that relates to our investigation? Can you be more specific?"

A pause while Ellis thought. "She was trying to track down

the source of Rohypnol into Cuba. She mentioned the clinic. Apparently some drugs went missing from a delivery there last week. And before then, too."

Sanchez had told Ramirez there had been no deliveries of Rohypnol into Cuba for years. *Another lie.*

SIXTY-SEVEN

Think, Celia, think. He had brought her to this school and it was not easy to find, so overgrown and desolate, so he must have known about this place before. It had to mean something to him. Sanchez must have been shaped into what he had become, in these buildings, in these woods.

Celia Jones tried to remember the training she had received with the RCMP so many years earlier. The first step was to make the hostage human. She could do that best by drawing her kidnapper out. Finding common ground. *When the hostage-taker gets to know someone, it is harder to kill them.*

She took a chance. She walked over to the steps of the school and sat down. Hoped he wouldn't shoot her for moving without his permission. Looked in his eyes as directly as she could, tried to pretend there was no gun. Kept her voice friendly, relaxed. She remembered her instructor's voice. *Always keep calm.*

"Do you want to talk about what happened in these buildings? Get it off your chest? There's no rush. No one is going to find me, you said so yourself. They won't even know I'm missing for another hour or more."

Prolong the situation. Stall.

"I can't go anywhere. And you have the gun. Take your time. I have the feeling that terrible things happened to you here. I'd really like to know what they are."

Sanchez considered this for what seemed like hours but was only a few minutes. Finally, he shrugged. He looked at the school and she could see him remembering.

"It started there." He pointed to the smaller building with the gun.

"This was a school, wasn't it?"

He nodded. "I was sent here when I was eight years old. My parents had no choice in the matter." Jones heard the tension in his voice. "The government had decided that children should be sent to rural residential boarding schools and indoctrinated into socialism properly. But it was really a child labour force for the agricultural sector. The Marxist-Leninist model. Children as working members of the proletariat."

He spat on the ground. "You must have heard the joke. A Marxist came up with a plan that would provide Cubans with all the food we needed, but it was rejected because it only worked in practice, not theory." He laughed bitterly. "We worked in those tobacco fields down there every day." He motioned towards the valley, hidden behind the trees.

"What was it like, Rodriguez?" *Focus the hostage-taker's attention on small details. Keep him talking. Always use the hostage-taker's first name.*

"What do you think it was like? We worked all day until we were exhausted. We were lonely, and the food was terrible. It was a government school run by Catholics. An American priest, O'Brien, was the principal. The other priests were mostly Spanish but there were some from other countries as well, even a few from Canada. They came and went over the years."

She had to keep him talking, draw him out. "And so what

happened to you here? Please. I'd like to know." *Use open-ended questions. Build a relationship.*

He took several deep breaths before he spoke again. "One night, Father O'Brien invited a few of the children to have dinner in that building. It was the rectory. We found tables inside set with white plates on clean linens with beautifully polished silverware. All cooked by older students of course. We were all so hungry, so thin. I had my first sugar cake, a taste of ice cream. It was like a dream."

"I can imagine," she said sympathetically. *Show empathy.*

"You can imagine nothing," he shouted, and waved the gun at her.

Keep the hostage-taker calm. Shit, what was she supposed to do now? He was anything but calm. She grasped at straws.

"There were schools like this in Canada once," Jones said. "Indian residential schools. There are thousands of claims against them now by former students for physical and sexual abuse." She guessed at what happened, willing to risk being wrong and making him angry. "Children were sexually abused here too, weren't they?"

It would fit the profile of these places. Young children, alone, frightened, far away from their families.

"These dinners you describe, it sounds as if the children were being groomed by pedophiles. Am I right? It's classic behaviour. They usually ingratiate themselves with small gifts, outings. Build up trust, so it's easier to take advantage of vulnerable children."

Be understanding. Use active listening. Feed information back so the hostage-taker knows he was heard.

Sanchez snorted scornfully. "Little help to know that now." He looked down at his feet, traced a line in the dirt with his shoe. He took out a package of cigarettes and lit one. Inhaled deeply, exhaled. The smoke curled above his head like a halo, where it was caught by the wind and carried away. She saw a shift in his body language, a sign that something traumatic had happened to him.

"Tell me, Rodriguez. You need to tell someone. You can't carry this burden alone."

He nodded slightly, his eyes distant. A few long minutes passed before he spoke again.

"You have no idea what we went through. The beatings we suffered, just for talking to each other. Or not brushing our teeth quickly enough or well enough for the priests. Worse. And believe me, we were angry that our families let the government send us here. We missed them at first, then hated them for not coming to get us. But the priests told us to forget our families. Told us only God loved us."

He looked up at the trees, gathering his words. "I was at the school for less than a month when I was told I would be allowed to sleep at the rectory overnight, away from the dormitories. It was my reward for being good. Can you imagine how thrilled I was? A little boy, alone, separated from his mother and father, from his brothers, from his home."

He spat on the ground again, his body language even more agitated. Something had happened here, she was sure of it now. Which would relax him the most: talking about it, or not talking about it? If she wanted to survive, she needed to know.

"You can tell me, Rodriguez. I won't tell anyone."

He paused, and she saw tears form in his eyes. He swallowed a few times before he spoke.

"There were three of us. After dinner, each of us was taken away by a different priest. Mine led me to a bathroom, to a hot tub. He washed me, made me clean even between my legs. He dried me with a soft towel, told me to put a nightshirt on. I can still feel it. The fabric was soft. All of our own clothes were second-hand, torn, faded. He took me to the bedroom. He picked me up and put me on my stomach on the bed, then pulled his pants down. He climbed on my back. He was heavy and he put his full weight on me. I remember, I could hardly breathe.

"I lay there, not knowing what was going to happen. Starting to get frightened. He pulled my nightshirt up at the back. He began to thrust himself against me. I remember his sweat dripped on the back of my neck." His voice cracked. "It hurt. I felt as if I had been torn in half. He moaned and rolled over. There was blood on the sheets. I started to cry. He slapped me and told me to be quiet. He made me get off the bed and kneel on the floor. He told me to beg God for forgiveness."

"You must have been so scared," Jones said softly, her eyes wet with tears. "I can't imagine how frightened and confused you must have been." *Never become emotionally involved with the hostage-taker. Don't cross the line.*

Too fucking late. So she'd blown it for a second time. That was where she had screwed up before, with the man on the ledge holding a baby. She had watched the child spiral through the air like a football, head down, the baby's jacket slipping through her fingers. And then he jumped.

Pay attention.

"After that, there was no cake or ice cream for me, or the others," he said. Tears streaked his cheeks. "Although sometimes, as I grew older, he gave me wine. Or cigarettes."

"The abuse continued, then? Not just that once?"

"Ah, no," Sanchez said, spitting out the words. "I was there for seven years, Señora. That is a lot of cigarettes."

"Were others abused, too?" But she already knew the answer.

Sanchez tossed the butt of his cigarette on the ground; let the gun drop just slightly. "We never spoke about it. Any one of us could be tapped on the shoulder at night and be taken into the darkness. The ones who were singled out would return later, trying hard not to cry. Sleep after that was impossible. One by one, we all became numbed to what was happening to us. Who could we tell? Our families were far away. These men were God's representatives. Our families trusted the church with their very lives, with their afterlives, no less. Who would ever believe the things they did to us?"

"What happened to you was unspeakably evil," said Jones. "You were children. They were adults. They were supposed to protect you; that was their *job*."

Just like it was her job to protect the hostage, to talk the man down, to get him to put down the child. And then he did what she asked, and her police career was over.

Sanchez ignored her, caught up in his own memories. "Years passed. When I turned fourteen and my voice began to deepen, the priest was no longer interested in me. It was the younger ones he wanted. And do you know how I felt?" he asked her, his brown eyes glistening. "Do you think I felt relieved? No, I felt betrayed. You understand? He replaced me with a younger child. Which meant I had no one, that I was completely alone in the world. Abandoned by my family first and then by the priest as well."

"What did you do?" she asked.

He stamped out the dying embers of his cigarette. "What do you think I did? I was a good student. I became a monster, too."

SIXTY-EIGHT

"Hector," Inspector Ramirez called out in English, "get me the number for the veterinary clinic in Viñales, please. It's probably the only one there. I need to find out if Señora Jones has arrived yet. Stay on the line, Señor Ellis," he said into the phone.

Ramirez pushed the second button on the wall phone for another line. He dialled the number Apiro handed him and identified himself to the manager of the clinic.

"Señora Diaz, did you see a Canadian lawyer named Celia Jones today?"

"Yes, Inspector, she was just here, actually. She asked about some drug shipments we received."

"Thefts of Rohypnol?"

"Yes. How did you know?"

"What did you tell her?"

"That we've had thefts over the years, and that we were short four capsules that should have been in the package in our last delivery. On December 20."

Ramirez put his hand over the receiver and repeated the information to Apiro. "Four Rohypnol capsules were stolen last week."

"That was not enough to kill Rubinder," Apiro said, shaking his head. "He had at least six doses in his system."

"Then there were more drugs stolen than just those four."

Ramirez took his hand from the receiver and asked the woman if the clinic had lost any supplies of Rohypnol before then.

"Funny," the woman declared, "that is exactly the same question Señora Jones asked. She wanted me to check our records going back as far as I could. I went back through all our records. We had several thefts between 2001 and 2005, then nothing until last week. That was the one that Señora Jones was most interested in."

"Do you have the forms there? The original manifests?"

"Yes, they are right in front of me."

"Can you check the bottom right corner for the name of the officer who reviewed the manifests at the airport? Was it Rodriguez Sanchez?"

"Yes," said Diaz, surprised. "How did you know?"

"When did Señora Jones leave your office?" Ramirez asked. He hoped he wasn't too late.

"Around ten minutes ago."

"Was she returning to the tour bus?" Perhaps Sanchez would miss her. Ramirez could always have a police car intercept the bus on the road.

"I don't think so, Inspector. I saw her get into a police car and drive away with someone. He was waiting for her outside. A detective, I would guess from his clothing. She seemed to know him."

Then Sanchez had her, which meant her chances of survival were non-existent. Ramirez thanked Diaz. He pushed down the button for Ellis, still waiting on the other line.

"Sanchez has her. She found evidence at the clinic that implicates him in these crimes."

"Then he's going to kill her," said Ellis. "For God's sake, why aren't you doing something to stop him?"

"I do not know where he has taken her, Señor."

"Well, where else would he go?" said Apiro, standing behind his friend. "It seems perfectly obvious to me. He will take her to the residential school outside of town that he attended."

"Why there, Hector? Surely a busy school is the last place Sanchez is likely to kill someone."

"It is closed down now, Ricardo, so there will be no one there. And the schools were always remotely situated to deter the children from running away. A perfect location for his needs; completely isolated. Do you not remember? Castro closed those schools years ago, after parents complained about how different the children were when they came home, how sullen and unhappy. There were suspicions even then that the children might have been mistreated, maybe sexually abused. The Pope agreed that parents should be free to choose where to send their children for school. Castro closed all the country boarding schools down, including the one outside Viñales."

A second's silence as Ramirez considered this information. Then he spoke to Ellis again.

"Did you hear any of that?"

"Yes. I heard everything."

"Dr. Apiro is right. That must be where they are."

"Listen," Ellis said. "We have to get there before he kills her. I'm going with you. She's my friend."

Ramirez thought quickly, then agreed. "Alright, then. Be in front of your hotel in five minutes, no more. We will take my car. It is faster than the patrol cars. I have a full tank of gas, so I probably have more fuel than any of them."

"Be careful," Apiro said as Ramirez hung up the phone. "This is a very dangerous man. Highly organized, highly intelligent. Unpredictable."

For a moment, Ramirez wasn't sure which man Apiro was describing: Ellis or Sanchez.

SIXTY-NINE

"You mean you started abusing children."

Rodriguez Sanchez nodded slowly. "The first boy was Rubén Montenegro."

"Arturo's brother?" Celia Jones guessed, drawing on the cigarette he had offered her. She coughed. She didn't smoke but she was going to die soon anyway; couldn't really see the downside. Cancer wasn't the most serious threat to her life at the moment.

"I didn't realize they were related until this week. Rubén Montenegro ran away from this place when he was fourteen or fifteen years old, many years later. His body is probably in that valley down below, in the fields. He had no way to get home from here. I am sure he knew that when he ran away. We all escaped in different ways. But he was only eight or nine when I first encountered him. He had been in school for about a week. We were both assigned chores in the barn. He was happy, always smiling, singing, stupid boy. He seemed to like the rabbits and the pigs.

"He hummed when he worked. It made me furious that he could be happy here, in this place, after what I was forced to do at his age. Then he told me he was going to have dinner that night with the priests, in the rectory. He was so excited to be going over to that building for dinner. He thought it would be fun.

"I grabbed him and punched him and threw him on the ground. I would show him what *fun* was. Even then, Rubén was strong and he tried to fight back. He landed a few hard kicks and started to cry. I hit him, told him to shut up. I told him, better me than them. That he should toughen up or he would die here.

"He was doubled over in pain, still crying, when I left. I said if he told anyone, I would kill the rabbits. He missed dinner that night. We all slept in the same dormitory; I saw him curled up in his bed. He did not get up in the morning, not even to go the bathroom. He made no more sounds."

"But he was alive," Jones said. Thinking of a lonely boy, hurting so badly, so far away from his family. Frightened, betrayed, abused. And then of the small boy he'd raped.

Sanchez nodded. "At breakfast, the priest who patrolled the boy's dormitory came to check on him. He was unconscious. That is when I first discovered how badly I had hurt him. I felt sorry, but it was too late. The priest pulled off his bedcovers. The sheets were saturated with blood. The priest told me to run for Father O'Brien and tell him there was an injured boy. O'Brien called the local *policía*. They took him away. A few days later, I was taken to another school for re-education. Rubén must have told them it was me after all."

"Where did they put you?"

He laughed bitterly. "Santa Clara. Some 're-education.' It was another school just like this one. Did you hear in Canada about the priest who was stabbed and set on fire in Santa Clara in 1998? The same year the Pope came? That, I believe, was in the international news. Back when we still had newspapers with real news in them, not just state propaganda. Students did that."

She did remember seeing something about it, a few lines,

nothing to convey the anguish of children who had killed a priest to save themselves.

"He was the same as the priests here. He liked little boys. That was the year that Castro finally closed the schools. He had kicked the Catholic Church out of Cuba years before but let some of the teachers stay. He threw them all out that year. These were not unrelated incidents."

"Castro *knew*?"

He nodded. "I think so. That was the same year Rubén ran away. I always considered it unfortunate, that if he had waited a little longer, he would still be alive today. But who could know that the schools would close? We all believed we were trapped here until we graduated. Or died."

"So when you graduated, what did you do? Is that when you joined the police?"

"I wanted to have some control in my life," said Sanchez. "I joined the Cuban National Revolutionary Police Force. I knew no one could hurt me again if I had a gun. I had no criminal record; I was too young to be charged for what I did to Rubén. I was smart, I worked hard, I passed all the tests at the top of my class.

"I was stationed in Havana. I spent several years working on street patrol, and then I was assigned to the International Airport. Ramirez worked on an investigation with me. He saw my potential. He had me transferred to his unit almost a year ago. He made me feel good about myself for the first time. And I proved him right. I am a very good investigator of sexual assaults and violence, Señora Jones, because I experienced so much of it myself."

SEVENTY

"You were just a child, Rodriguez. It wasn't your fault." Sanchez had not yet shot her and Celia Jones considered that progress. "Do you have any happy memories? Tell me about your family. What was it like before you went to school?"

She wanted his stress levels lower, so he wouldn't pull the trigger accidentally. She'd hate like hell to be killed unintentionally.

Sanchez looked at her for a moment. His eyes brightened. "I remember picking berries with my mother. I must have been five or six. I remember bright red berries peeking through the leaves. I can still taste the way they popped in my mouth. The bees seemed too heavy, too slow, to fly. I remember the air buzzing, there were so many of them. I tried to hold on to these things at night, whenever he came for me. They were the only memories I had left of home. By the time I graduated from Santa Clara, my parents were dead. I was too ashamed of what happened to me to look for my brothers. Ramirez should never have given me that job on the internet, you know. I had managed to control myself for a long time."

Sanchez pulled out his package of cigarettes, lit one. He

offered her another. She accepted, hoped the small gesture meant she had reached him. Because he had certainly reached *her*.

She had wanted to humanize herself to him. Ironic that what happened instead was he became more human to her. She could never forgive the crimes he had committed, but she could understand them now.

Somewhere, underneath all that pain, there was a small boy who had picked berries in the sun, who had shielded himself as much as he could from the evil of adults by holding their sweet taste in his memory, who had blocked out the sounds of his own abuse by listening to the placid humming of bees.

He wiped his eyes. "Well, now you know everything. You were right. I have carried this burden alone for years. Now it is yours, too. At least for a few more minutes. Do not worry; I won't make you suffer. I promise."

But she saw the gun waver in his hand. "Killing me won't change what happened to you," she said, as she tried to change his mind. "It just means another family will be destroyed. Mine this time. Shouldn't all this pain stop now?"

"I feel badly for that, trust me."

He pointed the gun at her head and cocked the hammer. She was running out of options. She tried a different tactic. The truth.

"You know, Rodriguez, there was an incident when I was with the RCMP years ago. I was a police negotiator back then. A man had barricaded himself on the top floor of a five-storey building. I managed to talk him into letting his wife go, but he kept their baby with him. She was only five months old. He went out on the ledge, holding her. She was crying, so terrified. I went out on the ledge after him. It was the middle of winter. Freezing cold. It was icy on that ledge, and it was snowing. I was supposed to talk him down. But I screwed up."

"He jumped?"

She nodded. "I kept asking him to let the baby go. But I didn't realize he would take me literally. He looked at me finally, like he was tired of hearing me say it. He spread his arms out like wings and let the baby go. I tried to grab her and I almost fell, but she slipped through my fingers. I lost her. Then he jumped."

"Did she die?"

"No. She landed in a snowbank. A fractured skull. A miracle, they said, but it didn't feel that way to me. I never found out what kind of disability it caused; I've just always assumed it was serious. Every time I see a disabled child, I feel responsible. I know it's irrational. It doesn't matter. I ended up quitting the force. I couldn't go through that again. I've never been good with heights since. Or snow, for that matter. My husband, Alex, will never believe that I went for a walk up the side of a mountain. He knows I'd never get that close to one voluntarily. He will find out what happened to me if it kills him. We're like a pair of old swans."

Sanchez nodded slowly and exhaled. He seemed more relaxed than before. "Yes, I know the net is tightening around me. I made stupid mistakes. Trying to cover it up."

Keep the hostage-taker talking.

"I'm guessing you made up the anonymous complaint about the man in the park. And then got Inspector Ramirez to search Mike's room so you could pretend to find that evidence. That was smart."

Sanchez nodded. "Ramirez is usually more professional than that, but recently he has been acting strangely. I can tell you this, Señora, it was nice to get new briefs. It can be difficult to find them here." He laughed. "You will never know, Señora, how close you came to getting Michael Ellis out of jail with that report of yours."

"My bloody report. Pun intended." She forced a smile.

"You know, I should kill you just for that joke." He laughed again. Incredibly, she found herself laughing as well. Maybe it will be okay, she thought. We're connecting; we're laughing. Maybe he'll let me go.

"I do feel sorry about the boy, you know," Sanchez said. "Arturo. He reminded me of Rubén, of what happened to me here. I admit, I beat the boy. I tried to frighten him from talking to anyone again. I told him that if he said anything, it would be worse the next time. But I didn't kill him. Nasim must have panicked and done that later that night. I have only ever killed one person in my life. And he deserved it."

"Nasim?"

Sanchez nodded. "To quote Lenin, he was a useful idiot. But if Ramirez had found him, he would have told him everything. He was a whiner, that one. No *cojones*." His eyes flicked away, but just for a moment. "I was not unkind, Señora. Arturo had no idea, never did, what was done to him. Better than what was done to me here, I can tell you that."

"Perhaps the panel will understand that and spare your life," said Jones, although she didn't believe it for a moment. There was only one reason to drug the boy: to make it impossible for him to identify his attacker. And to stop him from fighting back. "Maybe they'll only send you to jail."

"Do you really think I would let myself be arrested? A Cuban policeman in custody with a hundred political dissidents? I would be dead within a night. But you are the only person who knows about all of this. If I kill you, I can live a while longer, perhaps find some way to escape this island. My life has some value, if only to me. It certainly means more to me at the moment than yours. I'm sorry, Señora."

He pointed the gun squarely at her face and drew his finger down on the trigger. She blinked hard and tried not to flinch as she waited for the bullet. "So this is it?" Jones said. "I can't talk you out of doing this?"

"You don't beg. I like that. I never begged for anything either."

Sanchez released the trigger and stepped forward to sit below her on the steps. He looked up at her, one leg bent. He rested the gun on his knee, but still aimed at her. He reached into his coat pocket with his left hand. He brought out a tiny tape recorder and put it on the steps between them. Sanchez clicked the recorder on, hit "fast forward," played with the buttons. He looked at the beaded bracelet on his wrist for a long time. For the first time, he seemed ashamed.

"In my country, the statement of a dead person is admissible in court. Is it the same in your country?"

"Yes." She swallowed. "May I use that recorder to say goodbye to my husband?"

The final lesson in hostage-taking. *Negotiate. Offer to trade something small for something of value.* But she had nothing of value to exchange. He already had the forms.

Sanchez laughed. He pushed the button and the small machine whirred. He clicked it off and on. "I thought you wanted to hear everything."

"I'm listening."

"Padre Rey Callendes was his name. The Catholic priest. He was transferred to a school in another country for a while. Who knows? Maybe yours."

Then he fell silent again, thinking, she supposed, about the man who had betrayed him so callously, physically and then emotionally, by withdrawing what he had masqueraded as love.

Sanchez shook his head. "I thought I was safe, Señora Jones. I never expected you to pursue the drugs all the way to Viñales. You were supposed to be leaving tomorrow. You should have taken a different tour."

"I'm sorry now that I didn't."

"So am I."

"Please. Let me leave a message for my husband. You can hide the tape in my clothes. They may not find my body for years. I just want to tell Alex how much I love him. That I'm sorry I'm leaving nothing of the two of us behind. That we never had children."

"You see?" he observed. "Everyone begs eventually."

The small recorder beeped twice. Out of tape. "Too bad." He threw it on the ground and stood up, kicked it. "Made in China. A 'piece of shit,' as you might say."

He walked over to where he had kicked the small machine. He picked it up and rewound it, still holding the gun. She heard the tape click and waited for him to hand it to her. When he didn't, she knew her time was up, that all her police training had failed her again.

Jones forced herself not to cry. She wiped her eyes. She did not want Alex to imagine her weeping in her last seconds on this beautiful planet.

Sanchez turned his wrist to check his watch. "You never know. Perhaps they will find you sooner than you think."

He pushed the "record" button and raised his gun. She wondered how much dying would hurt. She was still trying to decide whether to close her eyes or not when Sanchez spoke into the tiny machine. He pointed the gun straight at her forehead, only inches away. He held his red and white beads in his fingers, twisting them like a rosary.

"This is Detective Rodriguez Sanchez of the Cuban National Revolutionary Police. May God forgive me for my sins, including this one. That is, if there is a God. I do not believe in one anymore. But best to make the request, just in case."

Sirens yelped in the distance. Sanchez pulled the gun up sharply and pulled the trigger.

SEVENTY-ONE

The blue car jumped the sidewalk as Inspector Ramirez turned it towards the Parque Ciudad. He drove down the centre of the pedestrian boulevard to save time. He blew his horn and tourists darted out of the way.

His car screeched to a stop in front of the hotel and Mike Ellis jumped into the passenger seat. They tore off as Ellis pulled the door closed, leaving a strip of black rubber on the road.

Ramirez took the highway to Viñales. He drove far over the speed limit, but smoothly, competently, managing to avoid the Cubans waiting for buses in the centre of the road. Several times, he wrenched the car sideways, spraying dirt and gravel, to miss the stray dogs that meandered across the highway as the sky darkened.

It was normally a two-hour drive to get to Viñales; they made it in just over an hour and a half. Ramirez was on the radio almost the entire time, speaking Spanish. He was calling for backup and support, he told Ellis. Notifying the other units that there was a rogue officer, armed and dangerous, with a foreign hostage.

He called ahead to other cars to block all routes leading to and from Viñales. More dramatic than it sounded, Ramirez explained, as there was only one route in and out of town.

"Sanchez," he said, shaking his head, trying not to allow his disappointment and shock affect what he had to do. "Rodriguez would normally be sitting in your seat, handling the radio. It is hard for me to believe this of him. In all my years as a police officer, I have never had to use my gun. I don't want my friend to be the first man I've ever killed."

"I know exactly what you mean," said Ellis.

Ramirez glimpsed the dead boy in his side mirror. The boy rolled around in the back. He hung onto the door handle as the car swerved around corners, smiling, as if he were on a roller coaster. Ramirez could tell he had no idea where they were going or why, but he liked the ride.

Police cars from the villages they passed pulled alongside and then dropped into line behind the small blue car. The noisy little car laboured up the coiled roads towards Viñales, but it held its own.

As they approached the crest of the Viñales mountains, there were at least twenty police cars reflected in the side mirror. Their flashing lights winked as they drove up the mountain road in single file. Ramirez used his hand-held radio to tell them to turn their sirens on. He wanted Sanchez to know he was coming.

But by the time they got to the school, it was too late.

Ramirez pulled into the overgrown yard of the old Viñales residential school and slammed on his brakes, leaving a cloud of dust. The other cars stopped well behind his. In a hostage-taking, the officers were supposed to contain the perimeter, but Inspector Ramirez had broken all the rules.

"Where is she?" Ellis demanded. "It's too dark here to see anything."

"Here." Ramirez handed him a flashlight and pulled another from the dash.

"I think I see a police car. Where the hell is she?"

"Quiet. There is someone on the steps." An ember, glowing in the dusk.

"Celia doesn't smoke," Ellis whispered.

Ramirez trained his light on the front of the school. "It's Ricardo Ramirez, Rodriguez," he called. "Give yourself up. We can work through this; you know that. No one else needs to die."

But when his light caught her, he realized it was Celia Jones. She sat on the wooden steps, blood smeared on her face, holding a cigarette.

Sanchez's body lay crumpled at her feet, a black gun held loosely in his fingers. Ramirez walked to her and trained his flashlight on the ground. The earth around Sanchez's head was stained dark. There was a hole in his temple.

"He shot himself. He couldn't bring himself to kill me. He was a policeman, Inspector. He just couldn't do it. I think he was afraid you would think less of him." She started to cry.

Ramirez held his fingers to his friend's wrist. No pulse. Sanchez was dead. He pulled the gun from Sanchez's fingers with his index finger and thumb. He pulled a plastic bag from his pocket and dropped it in. He noticed the beads wrapped around the fingers of Sanchez's other hand.

"Did he confess?"

Jones nodded, shaking. "He told me everything."

A confession. A final prayer to Chango for forgiveness. Ramirez shook his head sadly. Some crimes were too terrible to forgive.

The other policemen milled around, confused.

"Stay back!" he shouted. "Call the technicians. This is a crime scene."

Ramirez put his arm around the lawyer and helped her up. He

draped his jacket over her shaking shoulders. He helped her into the passenger seat of his car and closed the door softly. The back seat was empty; the boy was gone.

"I will drive Señora Jones back to the hotel later, but I need to debrief her in person, alone," Ramirez said to Michael Ellis. "The other patrol cars have to wait here for the technicians to arrive. The Viñales police division is responsible for this crime scene, not mine, so there is no car here that can take you back to Havana. I will ask one of the policemen to see if they can find you a ride back into town, but you may have to pay for it."

"I understand," said Ellis. "That's fine."

"Drop by the office in the morning. I'll return your passport then."

"Thank you, Inspector, for everything. I'll see you tomorrow."

SEVENTY-TWO

It was late by the time Inspector Ramirez got back to Havana, but the lights were on in Hector Apiro's office. He went upstairs to tell him what had happened.

When Ramirez poked his head in, a beautiful woman was sitting on a stool, drinking a cup of Apiro's fresh-brewed coffee. Apiro introduced her. Ramirez had never met Maria Vasquez before, although he knew her name from the investigation. He was even more surprised when he realized that the two were romantically involved.

Vasquez looked oddly familiar. "Just a minute," Ramirez said to her. "I think I have a picture of you in my file." He reached for the folder and flipped through it until he found the photograph that Candice Olefson had taken on the Malecón. "This was on a camera we found in Nasim Rubinder's hotel room."

She looked at the photo and laughed. "But that's not me," she said. "Look, that woman is wearing flat sandals. I only wear really *high* heels. But I was dressed almost like that on Christmas Eve when I met Señor Ellis. That woman must be his wife. Perhaps that is why he was so attracted to me."

She winked at Apiro, who grinned back, not bothered in the slightest by her comments.

Ramirez looked at the photograph again. "Lovely woman. And there is quite a resemblance."

He told them what had happened and lit a cigar, satisfied with the outcome of the day's events. He had done his job and then some. He had lost one friend but gained another. Not a bad week for a dying man. "I will have quite a story to tell Francesca when I get home."

"It *is* quite a story," Apiro remarked. "Quite a remarkable week, all things considered."

"And what of Señora Jones?" Vasquez asked. "Will she be alright? She must be terribly traumatized, after having a gun held to her head. Knowing she could die at any moment."

"She is enormously grateful to be alive, as you can imagine," said Ramirez. "But she told me on the way back here that she enjoyed being involved in a police investigation again, much more so than doing legal work. I've told her she can come work with us anytime. She plans to return to Havana soon, in any event. She saw some children in an orphanage in Viñales that she seems interested in."

"Is she thinking of raising supplies for orphans now, instead of puppies?" Apiro asked, smiling.

"Well, actually," Ramirez said, "I think she'd like to adopt one. There was a girl in a wheelchair she was quite taken with."

"A foreign adoption? Difficult," said Apiro. "But if she means it, perhaps we can help."

Apiro sipped his coffee and slipped his free hand into Maria's. Ramirez saw how comfortable the two were together.

"I confess, I was surprised, Maria, to meet you here of all places. I didn't know that you and Hector knew each other. Have you known each other long?"

Apiro turned to her. "How many years, my dear? Fifteen?"

"Hector, if I were to say, that would give away my age." She punched him lightly in the shoulder. "You know better than that."

"How impolite of me to ask," Apiro said, pretending to be chastened. "Maria is always reminding me of my manners. She is a real lady when it comes to such matters."

"Like my Francesca," Ramirez said. He took a deep breath and exhaled, then shook his head in wonderment. "*Dios mio*, what a week."

"And it is not over yet," the surgeon announced. "I forgot to tell you. Maria is moving into my apartment. We have decided that I have been an old bachelor for far too long."

"Congratulations to both of you," Ramirez exclaimed, genuinely pleased. "Give me a few minutes to go the station. I'll pay a visit to the exhibit room and find some fine old Havana Club so that we can celebrate the good news properly."

After he left, Maria turned to Apiro and squeezed the small man's hand. "Are we going to tell him?" she asked.

"No need," Apiro said. "Your new life began years ago. I see no reason for you to go back to it now."

"I have to go back to some of it. I have sisters I have never met."

"We will talk to your mother, then, together. Once she adjusts to the news that you are still alive, I think she will be very happy. She has lost a son and gained a daughter. And who knows, perhaps your family will want to live with us."

She slipped her arm through the surgeon's and he swelled inside with happiness.

His life had gone from being lonely to complete. And the fact that Maria had once been Rubén Montenegro? Well, that was a long time ago.

After Apiro repaired the boy's injuries, Rubén was returned to the school in Viñales, but that was not the end of their doctor-patient relationship. Almost six years later, there was a gentle knock on Apiro's office door. At first, he thought it was a girl standing in the shadows.

"Please," the boy said. "May I come in?"

Apiro waited quietly for the boy to tell him what he needed. Rubén took a deep breath. "I want you to turn me into a girl. I know you can do the surgery. You are a doctor; you can do anything."

Apiro tried not to smile. "How long have you been thinking about this?"

"All my life. Since I was five or six. Forever," said Rubén sadly, and Apiro heard something in the boy's voice that broke his heart. "I am not like other boys. I like to look pretty. I know I *am* a girl, inside."

Not sure what to say, Apiro brewed a pot of coffee. He was professionally intrigued. That the boy could become a beautiful woman when he grew up, even with only cosmetic surgery, was clear. Ironically, Rubén would be treated better as a woman than he ever would as a man. Life would be unpleasant for an effeminate boy in Cuba.

"What about getting married, having children, being with a woman?"

"I will never be with a woman," the boy responded firmly.

"Because of what was done to you before?"

"No," the boy said. "Because of what I am."

"How old are you now?"

"Fifteen next month."

"Fourteen is not very old to make this kind of decision. It is not unusual in adolescence to wonder if one is homosexual. Often the uncertainty passes."

"I am not like that. I need to do this to survive."

He would not patronize the boy, Apiro decided. This was Apiro's business, after all, re-engineering people. When it came right down to it, what was the difference between altering someone's nose and their genitals? Most medical literature supported the idea that sexual reassignment should begin in adolescence, when its chances of success were higher. But there had been only one transsexual operation in Cuba, in 1988, and that involved a mature adult, not a young boy who could be mistaken.

Still, in a little over a year, the boy would be old enough to choose. Apiro had seen the abuse Rubén had suffered, the sexual violence done to him. Who had a stronger claim than this boy to becoming transgendered if it helped him feel more comfortable in his own skin?

"What about your family? Have you discussed this with them?"

"I do not live with them. I live on the streets. It doesn't matter what they think. I don't belong in this body."

Apiro understood those feelings. He had lived with them his whole life.

"If you're serious about this, here is what I am willing to do," Apiro decided. "I will arrange to have a colleague meet with you. A psychiatrist who specializes in such matters. Gender confusion, I believe they call it. A term I dislike, because if you are at all confused, you should not do this. If she agrees, we will prescribe hormones to suppress some of your maleness as your development continues. You will have to live as a female for a least a year, and I mean that in all its senses. After that, once you are sixteen, if you still want to do this, we will see about surgery. But not before. Because once this surgery is done, it cannot be undone. Where can I reach you, once I arrange the appointment?"

"I have no address. I ran away from school months ago."

Apiro did not ask why Rubén had run away; it was none of his business. "Well, we can't have that. You can stay at the hospital tonight. And after that, we will see what can be done."

The consulting psychiatrist agreed with Apiro's approach after only a few meetings. The boy's initial psychological tests showed the emotional affect of a female of his age, not a male. But Rubén still had nowhere to live, so Apiro cleared away his pile of papers and made a space for the boy to sleep on the old damask couch in his apartment. It was a gross conflict of interest, but Apiro ignored the rules; after all, the child had to live somewhere.

Over the course of that year, Rubén Montenegro became Maria Vasquez. On Maria's sixteenth birthday, Apiro agreed to do the surgery.

During Maria's recovery, Apiro visited each day, sat with her late into the night, brought his chessboard so they could play, sometimes brought novels to read to her. On Easter Friday, he came with flowers to celebrate the fact that she was due for release, but her bed was already empty. She had left no message for him, had simply signed herself out of the hospital.

He realized he should not have become involved emotionally with a patient. He offered to work part-time with the police to atone for his mistake. As the years passed, his life took on a busyness that helped him, finally, to forget her. Until the body of her young brother was pulled from the ocean and wound up in his morgue.

Apiro thought back to Maria's revelations during their dinner at the *paladar*.

"The boy who raped me all those years ago became a patrolman in Havana, Hector. I heard a nurse mention his name the night I ran away from the hospital. He was on his way to the ward to interview someone for an investigation. I was afraid that if he recognized me, he would kill me to stop me from telling others what he had done to me."

"I never imagined," Apiro said, shocked. "You must have been terrified."

"I was. But it was foolish. I was afraid all these years for nothing. He is a detective now. Rodriguez Sanchez. I saw him this afternoon; I even spoke to him. And he didn't remember me at all."

SEVENTY-THREE

The inspector's phone rang first thing in the morning. It was Michael Ellis. He told Ramirez he'd be over shortly. A half-hour later, the guard called up and Ramirez walked down to meet him.

They walked up the stairs to the second-floor room where Señor Ellis had first been interviewed. It seemed as if that interview had taken place a million years before.

"I'm still trying to sort out everything that happened," said Ellis. "Can you spend a few minutes explaining some of the gaps in the story for me, before I leave? Did Detective Sanchez confess?"

Ramirez filled Ellis in on what Señora Jones had told him on the drive back.

It had taken Ramirez some time to put all the pieces together, but that was because, until recently, he'd been forced to puzzle it out in ink. He had smiled, entering his office that morning, to see the pencils Jones had left on his desk, along with a note saying, "Merry Christmas and Happy New Year. See you in a few weeks."

"How did Sanchez meet Nasim Rubinder?" Ellis asked.

"A Customs officer confiscated Rubinder's laptop when he arrived in Havana because it had child pornography on it. They called in Sanchez to question the suspect."

"So did Nasim kill Arturo? Or was it Sanchez?"

"It looks like Rubinder killed the boy. Maria Vasquez knew about him and was threatening to call the police. That's why he threatened her. When Rubinder left the bar, Sanchez took his seat beside you. He dropped a capsule of Rohypnol in your drink. Then he went looking for the boy. He found him begging at Plaza de Armas. But he told Señora Jones that he left the boy alive. Rubinder must have found him later on and killed him."

"How did Miguel Artez get involved in all of this?"

"Sanchez was responsible for monitoring all internet transmissions to and from Havana. Artez was known to Sanchez; he was very active on the sex tourism pages. Rubinder needed access to the internet after his laptop was seized at the airport. It appears that Sanchez introduced them online; Artez was quite happy to arrange internet access for a fee. But Artez didn't know Sanchez's name; he knew only that Rubinder had someone protecting him, not who."

"And the boy, Rubén Montenegro, the child that Sanchez assaulted in the Viñales school all those years ago. He was the dead child's brother? That's incredible."

"Yes, although the parents were never notified of Rubén's injuries. No doubt the Church was afraid of what would happen politically if a family found out their son was raped by another student at a Catholic-run school. But there is a marked resemblance in the photographs of the two boys, despite the age difference between them. Señora Montenegro told me she had another son who died in Viñales. I never thought to connect the two."

"It's quite the story, isn't it?"

"That it is," Ramirez agreed. "I hope I have answered all your questions, Detective Ellis. Here is your passport. I hope things go well for you in Canada."

"It's a small matter, but I don't suppose anyone admitted to taking the money from the safe in my room?"

"I think you should talk to your wife about that."

Ellis nodded. "Thanks."

As Ellis pushed on the door to let himself out, Ramirez spoke again. "One more thing, Señor Ellis? Perhaps you can answer another question for me, if you don't mind?"

"Of course," Ellis said and turned to face the inspector. "How can I help?"

"Why did you kill Steve Sloan?"

SEVENTY-FOUR

"I'm sorry?" said Mike Ellis. "I don't know what you're talking about. I didn't kill Steve Sloan; a suspect did. The same man who cut me up."

"Señor Ellis, we both know this is untrue. Please sit down. There are several hours before your flight leaves. The airport is not far."

Ellis sat down slowly on the same red plastic chair he'd occupied the first time the police brought him in for questioning. Ramirez seated himself on the other side of the Formica table.

"What makes you think I was responsible for Steve's death?"

"It's been bothering me for days, ever since I saw that medical report that referred to your blood type. A fertility test that concluded you were sterile. Not your fault, of course. I listened to your interview with Sanchez again this week as I prepared my case file for the prosecutor. You told him that your wife became pregnant six months ago. The test was dated well before then. I found birth control pills in the bathroom the day we searched your hotel room, which means your wife doesn't know of your infertility. Last night, Señora Jones mentioned to me that Señor Sloan died shortly after your wife found out she was pregnant.

You must have known it was not your child, that she was having an affair."

"So you think she was having an affair with Steve? And that I killed him over that?"

"We can only be betrayed by our friends," Ramirez said sadly. "This is something I was reminded of this week. Perhaps you could forgive your wife for an affair with someone else, but the depth of this betrayal, an affair with your closest friend, and then the carelessness of a pregnancy? I don't know many men who would wish to raise another man's child, planted in their nest like a cuckoo's egg."

"I told you," Ellis insisted. "Steve died during a police incident. I was injured, badly injured, by the same suspect who shot him. Look at the scars on my face where he slashed me. You think I made those up?"

"Not so, Señor Ellis. Dr. Apiro saw you during your interview with us the last time you were in this room, a week ago. We watched Sanchez question you together, through that very window." Ramirez pointed to the mirrored glass. "He wondered how you got your scars. According to him, you should have been slashed diagonally. Someone who swings a knife, left- or right-handed, swings it at an angle, like a golf swing. And your scars widen at the bottom. They should widen in the middle. Dr. Apiro is sure you cut your own face. Here, I have his report."

Ramirez pulled a document from his inside jacket pocket and put it on the table. "His conclusions are at the bottom. He used to be a famous plastic surgeon, known internationally for his analysis of skin injuries and facial wounds. You have seen for yourself how detailed his work is. Let me translate his conclusion for you: 'The tentative, hesitant, start to the cut down the subject's forehead and the lack of defensive wounds to his hands make it virtually certain that the wounds were self-inflicted.' I asked myself, Why would a man cut himself while his partner is bleeding to death? There is only one explanation. That is if *you* shot him and were covering up your crime."

"You're guessing," Ellis said. "You can't prove any of this."

"I don't need to, Señor Ellis. I can't charge you with a murder that took place outside of Cuba. I have no jurisdiction over this crime. We have no extradition treaty with Canada. And as I told you before, confessions are worthless in Cuba. I am just curious because I do not like unfinished business. But I am certain that you were responsible for your friend's death, make no mistake. You may feel better telling someone. Even Rodriguez Sanchez wanted someone to share his burden, to understand his actions. But it is entirely up to you."

Mike Ellis shook his head. He tried once again to wipe away the memory of Steve Sloan's face as they walked up the stairs to the "trouble with man" call. Hillary had told him that morning she was pregnant. He spent the whole day brooding about it, knowing the child couldn't possibly be his.

He sat back further on his chair, took a deep breath, and finally let it all out.

"I never told Hillary about the test results. But I told Steve. And then Hillary got pregnant. Steve and I were working the night shift." Ellis paused, remembering a night he had tried to erase with liquor for months. "It was about two in the morning. Communications, that's our Dispatch, told us to be careful. A man on the third floor was schizophrenic, off his meds. That was all the information we had. No one mentioned he had a knife. We were pulling up in front when I told Steve that Hillary was pregnant. I saw the guilt in his face. I couldn't believe it. That someone I loved so much had betrayed me."

They walked up the stairs to the dingy hallway leading to the apartment. Ellis rapped on the door with his flashlight. The hall smelled of urine. There were stains on the walls. The linoleum was cracked, filthy. The hallway light was out, the bulb broken. Ellis had his gun in one hand, his flashlight in the other. Sloan unbuttoned his holster and moved to the right-hand side of the door. He motioned Ellis to the left as he pulled out his gun.

Ellis stood on the other side of the door frame, facing the door, furious.

"Aw, shit, Mike. I'm sorry. It just happened, just that one time. She seduced *me*, honest to God."

The door swung open and a dishevelled man in his twenties lunged at them with a hunting knife. "Holy shit," Sloan said, "he's got a knife." Sloan shot the man once in the chest.

"Like hell she did." Ellis turned and shot Sloan in the groin, just below his police vest. Sloan groaned and slumped to the ground. Ellis saw the arterial blood spurt and knew immediately what he'd done.

It was pitch black, the only light the beams from the two flashlights. Sloan's had rolled on the floor, highlighting the pain in his eyes. Ellis knelt beside him. He saw how badly Sloan was hurt; already too late for paramedics. He took his partner in his arms, held Sloan's head in his hands.

"It didn't mean anything," Sloan said, his voice barely audible.

"It meant something to me. *Fuck, Steve*, what were you thinking? Why did you sleep with her? I can't believe you did that."

"I don't know. Just to *know*, I guess. I couldn't figure out why you couldn't just up and leave her. But we're even, buddy. I can't believe you just shot me either." He smiled weakly and then his eyes rolled back. Ellis was still holding him when his body went slack.

Ellis lifted his head up and looked Ramirez in the eyes. His hands were cupped in front of him as he once again cradled the back of Steve Sloan's head.

Ramirez nodded sympathetically. "We Cubans are Latinos. A cuckolded man, a faithless woman. It is an age-old story. Your rage is understandable. Most men in Cuba would have killed the wife, not the friend. But that is our Latino culture. How did you get away with it?"

"I knew I'd screwed up. I had one chance to save myself, whatever was left of my life, my marriage. And there was the baby to think of. That was all I had left. The suspect was dead: I took his knife and pulled it down my face. It was almost a relief that it hurt so much."

"What about the gun?"

"I switched mine with Steve's. Put his in my holster and mine in the suspect's hand, pressed his fingerprints on the grip and the trigger. I pulled out my portable and called Communications. I said we had a dead suspect and an officer down. I told them I was badly hurt, that I thought Steve was dead."

"No one examined the guns?"

Ellis shook his head. "They were test-fired, but no one checked to make sure they were the same ones issued to us."

"We would have done that," Ramirez said. "Apiro would have insisted on it."

"Yes. I've learned how good he is." Ellis took a deep breath. "What will you do about it, now that you know?"

"Me? Nothing. I told you, whatever happened to you in Canada has nothing to do with Cuba. But it must have been hard for you, keeping this to yourself. Our secrets destroy us from inside when we cannot speak about them openly."

"Yes," Ellis said. "I know exactly what that's like."

SEVENTY-FIVE

Inspector Ramirez handed Señor Ellis his passport and walked him to the front door. Then he returned to the second floor and opened the door to the anteroom. Hector Apiro stood by the window, still looking through the mirrored glass. He handed the small tape recorder to Ramirez.

"It's all there, Ricardo. Interesting. So it turns out the Canadian is a cold-blooded murderer after all."

"Even more cold-blooded than we imagined. Or perhaps more hot-blooded."

"But I never examined his scars professionally," said Apiro. "Where did you come up with all that nonsense about the width of the scars and the swing of the knife? I know nothing about golf. I have never once played it."

"I made it up," Ramirez admitted. "There was no expert report. I used a copy of the departmental order form for supplies. He can't read Spanish. I knew he couldn't tell the difference."

"You are a rascal, Ricardo," Apiro chuckled. "Some day that trick won't work, and you will get caught. But you know, I could have fixed those scars for him, and made him rather handsome.

You were right; when it came to the knife, he was an amateur."
He laughed his staccato laugh. "Can the Canadian authorities use
that information?"

"I'll find out soon enough. I forgot to tell you," said Ramirez.
"I had a call last night from the Rideau Police in Canada. Chief
Miles O'Malley. His government is trying to get a special authorization for me to go to Canada to assist in an investigation. They
think that some of the perpetrators of abuse at our residential
schools were transferred to theirs, as part of a cover-up by the
Catholic Church. The Catholic brother that Sanchez named may
have abused children in Canada also. Chief O'Malley says he
was arrested recently for possession of child pornography at the
Ottawa airport."

It was the least Ramirez could do for Rodriguez, his poor,
tormented friend. He would help the Canadian police and see
the man face justice. A short trip, Chief O'Malley had promised,
no more than a week. Ramirez didn't want to lose any more time
than that with his family, not when he wasn't sure how much, or
how little, he had left.

The second call, the one he didn't disclose to his small friend,
was from the Minister of the Interior.

"Castro has heard a policeman died in action," the minister
said. "He wants a full military funeral. It will be good for
morale. Your report will emphasize Detective Sanchez's courage
in exposing the prior abuses of the Catholic Church towards
Cuban children. It will conclude that he died accidentally in
an abandoned school while searching for evidence to support
an international investigation into historic crimes against our
children. He was accompanied at the time by a Canadian lawyer
who personally witnessed his heroism. She will attest to this, in
writing. You will get your special authorization to ensure that
this story is told. Do you understand, Inspector?"

Ramirez understood exactly how much his trip to Canada would cost.

"That's exciting," Hector Apiro exclaimed. "You have not been off this island since you went to Russia."

"No, I haven't, although I imagine Canada will be much the same as Moscow when it comes to weather. It's winter there now. Chief O'Malley wants me to come as soon as possible."

"How will the unit manage with both you and Sanchez gone?"

"They will be busy," Ramirez agreed, "but we have a new member. That officer from Patrol, the one from the first day of the investigation. The clever one. Espinoza. I had him transferred today to replace Sanchez."

"The lad must be thrilled."

"He is very happy about the raise in pay, yes." Twenty-five dollars a month was a lot of money, even more than the salary of a plastic surgeon.

"Will you turn the tape over to Señora Jones when you go to Canada, then?"

"Most likely," Ramirez said. But not right away. When he needed to secure her written statement, the small tape in his pocket could be helpful. He had learned that from Señora Jones on the drive back to Havana. In negotiations, you had to have something valuable to exchange.

"It's funny that the Canadians have homosexuals on their police force," Apiro mused. "They must be far ahead of us in that sense."

"Who do you mean, Hector?"

"Señor Ellis, of course."

"You think Michael Ellis is gay?" asked Ramirez.

"It seems obvious. Most men whose wives have been unfaithful get divorced rather than shooting their wife's lover in the *cojones*. And to show such concern for his friend's baby? Describe it as all he had left? All he had left of Señor Sloan is what I think he meant. I think it was not the fact that Hillary Ellis slept with another man that enraged Señor Ellis but *who* she slept with. His own lover. Steve Sloan."

SEVENTY-SIX

It was just after 11 P.M. on New Year's Eve. After his discussion with Hector Apiro, Inspector Ramirez spent the rest of the day preparing his reports for the Attorney General and the Minister of the Interior.

He dropped by Apiro's office, hoping to discuss the political trade-offs he'd negotiated, but Maria Vasquez was there. It could wait, he decided, smiling at the pink lipstick on Apiro's face. The pair seemed very happy in each other's company and that made him happy. Apiro poured them each a glass of rum and they toasted each other and the coming New Year. Ramirez lit a cigar.

"So I'm not sure you ever did tell me how you met," Ramirez reminded them.

"I was a patient of Hector's once, long ago," Maria explained. "And then the night that Señor Ellis was released from your custody, I came here to see him. Señor Ellis had mentioned Hector's name to me in connection with your investigation and I realized he was still working in Havana."

"Yes, Maria came by for coffee. And one thing led to another," Apiro said with a wide smile.

Ramirez felt the small boy's presence again. The dead boy

stood behind Maria's chair, his arms around her neck. Looking closely at the two of them together, Ramirez realized Maria Vasquez could easily pass for Arturo's mother. The resemblance was striking. But Señora Montenegro had mentioned no older sister, only the son who went missing in 1998.

Ramirez remembered the photograph of Rubén Montenegro in his file. "The priests told us he fell down the mountainside trying to get home," the mother had said. But there had been no body, no burial. Ramirez looked at the two of them together again, and then he saw it. He realized for the first time just how good a plastic surgeon Apiro really was.

So the street child that Maria Vasquez protected was her own little brother. She could not have told Arturo who she really was. He was just a child and would not have understood how a brother he had never known could somehow be his sister. But Maria knew where Arturo Montenegro lived. She knew exactly who *he* was. No wonder she had been so worried for his safety.

Señora Montenegro believed her older son was dead; that Rubén had vanished, had died in the hills years earlier. She had no idea that he was alive, that he now lived as a woman. But the similarities between the two siblings, once one saw through the surgery, were startling, unmistakable.

The boy walked over and put his small hand in Ramirez's. The boy nodded, then smiled, and Ramirez saw the dimples for himself. He felt the small fingers slipping from his hand as the boy once again showed the inspector his empty palms.

Why was he still here instead of playing wherever dead boys played? thought Ramirez. Ramirez had apparently missed something important, but what? And why does he keep showing me his empty hands? And then Ramirez finally understood what the boy was trying to convey.

Michael Ellis gave Arturo Montenegro a lot of money. It wasn't on the body. Where had the boy spent it? He'd never thought to check.

The boy smiled a final time and skipped away, as if someone waited outside the door.

"I am very pleased for both of you," Ramirez said and raised his glass to Hector and Maria again. "Trust me, there is nothing like having a strong woman on your side. The secret is learning how to fight and how to forgive. It is time, Hector, that you visited my home. Francesca will welcome having another girlfriend to complain to about my bad habits. Like me coming home late again, on New Year's Eve."

Ramirez looked at his watch and stood up. It was almost midnight. It was time to go home and have a difficult discussion with his wife. He owed it to Francesca to finally tell her about his illness. To share with her the bad news he had tried to protect her from for too long.

Francesca would be terrified, livid that he had kept such a secret to himself. He rubbed the side of his face, anticipating her slap and the angry tears that would follow. But together, they would face whatever happened. They always did; they had no choice.

"Thank you," Apiro said, inclining his head. "You are absolutely right. I have lived like a hermit crab for too long, cramped in my small shell. I swear, Ricardo, I have grown a few inches already."

"And that's just his height," Maria said, and the three of them laughed, Apiro the loudest, with his raspy caw.

Ramirez put down his empty glass. As he did, his hand quivered. He saw Apiro, always thoughtful, swivel his head like a parrot to focus on the movement.

He was several steps down the narrow hallway when he heard Apiro's door squeak open, the sound of Apiro scuttling after him. He turned to see his small friend waving a piece of paper.

"I have something for you, Ricardo. My sincere apologies: I completely forgot with all the excitement this week. Our medical records are computerized now. I finally found the results of that autopsy that I promised to get for you so long ago. Your grandmother's. Here." He handed Ramirez the sheet of paper. "Look. Not a single Lewy body in her brain; no signs of plaque. No dementia of any kind. She died of old age."

Ramirez skimmed through the document. The autopsy report listed "natural causes" as the reason for his grandmother's death. "There was nothing wrong with her?"

"Not quite," said Apiro. "She suffered from hyperthyroidism, a hereditary illness. I couldn't help but notice your hand was shaking again tonight. And how out of breath you were this week. These can be symptoms of that disease. I'd like to arrange an iodine scan for you. If I'm right, a single dose of radioactive isotope will put you back to normal in no time. And the good news, Ricardo, is that we have the supplies."

SEVENTY-SEVEN

Ricardo Ramirez walked slowly through the lobby, savouring the news. The burdens he'd carried for so long lifted from his shoulders. Hector Apiro had given him the greatest gift of all for Christmas: a future. But if I'm not dying, he thought, then what in heaven's name have I been seeing all these years?

He cast his mind back to his grandmother's last words. Could his visions truly be spirits, sentinels from the other side? He had treated them as mere distractions, as games played by his subconscious. He had even ordered the apparitions out of sight when they annoyed him.

As Ramirez thought back on it, the dead man had provided him with all the clues he needed to solve the boy's death, if he had just paid more attention.

In the hotel room, the dead man tried to warn him that Sanchez had planted the capsule. When Sanchez pointed to it, the dead man pointed at him. He had shown Ramirez just how Sanchez had pulled the photographs and CD from his pant pockets, but once again Ramirez misunderstood.

In the back of the car, he had pretended to hold a collection plate, representing the Church. The dead man had even demonstrated how Sanchez would kill himself with a bullet to his own head, with his own gun.

Ramirez's subconscious mind could not possibly have invented those details. The man was real, Ramirez realized, astonished. Or at least as real as any ghost could ever be.

Ramirez recalled the other clues the dead man provided. The circles he drew with his hands when they drove past the Ferris wheel as children screamed. The boy had done the same; Ramirez had seen his fascination with the hamster wheel but paid it little attention. What did all that mean? And why had the dead man appeared in relation to the child's death instead of his own?

The man had drowned; Ramirez was sure of that, he had seen foam spill from his mouth. Yet if he was murdered, Ramirez had no way to solve his death. He still had no name for the man, not even a missing persons report.

Two shapes emerged from the shadows. A man and a small boy, side by side, walked towards the Malecón. The man clasped the small boy's hand tightly in his own, keeping him close. He held his battered hat in his other hand.

They were heading to the Ferris wheel, Ramirez guessed, from the way the dead boy skipped joyfully beside the ghost that had followed Ramirez all week. A man who had waited patiently for Ramirez, twisting his hat, wistfully hoping for a few moments of the inspector's undivided attention.

The dead man turned his head to look back at Ramirez. He smiled widely for the first time. Ramirez saw the dimples and finally grasped who the man was, who he once had been.

Arturo's father.

After he took his son to the Ferris wheel for the last time, Señor Montenegro would return Arturo to the ocean, where they both belonged. Yemayá, the ocean *orisha*, would care for them from now on. They were leaving Ramirez's jurisdiction.

The dead man tipped the brim of his hat. Ramirez raised his hand slowly and waved goodbye to Eshu's messengers.

SEVENTY-EIGHT

Ramirez had practically forgotten he had New Year's Day off, his first in years. Once he got home, he could actually sleep in for a change. Make love to his wife, play with his children, and finally listen to that CD of Lucy Provedo that Francesca had given him for Christmas.

He wanted to do something special to celebrate their future together, a future now as uncertain, and thus as hopeful, as that of anyone else. Perhaps they would have another child. The world was full of possibilities.

The Beggar's Opera was playing at the Gran Teatro on Sunday afternoon; he had seen posters for it all week. When he got home, he would take a surprised Francesca in his arms, dance her around the apartment, and tell her of his plans to make it up to her for working on Christmas Day.

It was their favourite. An opera about political corruption, with a lively cast that included well-bred whores with impeccable manners, men disguised as women, beggars, even prisoners. It was a story of poisoned chalices, violence, and revenge; false charges, even a threatened execution. But it was also about love and loyalty and, above all, friendship. It seemed to fit the events of the week.

The original opera ended with a hanging, but the audience demanded a happy ending, and so its ending was rewritten. And so was his.

Ramirez whistled an aria as he walked to the parking lot, a bounce in his step. He opened the door to his small blue car and was about to climb in when he saw her. A dignified elderly woman walking slowly towards him as she tried to ignore her ruined dress and the knife protruding from her chest. A giant fabric flower was pinned to the white bandana wrapped around her head.

"It's my day off," he said kindly, as he escorted her back into the shadows. "But it looks like I have tomorrow."

EPILOGUE

A week had passed but the ride operator still trembled, still jumped whenever he heard a police siren, felt his heart race at the mere sight of a *policía*.

He was haunted by thoughts of the dead boy, could not forget how the boy had shown up at the park at midnight, just as Christmas Eve turned into Christmas Day. The bells and horns were still sounding; even a distant bagpipe honked in the night air. But the rides were not running when the small boy slid beneath the metal gates the ride operator had just locked together and materialized at his side. "Please," the boy begged. "Please let me ride the big wheel. Please."

"We are not open, little one. Come back on Monday."

The boy looked terribly disappointed. "Please. I have never been on the rides. Just this once. I have money." He showed the man five pesos that he pulled carefully from the pocket in his shorts. He held the coins out on the palms of his two hands.

He seemed so downcast that the ride operator smiled. Perhaps it was not a problem to open the ride this one time. He took the little boy by the hand to the bottom seat, strapped him in, then

pulled the bar down. After making sure the boy was secure, he
started the ride.

But as the wheel moved higher, the boy squirmed in his seat,
then lifted the bar to stand, and sweet Virgin Mary there was no
time to tell him to sit down before the boy fell over the side. It was
that quick and that sudden, the ride operator could not believe
it. Not even a scream, just a small noise as the boy hit the metal
post that held the Cuban flag with the back of his head, then fell
on his back on the ground.

And there the boy was, not moving, already limp and empty.
A small amount of blood, a few drops, trickled from his ear.

The ride operator knelt beside the boy, but he was dead. Some
children became dizzy on the wheel. It was not his fault. But there
the boy was, his head soft on the hard cement.

"Jesus," the ride operator whispered, "Jesus, forgive me, what
have I done?"

He felt the boy's neck, his wrist, put his face against the boy's
face looking for breath, searched desperately for signs of life. He
felt the panic rise in his chest, his heart beating quickly like that
of a bird.

He was crying, but he had to stop, he had to think what to do.
The bells were ringing; it was Christmas Day already, midnight,
madre mio, Christmas Day. He was alone at the park, no one else
was there, everyone at church or at mass. Thank God at least for
that.

Jesus, he prayed to his saviour, and then to Yemayá, the *orisha*
who was supposed to protect children, who he had angered in
some unknown way. *Forgive me, I did not mean to harm him, he
was just a child.*

But the child was dead. And all his prayers could not change
that one fact.

The ride operator thought of running to the policeman who

always stood on the Malecón, a bored young man in a light blue shirt, little more than a boy himself. He should confess, tell the officer that he shouldn't have opened the park when it was closed, that he was trying to be kind, that the boy simply fell. But how could he explain that a little boy could afford the price of a ride? Too much money for a small boy to have. Five tourist pesos, and there was no way to account for that.

He hadn't asked how or where the boy got the money, he had just been happy to see the child smile, and now the boy was dead and somehow, one way or another, he would be blamed for it, of that he was sure.

He thought of his wife and his three children and all the lives that would be ruined if the police put him in jail. He made his decision. He hoisted the boy up like a sack of potatoes and carried him to the back of his truck, where he laid the boy gently on his back, then covered him with a tarp. He went about his business of closing up of the park. No one had seen him; no one had seen the boy.

He drove his family to late mass, his wife completely unaware of his small cargo. Later that night, as she slept, and the sounds of partying along the Malecón quieted, when the last trumpet and guitar that filled the night air ceased their music, he got up, dressed himself, and drove to the Malecón. He parked across from the medical towers, the darkest part of the seaway, where there were no working lights.

The boy's body was no heavier than a bag of yams. He carried his light load to the stone wall and let the boy go. Dropped him over the seawall. Heard the small splash on the edge of the shore. He prayed that Eshu, the god of misfortune, would give safe passage to the boy.

He could not see the body in the dark, but the tide would move it out overnight. The boy would be found, he was sure, by the fishermen in the morning, and then the boy's parents would believe he had slipped while playing on the rocks, where all the boys fished and waded. They would be sad, devastated by his death, but no sadder than if they knew how he really died. An accident, either way. No one's fault.

A dead child, he thought, is a dead child, there is no greater loss, but how he died is less important than *that* he died and I am sorry that this happened, but I cannot change fate. This little boy will never grow old, but it was not my fault. How could I know?

He said a prayer for the boy and the waves that caressed him. *Grace be to God and may his soul be carried to Heaven.*

And then he made the sign of the cross, and carrying a weight in his heart as heavy as the Christmas cross itself, he walked slowly across the Malecón, gripping the boy's five tourist pesos, which his own family needed as much as any other.

He went home to his wife and his young children, but first he folded up his tarp carefully, because it was hard to find good tarps in Cuba, and had been since the revolución.

ACKNOWLEDGMENTS

I've never lost sight of the fact that I wouldn't have been published at all if I hadn't been standing in the bar on the last night of Theakstons Old Peculier crime writing conference in Harrogate, U.K. (having lost the Debut Dagger the night before), at the very moment that the Scottish author Ian Rankin walked by.

The bar was almost deserted. Everyone else was in a session. I was having a last glass of wine before I went back to my hotel room to pack for my red-eye trip home. I asked him if I could take his picture, which I almost never do—if I see a celebrity, I usually leave them alone. But I'd promised the Crime Writers of Canada that I'd take pictures for their website if I saw anyone famous.

He was kind enough to say yes. He asked me where I was from. I said Ottawa. It turned out he had just returned from Ottawa's Bluesfest the week before, where he'd been with his son. Now how weird is that?

If we hadn't had that five-minute chat about the crazy forty-degree heat the previous week in Ottawa and how great Bluesfest was despite it, I doubt he would have asked me why I was in Harrogate, or if I had an agent or a publisher, which I didn't.

But he did. And he generously offered to let me use his name
to contact them. Thanks to his referral, I found my U.K. agent,
Peter Robinson, and through him my Canadian agent, Anne
McDermid, both of whom I adore.

"I worked so hard that I got lucky" is the phrase that comes
to mind. But some things about this book (and this series) seem
to be tied much less to hard work than to a very benevolent Lady
Luck indeed.

So many wonderful friends have stepped up to the plate to
read *The Beggar's Opera* (sometimes several times) and offer
advice. Thelma Farmer takes the absolute record: I think she read
the manuscript at least a dozen times. Then there's Bill Schaper,
Lou Allin, Debbie Hantusch, Mike Hutton, John Lindsay, Ken
Stuart, Brian French, Beth McColl, Mark Bourrie, E. Kaye
Fulton, Paul Olioff, and, of course, my daughter, Jade, who not
only helped me think through the plot of the story in its earliest
stages, but had a hand in designing the book jacket. Guillermo
Martinez-Zalce helped me make sure the Spanish words I used
were accurate; Alex Schultz ensured that the same could be said
of the English ones.

Thanks to all of you. And profound thanks to the Crime
Writers' Association of the U.K. for starting me on this adven-
ture by shortlisting me for the Debut Dagger. A final thanks to
Adrienne Kerr at Penguin Canada for believing in me.